Book 1 in Bloodlines of Destiny

RAVEN AND THE WITCH

WENDY PYM

Queensland, Australia

Please be aware that this novel has been written in Australian English and uses Australian language, spelling, grammar and punctuation conventions. These are notably different to American, Canadian and British language conventions.

Disclaimer: *Raven and the Witch* is a work of fiction that draws inspiration from Native American themes, characters, folklore and settings. The story is born from the author's deep admiration for Indigenous culture and people. However, this is a fantasy novel shaped by imagination, featuring mythical beings with supernatural abilities. It is not intended to depict real historical events, figures or struggles. Any resemblance to actual persons, places or traditions is purely coincidental. This novel does not claim to be an accurate historical account of Native American history or lived experiences. The time periods featured in the novel are also for atmospheric and scene-setting purposes and are not an historical account of those eras.

Cover design by Judith San Nicolas
Typeset in Garamond 12pt and Apple Chancery 28pt
Printed and bound in Australia by IngramSpark
Prepared for publication by Dr Juliette Lachemeier at The Erudite Pen

A catalogue record for this book is available from the National Library of Australia

Raven and the Witch – Book 1 in the Bloodlines of Destiny Chronicles 1st ed.
ISBN 9781763869905
E-ISBN 9781763869912

For Tessa-lee Rose. With boundless love, this book is for you.
Never stop believing in magic.

Author's Note

For as long as I can remember, I have been captivated by storytelling and the art of world-building. Inspired by Native American history, mythology and magic, I have poured my creative vision into *Raven and the Witch*, the first book in my debut series, Bloodlines of Destiny. This story is particularly close to my heart, as it fulfils a promise I made to my late brother, Brent, to share my stories with the world.

I have always been fascinated by Native American culture – their deep connection to nature, respect for the animals they hunted and their rich spiritual traditions. As a child, I would collect bones and feathers to craft ornaments, long before I understood their cultural significance. That passion eventually led me to travel solo to America, where I visited reservations and brought home treasured jewellery and carvings that continue to inspire my work today.

That said, *Raven and the Witch* is a work of fantasy. While it draws inspiration from Native American themes, characters, folklore and settings, it is in no way intended to reflect, capture or accurately portray Native American culture, struggles or mores, nor the historical realities of the 17th and 18th centuries. The world, characters and supernatural elements are entirely fictional, shaped by imagination rather than historical fact. Any resemblance to actual persons, places or traditions is purely coincidental. The time periods featured in the novel are included purely for atmospheric and scene-setting purposes and should not be interpreted as historically accurate representations.

I hope you enjoy this journey into a world where identity, magic and the eternal clash between light and darkness take centre stage.

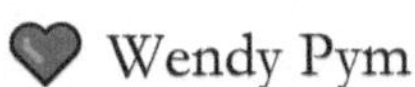 Wendy Pym

Contents

Prologue

They year 1642 in Lancashire, England, was plagued by dark times and engulfed in a frenzy of witch hunts. Hunters were generously rewarded by both the Catholic and Protestant churches for identifying and delivering individuals suspected of practising the occult.

Countless innocent women, including mere healers, were uprooted from their homes and transported to hidden chambers deep beneath the churches, where they endured unspeakable torture. The haunting sounds of their anguish and suffering reverberated through the streets, instilling fear in the inhabitants of Pendle Hill, as desired by the ordained ministers.

Eventually, those accused, on the brink of death, were paraded through the grimy thoroughfares to meet their fate at the merciless hand of the pyres. Barefoot and bloodied, with rotten food and stones hurled at them as they were forced forward, the accused were subjected to a barrage of slander from the terrified townspeople who clamoured for their burning.

Their scantily covered bodies were tarnished, their clothing tattered and torn, and stained with dried blood. Their lacerated feet left a trail of dried blood as they limped behind their captors, suffering with each step.

Thick ropes were cruelly fastened around their necks, causing searing pain as the fibres cut into their tender flesh, the grip of death tightening long before the final moment of hanging. The church congregations instilled fear and intolerance among the townspeople, vehemently suppressing those who deviated from their beliefs. They proclaimed that only a selected few had been chosen by God for salvation, while the rest of humanity was destined for eternal damnation due to their sins. Uncertainty shrouded the fate of many individuals, leaving them in a state of perpetual dread and apprehension. Striving to cleanse the streets of impurity and rid the land of perceived evil, a curfew descended upon the once vibrant town, casting a pall of restriction over its inhabitants.

Numerous harmless citizens endured harrowing fates and perished under the religious pretext of divine intervention. Faced with such persecution, many witches opted to escape, taking flight under the cover of the full moon, soaring high above the clouds on their brooms in search of new lands where they could conceal themselves and practise their arts without fear. Some opted to relocate to secluded areas within dense woodlands, choosing to remain deeply concealed and hidden from the prying eyes of persecution.

However, *some* witches were indeed practitioners of the dark arts. The townspeople and the church had every right to fear these witches, and their formidable reputations and evil powers condemned all witches, healers and many ordinary women to the pyre.

Flying through the night and into the break of dawn, two evil blood witches journeyed to the remote and shadowed reaches of the Canadian wilderness, where they discovered an idyllic location to establish a new life. In this secluded sanctuary nestled within the depths of the forest, they not only found refuge and a place to call home, but also selected this spot for its isolation from civilisation, ensuring their concealment without the looming threat of exposure.

Despite their seclusion, they remained close to the neighbouring indigenous tribes comprising the Huron and Iroquois Confederacies, later recognised as the Six Tribes.

These blood witches, however, wielded formidable magic, and united as mother and daughter, they immersed themselves in malevolent sorcery and wicked deeds. Under the veil of night, they engaged in human hunting and nurtured a garden of poisonous flora around their abode.

The mother imparted her dark knowledge to her sole progeny, instructing her in the sinister arts until they became proficient in hunting and eliminating the neighbouring clans. Across a generation, these witches conducted sacrificial rituals to honour their dark master, the devil. They engaged in blood rites and the consumption of their victims' organs and blood to absorb their strengths.

Their sinister objective culminated in the delivery of captured souls to the underworld's evil ruler, ensnaring these essences in eternal darkness and torment within the devil's domain, forever severed from the realm of light and peace.

United in their dark endeavours, the blood witch duo thrived in secrecy within the hidden depths of the forest, weaving potent binding and protection spells to shield themselves from discovery. Their familiars dutifully carried out their bidding, gathering intelligence on their neighbours and conveying whispered messages to the sorceresses. As years flew by, amidst the arrival of a blood moon in 1662, the mother aided in welcoming her sole granddaughter into the world before departing to the dark spirit realm when the babe turned fifteen to reunite with her forebears, leaving her legacy for the next generation.

This new blood witch granddaughter had been predestined long before her arrival. Branded by Satan with a vivid red ivy leaf on her cheek, it served as a perpetual emblem of her allegiance to him.

She was named Ivy, in honour of her distinctive birthmark, and was meticulously tutored in the dark arts by her mother, until her mother's passing. Ivy matured into the most dreaded and formidable blood witch across the confederate lands, renowned for her mastery in the art of poisons.

In her garden stood her cherished possessions: the deadliest flora that she used in her potions to incapacitate and mutilate her prey before ultimately dispatching and consuming them.

But now, in the depth of the ancient forest, amidst the towering trees and twisting vines, Ivy – a once fearsome necromancer who could tap into dark forces at will – now grappled with the fading embers of her powerful magic.

At sixty-two years old, she felt the weight of time pressing upon her, whispering of days past and the inevitable approach of her own mortality. For all her powers, she could not achieve immortality. Satan had all but abandoned Ivy since she had stopped offering him human souls. He would watch her from time to time, his amusement growing as strong as his desire for redemption.

As her powers weakened, Ivy realised she had been cast aside when as a necromancer, she could no longer command his evil spirits to do her bidding. For the devil gave nothing for free and of course abandoned her once she could no longer provide him with human souls to torment.

Secluded within her fortress of stone and shadows, she tended to her garden of poisonous flora, the only companions to her solitude apart from her loyal familiars, with meticulous care.

Ivy's familiars were a unique and diverse group of companions, each bringing their own special qualities to her blood sorcery world. Luna, her cat, was her oldest and most trusted companion, with bright green eyes that seemed to hold ancient wisdom. Silas, her snake, slithered gracefully around her, his scales shimmering in the dim candlelight, a symbol of transformation and rebirth. Eve, her spider, wove intricate webs of protection and creativity, her delicate movements reflecting Ivy's own complex thoughts and emotions. Moonshadow her majestic snowy owl, spied on the surrounding tribes, carrying whispered tales and ancient prophecies back to her mistress.

Together, these familiars formed a mystical bond with their dark mistress Ivy, guiding her through the unseen realms with their insight and prowess abilities. As a blood witch, Ivy shared a telepathic bond with her familiar, Luna. Through this connection, Luna communicated with Ivy using a language of emotions, images and intuitive insights that only Ivy could understand.

One fateful night, as the moon cast its silvery glow upon the land, Ivy's faithful owl, Moonshadow, returned from her nocturnal flight. With snowy white wings beating silently, the owl alighted upon Ivy's shoulder, bearing a message that stirred something deep within her soul. A longing desire, a spark of hope, ignited within Ivy as Moonshadow whispered of a prophecy foretold.

It spoke of a newborn, a child of the Iroquois clan, destined to possess potent shapeshifting magic. The baby, a girl of Mohawk descent, would inherit the legacy of her ancestors, wielding powers that transcended the realms of the living and the dead. With the ability to transform into a raven at will and don an invisibility cloak, she would walk the path of mysticism and mystery, her connection to the spirt realm profound and unyielding.

As the prophecy of the newborn with untold powers echoed in Ivy's ears, a fierce determination blossomed within her, reigniting the flames of her once formidable magic. The spark that had been kindled by Moonshadow's message now blazed into a roaring fire, fuelling Ivy's primal desire to reclaim her former glory and establish herself as a force to be reckoned with once more.

The blood witch, driven by a dark and covetous desire, bided her time with calculated patience as she observed the growth of the newborn – Raven. Ivy eagerly anticipated the moment when the young girl's powers would reach their full potential, and she dreamed of hunting and seizing Raven's youth and magic for herself.

While she waited over the years, Ivy enjoyed taunting young Raven. She mastered the art of entering her dreams and loved nothing more than to cast fear in the young girl's mind, all the while keeping a watchful eye on her developing skills.

Concealed within the impenetrable walls of her fortress, Ivy deftly hunted the forest animals for sustenance, while she worked tirelessly to create a powerful dragon ally. With intricate spells and potent potions, Ivy meticulously crafted the perfect companion to aid her in her sinister endeavours. For the time would soon come to feast once again on human blood and flesh. Eternity and power would be hers, or she would die trying, for possess it she must, if Satan would not give it to her after everything she and her lineage had done for him.

Ivy's patient anticipation reached its culmination at the age of seventy-eight, coinciding with Raven's sixteenth birthday, a timely convergence. Raven's magical prowess had matured, and Ivy found herself on the brink of witnessing the blossoming of her most powerful creation – the poisonous and enigmatic devil's horn flower. A radiant and luminous blossom that graced the witch's garden with its vivid glow once every decade. But beneath its dazzling exterior lay a deadly touch that could paralyse those who were unlucky enough to encounter its enchanting beauty and narcotic bloom.

Raven would be hers. She was leaving nothing to fate this time.

Shikoba 'Little Feather'

Lake Ontario, Canada, 1740

Raven Shikoba swiped at her sweat-covered brow with the back of her hand, feeling somewhat disgruntled and a little defiant that she was training on this perfect summer's day.

'Again,' her mentor instructed. She shot him a dark glare, her amber-coloured eyes flashing with annoyance before she dropped and heaved out twenty push-ups. It was hot, and the more she moaned and groaned in defiance, the more he pushed her.

Raven bit down hard on her lip to stop herself from whining, just in case he gave her another twenty. It felt like she had trained for a good part of the day having already completing four sets of twenty gruelling exercises. However, it was nothing new, nothing she wasn't used to.

Upon standing, she stood tall and stared her mentor Silent Wolf straight in the eyes. His pale eyes – one blue and one brown – remained, neutral. Unreadable. He passed her a heavy waterskin, and she guzzled it thirstily before pouring the rest over her steaming hot face. The cool water was a refreshing change to the sweat that stung her heated cheeks.

'To finish off, you can go for a six-mile run, and before you complain be grateful it's not ten.' On a good day, she could easily run the full distance. But tiredness stifled her efforts today, making every exercise harder than usual.

Raven's nights were full of dreams of late – dark foreboding dreams filled with uncertainty niggled at her. It was like something was trying to claw its way in, searching for a space to permanently reside within her mind. These dreams kept her awake as she tossed and turned, like crashing waves caught between two realms of dreaming and waking.

'Argh,' she retorted, rolling her eyes. 'Why should I run when I can fly?'

'Because I said so, now get going.'

She pursed her lips together, feeling utterly drained already. Raven had just turned sixteen that summer, and she thought her mentor may cut her some slack, and that maybe, just maybe – she could reduce the amount of training Silent Wolf demanded of her. Sick and tired was an understatement of how she was feeling about the relentless regime. Her mind flickered a little, like the heat waves she could see rippling across the sun-baked ground. It was a scorching summer's day, and she could be swimming in the lake or doing countless other things. But no – today was not one of those days.

Taking a deep breath, she sighed heavily, resigning herself to the fact that she would not be given the rest of the day off. Silent Wolf would be timing her run as he always did. And she wanted nothing more than to beat her personal best. But she doubted that would happen today, the way she was feeling. There was no cheating either, or simply shapeshifting and flying the distance, as her mentor also ran the trail close behind her. However, he had an advantage over her, running in his wolf form, usually behind, nipping at her heals and pushing her to go faster and harder.

Silent Wolf's human transformation into an actual Dire Wolf turned him into a powerful force, making him an intimidating competitor in any scenario. Raven was relieved that he was her ally, but he was a tough teacher.

Raven's legs throbbed, her muscles protesting as she sprinted up the steep hill and navigated the winding forest trail. Despite the burning sensation in her throat, she pushed herself to run faster. As the urge to stop intensified, her pace gradually decreased.

Silent Wolf growled, emitting a low rumble from his throat that spurred Raven on to push through to the finish.

In the distance, she finally caught sight of the red ribbon, signalling the spot where she could finally rest. Digging deep, she sprinted through the final excruciating steps. As she came to a stop, she immediately doubled over and vomited. Breathing heavily, she collapsed against a tree trunk, her back finding temporary relief. Nearby, Silent Wolf stood, panting heavily, his long tongue lolling out of his mouth, salvia dripping. At least he appeared to be slightly suffering along with her. She wasn't alone in her torment after all.

When Raven finally regained her composure, she spoke. 'Well, was it my personal best?' Her amber eyes searched his. She felt it was, as she had pushed herself today, and she was only sick when she did.

Silent Wolf was fit, and although in his human form he had a full head of shaggy grey hair, he was in his prime at forty years of age. He had really done that run with ease, and she knew it. He had been her mentor since she was eight years old. It had been an exceptionally challenging year. Beyond enduring the rigorous training that had commenced, she had also suffered the loss of both her parents – Little Wing and Silver Oak – to the coughing sickness. Consumed by grief, she'd found herself devoid of the desire to train, to wield her magic, and certainly devoid of any desire to fulfil the role of a prophesied saviour. Yet, this destiny had been relentlessly impressed upon her since birth, to the point where the very mention of it made her feel nauseous.

'Damn the prophecy to hell,' she had muttered under her breath, on more than one occasion.

It didn't matter how much she detested the whole thing, loathed it at times, for there she was, eight years later and still training. She trained more often than she cared to admit. For twenty-five days in each moon cycle, she was put through gruelling exercises, both mentally and physically. Silent Wolf's repetitive words echoed in her mind, emphasising that to fulfil her destiny, she must strive to excel. Excel not only in mastering her craft and power, but also in the art of combat and taking lives.

Evidently deciding that Raven had recovered enough from her run, Silent Wolf approached her and nudged her with his wet nose. A sign she knew all too well.

'Okay, okay, can I at least fly home?' she pleaded, batting her long eyelashes at him, knowing the question would fall on deaf ears before she even asked it.

He only nudged her again, harder this time.

Raven released a deep sigh through her nose and rose to her feet, her shirt drenched in sweat. Taking one step after another, she cautiously began her decent along the winding path, her weary legs trembling slightly. Silent Wolf nudged her on with a gentle nip on the back of her elbow, spurring her to start running.

Laughter and splashing resounded from the lake below, indicating the presence of the giggling group Raven recognised all too well – the girls from her village relishing the summer sun. Envy coursed through Raven, and a fleeting impulse crossed her mind to sprint down the hill and plunge into the cool, dark depths of the cold lake, possibly startling the girls and disrupting their carefree day.

Silent Wolf remained close behind her, making her escape to the lake impossible. She felt indifferent towards the company of the village girls, knowing they despised her and harboured nothing but jealousy towards her magical abilities and striking appearance. But if given the chance, she would have traded places with them in an instant. Instead, she sprinted past the sounds of joy and freedom, pushing herself to the limits, almost stumbling over her own feet as her body struggled to keep up with the pace of her legs.

Upon reaching Silent Wolf's teepee, she collapsed in a sweaty heap outside, gasping for breath, utterly exhausted.

Silent Wolf retreated into his teepee and transformed back into his human form. As the respected medicine man of the village, he always had a tonic or herbal concoction prepared for Raven to drink after their training sessions. Maintaining his usual composed demeanour, he offered her a bone cup.

Raven wrinkled her nose, fully aware of its contents. Downing it swiftly was her only option. She reluctantly pinched her nose before swallowing the liquid. 'Err, yuck,' she exclaimed in distaste.

Her mentor simply smirked before returning to the comfort of his teepee, calling out, 'Training resumes at sunrise tomorrow. Rest up.'

Realising there was no use in arguing, she stayed lying on her back for a while, gazing up at the clear sky. The day would soon come to a peaceful close. The urge to swim and soak up the sun had vanished. With a heavy sigh, she got up and made her way to her quarters, limping slightly. Exhausted from her intense training, she knew she would sleep soundly. Too fatigued to even change her clothes, she settled onto her soft fur bed and closed her weary eyes, drifting off to sleep almost instantly.

The next day, training resumed promptly at sunrise as scheduled.

'Concentrate, Raven,' Silent Wolf growled, displaying impatience with her progress after being at it all day again.

'I thought you promised we would visit the seer once I turned sixteen?' she questioned, mirroring her teacher's irritation.

'Only after you have perfected the use of your invisibility cloak,' he replied sharply.

Raven rolled her eyes, fully aware that it irritated him, yet she continued to do it regardless, even if it meant enduring additional lessons.

'Do it again,' he almost barked the command.

Raven persisted in her questioning. 'I thought you mentioned we would go soon. And when precisely is soon, may I inquire?'

Silent Wolf sighed and shook his head. 'Very well, if you are insistent on going, we will depart at first light in the morning – provided you can demonstrate improvement and speed in your magical abilities.'

Raven Shikoba could hardly believe her ears. She had thought this day would never arrive, that her magic would never reach the required level, and she would be stuck in an endless cycle of tedious training.

'Yes, yes, I can do that,' she stammered excitedly, struggling to contain her bubbling excitement. Focusing all her energy, she shapeshifted effortlessly, transforming into her raven form. Taking flight, she landed gracefully on a nearby tree branch before swiftly cloaking herself in invisibility.

'Excellent, Raven. Why couldn't you do that the fifty other times you tried today? That was much better!' he called out to her.

Raven gracefully descended into the privacy of Silent Wolf's teepee and reverted to her human form. Swiftly dressing herself, she stepped out to face her teacher. 'Can we truly leave in the morning?' Nervously she bit her lip in anticipation of his response.

'Yes, Raven, as you wish.' He smiled, revealing a perfect set of white teeth. 'I may not have mentioned it lately, but I am proud of all the hard work you've been putting in. I know it hasn't been easy,' he expressed with admiration, patting her affectionately on the back. This gesture was his way of showing her that he did care about her.

'I'm going to pack then,' she declared before hurrying off, eager to get ready before he could possibly change his mind.

'Pack lightly!' he yelled after her, as she vanished along the familiar trail leading through the village.

With determination in her eyes, Raven hastily packed all the essential items and clothing she could into a spacious buffalo skin bag. Standing amidst her teepee, a sense of readiness enveloped her. Gazing at her surroundings, she couldn't help but ponder the uncertain future that lay ahead. Perhaps, upon her return, she would have fulfilled her destined path, or perhaps she would meet her end in the pursuit of it. The weight of the unknown hung heavy in the air as she prepared herself for the journey that could shape her fate.

That night, Raven was filled with excitement and could hardly sleep a wink. Tossing and turning, she couldn't believe she would finally get to see Otter again, as well as Saskia the Seer, at Laughing Bear's camp. Otter was her childhood friend, her only true friend aside from Silent Wolf. Her mentor was more like a father figure, taking on the many lessons Silver Oak would have taught her.

Two years senior to Raven, Otter, at the age of eighteen, had earned the esteemed title of warrior following a successful initiation ceremony. Accompanied by a hunting party, he'd embarked on a journey to engage in trade activities with their allies from the south.

The journey to Raven's extended family's village, or camp, spanned six days of travel. In this village resided Saskia, the revered seer of the Oneida clan, known for her profound insights into unfolding events and her gift for making predictions. Saskia frequently played a pivotal role in guiding the clan through dreaming rituals and ceremonies, offering her wisdom and foresight to aid in their spiritual endeavours.

Raven felt butterflies welling up in her stomach at the thought of formally meeting with her at long last.

The following morning, with the sun rising bright and early, Silent Wolf discovered Raven standing outside his dwelling, prepared and equipped for the journey ahead. By her side stood her loyal horse, Crow, as they both awaited the start of their adventure. The air was filled with a sense of anticipation and determination, signalling the beginning of a new chapter in their shared quest.

'If only you were as diligent with your training, we might have departed from this place months ago,' Silent Wolf remarked with a hint of amusement in his voice, chuckling softly as he rubbed away the remnants of sleep from his eyes. 'Guess we're finally hitting the road then?'

Raven simply beamed a radiant smile at him, conveying her excitement without the need for words. With swift efficiency, Silent Wolf completed packing, staying true to his promise. Together, they set off. As they left the confines of their small village behind, Raven felt a sense of finality settle within her. She didn't spare a glance back, convinced that she had seen enough of her humble abode to satisfy a lifetime of memories.

Throughout the day, they journeyed along the forest trail heading southward. As the sun began its descent below the horizon, Silent Wolf selected a secluded spot for them to establish their campsite. Dinner was consumed in silence, a routine that felt familiar and unremarkable. Raven's mentor was known for his taciturn nature, often expressing himself through actions rather than words. Together, they constructed a modest shelter for the night using buffalo skins and white cedar branches, creating a cosy sanctuary under the stars.

The rhythmic sound of her mentor's snoring, though slightly bothersome, provided a sense of comfort in the wilderness. With a contented smile, Raven settled into her fur blanket, drawing her jacket hood snugly around her face before drifting off into a peaceful slumber, the tranquillity of the forest enveloping her.

Raven's Call

Raven was dreaming, soaring through the forest trees, calling to her kin. There was no answer. She called again and again. Where were they? Lost in the void, she feared this place. The immense darkness. The evil sickness that lingered, waiting to seep its way into her blood. With her heart racing, she called out loud, but her throat made no sound. Just then, Raven started descending.

'No!'

She tried to cry out as she did not want to wake up. Sensing death and immense sorrow here, Raven called out again, one last desperate call. There was still no answer. She was waking up. Raven flapped her wings with all her strength, but it was no use. Landing on the forest floor, she felt the pine needles under claws.

The dream felt so real as she awakened to the sounds of the forest coming alive, birds chirping loudly, disturbing the peace. Slowly rolling over onto her side, she observed Silent Wolf sleeping soundly, his chest rising and falling in a peaceful rhythm.

Sitting up, she opened the flap of the shelter, wiping the tears from her face. She shivered. That was such a terrible dream, and what did it mean? Raven fastened the flap open to the outside of the shelter and lay back down so she could watch the tops of the tall pine trees gently swaying in the breeze.

The sound of a persistent woodpecker beating its song out, like a drummer on a tree, resonated in the distance. A sweet pine fragrance filled her senses, and she inhaled deeply, enjoying the crisp, clean smell of the forest and trying to ignore the sense of foreboding that lingered after her dream.

The morning was cold and grey, and a heavy fog hung in the air. It had been a chilly night, and it was even colder now with the flap open. Sitting back up, she looked to the tops of the tall trees that were swaying gently with the breeze and listened to the tunes of the winter winds whispering their sad, lonely songs.

Time to get up, get a fire started and make a hot brew, she thought to herself. As she made her way out of the warmth of her shelter, the cold winds kissed her face lightly, and she thought of Otter. She wondered if he was thinking of her, and if he too were just waking to greet the dawn.

Raven grabbed her buffalo skin and draped it over her shoulders. She pulled the jacket hood underneath the skin over her head and felt the soft rabbit fur caress her face. Raven's mother had made this jacket, a long time ago now, and it was well worn and soft with age. Raven had inherited her parent's belongings when they had passed. Among them was the jacket that had once belonged to Little Wing, a cherished possession now.

The jacket had been crafted from the skin of a beautiful red deer, lovingly made by her mother, adding to its sentimental value in Raven's eyes.

Little Wing had been well known in their Iroquois clan for being exceptionally skilled in the art of bead work. She had painstakingly inlaid sections of the jacket with hand-picked turquoise and red coral beads.

To provide additional warmth, the entire interior of the jacket was meticulously lined with soft rabbit fur, extending from the hood to the front panels, arm cuffs, and even the bottom, ensuring comfort and cosiness.

It was undeniably the most beautiful item that Raven possessed, with its intricate details and familiar scent, serving as a tender and evocative tribute to Little Wing. Every touch of the soft fur lining and every glimpse of the well-loved garment brough forth a flood of memories, wrapping Raven in a warm embrace of nostalgia and love, keeping her mother's spirit close to her heart.

Before long, Raven had a crackling fire burning, its flames dancing and hissing in the crisp morning air. Using pine needles and cones as a fire base, the fire quickly ignited to life, sending out waves of comforting warmth that pushed back the chill and wrapped her in a cosy embrace amidst the serene surroundings.

Raven threw off her buffalo skin and untied her jacket. She sipped a hot brew of mint leaf and honey. As the fog slowly disappeared into the morning light, so too did many shadows dart back into the deep blackness of the forest.

Crow gently rubbed his warm nose on her shoulder, nickering softly, gesturing to her to give him something to eat. Raven dug deep into her rabbit skin bag and pulled out a large corn cake. Her horse devoured it, sniffing the bag, looking for more.

'Better save the rest for later, eh?' she said, as she put the bag behind her out of sight. Crow looked at her longingly for a minute to see if she would change her mind, then turned and sniffed his way over to a new-looking patch of grass to continue his morning meal.

Silent Wolf finally stirred awake, pushing off his fur blanket and slowly emerging from the snug confines of his sleeping space. He joined Raven by the fire, and they sat quietly enjoying the serenity of the forest. He watched Raven, her facial features conveying she was troubled.

'Did you sleep well?' he asked.

Raven gave him a side-long glance, trying to find the right words before answering. 'Lately, my dreams have been full of haunting shadows, drawing me back time and again to a suffocating abyss.' She paused for a moment, staring at the flames. 'Sinister whispers swirl around me, and I sense a malevolent presence that tries to grip my very soul. My throat constricts, making me voiceless, and I find myself questioning the mysterious pull of this ominous void. Could there be a deeper, hidden purpose behind my repeated descent into this nightmarish realm?'

As Silent Wolf studied Raven, her brow furrowed. He threw a few dried branches on the fire as he spoke calmly, trying to reassure her and extinguish her fears. 'Our dreams can sometimes be whispers of our subconscious, revealing hidden truths and untold fears. The shadows that haunt you in your sleep may be reflections of challenges yet to come or the echoes of mysteries waiting to be unravelled. Embrace them as messages from the depths of your being, for within the darkness lies the key to unlocking your inner strength. Trust in yourself, and the answers you seek will reveal themselves in due time.'

Raven pondered Silent Wolf's words. He was right of course, all would be revealed in time. As she watched the flames, mesmerised by the colours jumping in and around the fire, the stories her people had told came dancing around in her head.

…Raven had been her chosen name. It had been decided before she had even been born. When she had been dreaming and growing inside her mother, Silent Wolf, the medicine man of her people, held a birthing ceremony. On the full moon of the popping seeds, the sweat lodge was prepared. Raven's mother, Little Wing, was instructed to sit down on the buffalo rug nearest to the fire. Silent Wolf carefully selected a few handfuls of dried herbs and flowers from his stored containers and placed them in his mixing bowl. He removed a leather pouch from his sash, which was tied around his waist. Untying the pouch, he added an amount the size of an acorn to the bowl's contents, so a blue-black powder covered the herbs. Retrieving his ceremonial knife from amongst several knives he had lain out on a piece of suede, he grasped the handle. It was carved from a beautiful big deer antler. Animal bones of various shapes and sizes were threaded, along with turquoise and coral beads, onto long leather strips, which were tied around the butt. Two snowy owl feathers swung off the end of the leather, swaying with the movement, their beauty tied tightly, lovingly, forever.

Silent Wolf ran the blade down the length of his palm. Blood quickly saturated the contents of the medicine bowl. He then told Little Wing to lie down, placing a circle of raven feathers around her and chanting a slow, methodical song. As the mixture brewed over the fire, Silent Wolf untied another leather sash and selected the primary wing feather of a raven he had specially selected for the ceremony.

The now-thick consistency of the brew started to expel vapours of beautiful blue-black smoke. Removing the mixture from the fire, he painted several sacred symbols on Little Wing's forehead and cheeks. He inhaled the smoke deep into his lungs, passing the bowl to Little Wing and instructing her to do the same. The smoke became thick and hung heavily in the air. His chant continued, the melody droning softly, while he rubbed her swollen belly in a circular motion. The smoke engulfed the lodge and surrounded them both. The thick scent of the mixture would remain on their clothing, furs and lodge walls for many moons to come.

After the ceremony was over, Silent Wolf sat and stared intently at the fire. He told her that she would soon give birth to a beautiful girl. That her baby would be born of raven medicine. Raven's magic would be powerful, and she would bring a new consciousness to the people, leading them out of a great void of darkness that they would one day fall into. This would be the babe's destiny, just as it was Silent Wolf's destiny to be her teacher and guide.

The girl's hair would be a thick, lustrous and shiny blue-black colour. Her eyes would see far, like a raven, and be a pale amber. She would also be petite like a raven, but well-proportioned and strong, with a small birth mark of pure white on her throat. Otherwise, her skin would be like her mother's, a beautiful light honey colour.

Silent Wolf had used his own blood in the ceremony to pass on his vast knowledge of magic. 'Ravens are of the highest intelligence,' he said, 'and perhaps are considered the smartest bird. The special bond between your daughter, who will also bear the name Raven, and me will be woven with threads of knowledge and magic, connecting us in a unique and profound way.'

Little Wing nodded in acceptance. 'So, she will fly, and become the raven?' she asked.

Silent Wolf smiled a wide grin, showing off a beautiful set of perfect white teeth. His flecked grey hair fell softly around his face, sheltering it like a hood of new fur, cocooning its occupier. His eyes were two unusual colours. One pale brown, the other the same in lightness, but blue. They watched the remainder of the fire burn *down into luminous red embers, slowly smouldering and dying away to become ash and return to the earth once more.*

Crow snorted and stamped his hind hoof, bringing Raven out of her daydream. The fire had almost completely gone out, and smoke was wisping away, disappearing with the wind into the morning light. Her horse was looking at her, his big black eyes drooping slightly, prepared to stay put for the day. Raven tipped the remaining hot water over the smoking fire. Silent Wolf had already dismantled their shelter as she was daydreaming and struck out any evidence of anyone ever having been there.

Raven softly whistled a haunting tune she recalled from a dream, its melody lingering in the air like a whisper of hope. Though she knew it might be wishful thinking, the music reassured her and kindled a belief that everything would be alright. With determination in her heart, she held onto the conviction that she would be the beacon of light to lead her people out of the long-standing shadows of sorrow and darkness that had overshadowed their lives for decades. With un-wavering resolve, Raven embraced the belief that she would fulfil the prophecy foretold.

As the beautiful summer days drew to a close, the arrival of autumn was heralded by the chilling winds that swept through the land, sig-nalling the changing of the seasons. The morning dew was dripping off the supple green leaves of a bluebell. Sparkling droplets fell from a beautiful big cobweb, as a most hairy critter came out from its cover to warm itself in the morning sun. As they departed the forest, she could feel a presence. Raven could usually sense magic, good or bad. But this feeling she was not sure of.

'Okay Crow, let's go.' Raven nudged him gently with her heel, and he gave that look he always gave, spirited and sure of himself, quick-ening his pace to a steady trot.

Silent Wolf morphed into his wolf form and vanished into the dense forest, likely on the hunt for a rabbit or prey. They would meet up again later in the day. Raven followed the winding trail deeper into the forest before she heard running water in the distance and let Crow guide them to a welcomed sight. Giving a neigh of approval, he started drinking, not seeming to mind the coldness. The creek was gently flowing and cascading over rocks and fallen logs, forming small pools. The water was slightly icy in parts, and Raven felt the chill of it, all the way down to the depths of her stomach. She filled up her waterskin while Crow continued to guzzle enormous amounts, hesitating only once to listen to the forest creaking and rustling with the gentle wind. Raven looked through the dense forest towards the snowy mountains in the distance and felt a sense of bewilderment about not knowing what faced her in the depths of the mountains. Otter and the other warriors had told stories of Zaltana, the high mountains.

The men of her tribe were known for their storytelling, often changing the story when it suited them. They could then become the warrior who had killed the most enemies or rescued the most young and old from certain death. The young women's faces would flush red as they giggled behind their hands, whispering to one another and flashing their long dark eyelashes at the strongest and most skilled warriors.

As Raven made her way through the thick of the forest, she came to a large clearing. The sun was full in the sky, radiating its warmth upon them, feeding the earth. Crow's lustrous black coat was glistening, and blue-black flecks of colour shone off him, shimmering in the sun. Crow and Raven shared this colour, a shimmering blue-black iridescence that spoke of magic.

Raven motioned Crow to stop, dismounted, then gave him most of the corn cakes, having just enough herself to take away the gnarly feeling deep in her stomach. She thought about using her magic and taking flight to see how far away from Laughing Bear's camp she was. But this took great concentration and much energy, too much energy to use now. It was also getting harder and harder to shape shift back to human form, so she only used it when necessary.

In the beginning, it had been hard for Raven to change into her bird form. But Silent Wolf had helped her master the art of shape shifting. As she grew, so did her magic. Shape shifting came easier then. It almost felt like she was meant to stay in bird form, where flying was the greatest magic. Everything was so clear, and with her sight she could see far and would one day cast fear upon those who sought to use magic for evil. The invisibility cloaking was harder to master but she was getting there.

But Raven knew one day she would not return from flight. She would stay just like that. A bird. A beautiful, powerful black bird. A raven with the magic to foresee the unknown and bring messages of hope and new beginnings to her people. When that time came, she would accept her fate, shape shift for the last time, leaving behind this human form and the people she had grown to love. But for now, her magic was needed; her people depended on it. Her human form would have to wait before coming to its lovely end. How she longed to soar on the thermal updrafts once again, feel the coolness of the air beneath her feathers, the warmth of the summer sun on her wings and fly totally free, away from all the worries and wants of humankind.

Laughing Bear

Raven sat quietly in the warmth of the autumn sun, appreciating the fact that she wasn't training for a change. However, she was keen to continue on and reach Laughing Bear's camp.

'Come on, Crow. Time to go.'

He looked up at her with his knowing eyes and ambled over to where she was sitting. Crow nudged her on the top of her head with his wet nose, and the smell of freshly cut grass filled her own nostrils.

'I think you've had enough, hey?'

He snorted as if to agree with her, and she chuckled at his approval. They headed out of the clearing and back into the thick of the forest, following a winding track through the pines that surrounded her on all sides. Large tree trunk roots had made their own path pushing their way to the surface of the forest floor. They were so beautifully gnarled and twisted together, with some parts covered in a thick blanket of green moss. Fungi pushed its way up out of the darkness of fallen logs and grew in little patches, and beautiful giant tree ferns adorned the undergrowth.

Clusters of petite ferns littered the pathway, rendering this enchanting section of the forest the epitome of magical charm.

In anticipation of the impending leaf-fall that would soon blanket the forest floor, she decided to revel in the lush greens and vivid hues of the foliage and flowers that currently adorned the enchanting woodland surroundings. Raven caught sight of a cluster of sapphire blue mushrooms nestled in a decaying section of a fallen tree off the beaten path. Recognising these as a rare discovery, she dismounted from Crow's back and gathered a generous handful. These prized mushrooms played a vital role in their sacred dreaming rituals. With stems and caps emitting a brilliant iridescent blue glow, they stood out vividly against the diverse colours of the forest. Upon plucking, the stem transitioned to a deeper, more sombre blue-black hue, serving as the distinguishing factor between the coveted dreaming mushroom and a common toadstool.

Effortlessly mounting Crow's back, Raven pressed on, feeling a sense of relief that their journey was nearing its end. After six days of travel, marked by the passing sun, Silent Wolf had assured her that once they traversed the expansive, thick forest, Laughing Bear's village would be within reach by nightfall. Spotting a familiar landmark, Raven's eyes fell upon the towering giant redwoods ahead.

'We're almost there, Crow. Just a little further,' Raven encouraged as Crow quickened his pace, eager to reach their destination as well. At the end of the lengthy pathway, beams of light filtered through the trees, illuminating the way. Towering pines flanked the track like ancient sentinels guarding the entrance to the village. Emerging from the forest, a gentle breeze brushed across Raven's face, carrying with it a familiar scent that instantly caught her attention. Otter!

Crow broke into a trot as they made their grand entrance into the camp. It was alive and bustling with activity.

In the midst of the camp, two courageous young men let out a powerful cry, signalling a call to alert their fellow tribespeople. These adolescent males, known as braves, bore this title until they came of age at sixteen. Upon successfully completing their rites of passage, demonstrating courage and strength, they were initiated into manhood and revered as warriors among their people.

They now sprinted alongside Raven and Crow, whooping and brandishing their spears high above their heads. Raven felt immense joy in the company of her extended Iroquois kin. During special gatherings, they would convene and partake in ceremonies, often coinciding with the solstices. These occasions were marked by feasting, singing and spirited dancing around roaring campfires, where stories were shared and dreaming rituals were conducted to guide the young braves through their rites of passage. Raven eagerly anticipated learning about their initiation, as it had been a while since she last witnessed such a significant event.

Among the various initiation tasks, Raven particularly enjoyed the quail egg challenge. Each young brave was entrusted with a delicate quail egg, and the objective was to navigate through treacherous mountain terrain while safeguarding the egg from breaking. Early on, the braves realised that the safest place to store the fragile egg was in their mouths. As the group of aspiring warriors embarked on the challenge, they had to showcase great skill and cunning to succeed.

In their race to the mountaintop, where they were to retrieve a rabbit tail and return to camp with the egg intact, the braves engaged in a strategic game of outsmarting one another. Speed was advantageous, as the fastest runner could gain a significant lead and even set up surprises for competitors along the trail. Some resorted to knocking or tripping their rivals, hoping to eliminate them from the challenge. However, such manoeuvres often led to the unfortunate outcome of the egg breaking upon the fall.

The ultimate victor of the task was the first brave to reach the mountaintop, secure a rabbit tail, and return to camp with the quail egg unscathed. This demanding trial required not only swift feet but also sharp wit and keen observation skills from the participants. Raven surveyed the lively camp, her gaze flickering in search of Silent Wolf. Yet, he remained elusive, nowhere in sight. Undoubtedly, he would appear as arranged.

Riding through the bustling camp, they made their way past numerous teepees and flickering campfires, their destination set on the central longhouse. Brining her mount to a stop, Otter's eyes locked with Raven's, his captivating smile enhancing his rugged features. His deep brown eyes studied her as he took hold of Crow's reigns, gently patting the horse's nose.

'Hello, boy,' he greeted tenderly. 'You've arrived swiftly, Raven,' he complimented, guiding Crow towards a clearing close to the lodge. Assisting her in dismounting, he then directed her towards the spread of food and drink he had arranged beforehand. Taking her hand, Otter led her to a glowing fire.

Standing before the flickering flames, she rubbed her hands together to chase away the chill.

Raven was captivated by the bustling activity of the clan members around her. Anticipation of the evening's feast gripped her, heightened by the tantalising aromas drifting through the camp. Suddenly, her uncle Laughing Bear approached, renowned for his enveloping bear hugs. His muscular arms effortlessly encircled her petite form, delivering a tender yet strong embrace before gently releasing her. His deep, commanding voice reverberated as he addressed her, 'We are delighted to have you here, Raven. It has been far too long. The sweat lodge is ready as instructed by Silent Wolf.' He cast a searching gaze around, half expecting to spot her mentor in the vicinity.

Laughing Bear cut an imposing figure with his sturdy build and towering height, commanding attention with his broad shoulders and powerful presence. As the esteemed chieftain of the clan, he exuded a sense of authority and strength, yet his leadership was tempered by fairness and a deep sense of justice. Known for his unwavering dedication to his people, Laughing Bear made it a point to attentively listen to their concerns and perspectives before making any decisions that would impact their well-being. This approach endeared him to the clan, fostering a strong sense of trust and respect among its members. To Raven, his resemblance to her late father, Silver Oak, was striking, evoking a sense of nostalgia and comfort in his familiar demeanour.

While Raven was filled with joy upon her arrival, a hint of apprehension lingered in her heart regarding the upcoming dreaming ceremony scheduled for that night. Otter, ever perceptive, noticed the subtle signs of her unease. Without hesitation, he approached her and gently clasped her hand in his own. The touch bought a sense of comfort and security as his large, powerful hand cradled hers with ease.

'Come, Raven. Crow will be well cared for,' Otter assured her, sensing her reluctance to leave her horse behind. With a beckoning gesture, he caught the attention of a nearby young lad and signalled for him to approach. A spirited boy, eager to please, hurried over in response to Otter's call.

Otter instructed the boy to lead Crow to the shelter where the other horses were kept, and ensure he had water. The boy grinned, clearly pleased with the responsibility entrusted to him. As he attempted to guide Crow away, the horse stood resolute, refusing to move despite the boy's repeated tugs on the reigns. Undeterred, the boy resorted to a more assertive approach, raising his voice in a failed attempt to coax Crow into motion. Otter and Raven observed the scene with amusement, struggling to stifle their laughter at the comical sight. Despite the boy's persistence, Crow remained unmoved.

With a puzzled expression, the boy paused to assess the situation, his flushed face betraying his confusion. After a moment of contemplation, he gently rubbed Crow's nose and spoke soothingly to the horse. Gradually, Crow's demeanour softened, his eyes growing weary and relaxed. Siezing the opportunity, the determined young lad made another attempt at leading Crow away. With a gentle tug on the reigns and a soft click of his tongue, he tried to encourage Crow to move. However, the horse remained steadfast, his powerful legs rooted to the ground, unmoved by the boy's efforts.

Raven and Otter burst into laughter, unable to contain their amusement at the scene unfolding before them. Sensing their mirth, the boy turned to them, realisation dawning that he had unwittingly become the subject of a playful prank. Taking the revelation in good humour, he joined in the laughter, his good-natured response earning a smile from Raven who decided to give the boy a hand, and she gestured for Crow to accompany the boy.

'Good boy, Crow,' she said to him, reassuring him to go.

He turned and ambled away, looking back over his flank at her as he reluctantly left.

Otter draped his arm around Raven's shoulders, guiding her gently towards his teepee. By the flickering light of a small campfire, a cast iron pot hung, its contents simmering and sending forth a tantalising aroma. Raven's keen senses immediately caught the scent of a fragrant blend of mint and sage wafting through the air.

With a thoughtful gesture, Otter filled a bone cup with the bubbling concoction, its warmth seeping into Raven's hands as she cradled the vessel. She closed her eyes and inhaled deeply, letting the aromatic steam envelop her senses. The sweet fragrance of honeysuckle danced through her nostrils, carrying with it a sense of comfort and familiarity.

As Raven sipped the brew, its soothing warmth spread through her, bringing a sense of peace and contentment to her soul. The simple act of sharing this moment with Otter in the quiet of night created a feeling within her that transcended words. After satisfying her hunger and regaling Otter with tales of her six-day journey, he led her to his teepee. Gesturing for her to enter, he lifted the flap to reveal a meticulously arranged and tidy interior. Several buffalo hides were spread out on the ground, serving as comfortable bedding.

In one corner, his hunting gear was propped up, including a spear, bow and arrows, and a collection of knives. The spear stood out with its intricate adornment of rabbit fur, beads, leather and a feather from Raven. In the dim candlelight, the spear shimmered with a subtle blue-black hue, casting a captivating sheen throughout the space.

'Rest here, Raven,' Otter said softly, gesturing for her to recline on the luxuriously soft and warm fur. As she settled in, she gazed up at the apex of the teepee, taking in the intricate patterns and shadows created by the flickering candlelight.

Otter draped another fur over her, tucking her in with care, before leaning in to plant a tender kiss on her forehead. 'I'll return once everything is prepared,' he murmured before rising to his feet and stepping out of the teepee. With a graceful motion, he closed the flap behind him, leaving Raven to bask in the tranquil ambience of the toasty shelter.

Raven looked around the orderly space before closing her eyes. She took a deep breath, smelling Otter all around her. His familiar scent made her feel safe. Burying her face in the covers, she drifted off into dreamland, ready to take flight once again. It didn't take long before she realised she was flying through the same darkness once again, calling and calling to her kin. Why wouldn't anyone answer? She couldn't see far ahead as it was so black there.

'Silent Wolf!' she called out in her tongue, to no answer. 'Otter! Where are you?' There was only silence.

Fear took hold and she tried to cry out, but it was no use. She had no voice; no sound escaped her throat. She started to fall.

'No!' she cried out. 'Not yet.'

But it was too late. She was descending fast. She was awake. It had been the same dream, again. Tears rolled down her cheeks and she wondered if her fears were a premonition of what was to come.

All three would soon go into a dreaming ceremony, where she would meet Silent Wolf and Otter in spirit. Raven knew she had to be careful as it was easy to lose herself in the dream realm. The deeper she ventured, the more the shadows lurked, twisting into sinister forms that whispered of forgotten fears and twisted desires, beckoning her to lose herself in the labyrinth of darkness.

Silent Wolf had given Raven a very powerful and rare blue quartz crystal. He told her if she carried this stone, it would protect her from dark magic; however, she could use the crystal for healing also. She asked him how this was possible. He said it would all be revealed at the dreaming ritual with the guidance of the seer.

'Remember your teachings, Raven,' he'd said to her.

Now fully awake, she was listening intently to all the voices and bustling commotion going on outside.

Just as she was preparing to rise, the door flap of the teepee swung open, and Otter entered.

'Everything's ready, and Silent Wolf has arrived right on time for the feast,' he announced with a smile, his playful grin lighting up his face. He noticed the traces of tears on her cheeks, a silent testament to the depth of emotion her dreams stirred within her. Raven's powerful gift of shapeshifting, while extraordinary, also exacted a heavy toll on her both emotionally and physically. Lately, he had observed her growing more emotionally fragile, a trend that troubled him deeply.

'Another one of your dreams?' Otter inquired gently, his concern evident in his voice.

Raven simply nodded, her expression a mix of vulnerability and resolve. 'The same one. I just pray it's not a forewarning of what's to come. If it is, I fear I may not have the strength to protect our people. What if the prophecy isn't right? What if I'm not the chosen one destined to guide our tribe through these trials?' She voiced her inner turmoil, her doubts laid bare in the flickering light of the teepee.

Raven had become all too familiar with this realm, where shadows coiled like serpents and whispers echoed like distant thunder, the unknown beckoning with a seductive yet chilling allure. Within the veil of darkness, where starlight dared not tread and silence reigned as a haunting melody, secrets slumbered and mysteries stirred, waiting to be unveiled by courageous hearts.

Otter gently cradled Raven's face in his hands, his gaze unwavering as he locked eyes with her.

'Silent Wolf's wisdom has never faltered, so trust in his guidance and have faith, just as we all have faith in you. I have no doubt that you will soar with unwavering precision and purpose,' he reassured her, his voice filled with conviction and support. With a gentle motion, he beckoned her to rise.

As she stood, Otter enveloped her in a tight embrace, a silent reassurance she needed. Raven grabbed a fur as they exited the inviting warmth of the teepee, stepping into the crisp evening air. The cool breeze sent a shiver down her spine, causing the hairs on the nape of her neck to prickle.

Anticipation filled her as she sensed the promise of a memorable night ahead, brimming with feasting, dancing, captivating storytelling, and the enchantment of magic woven into the fabric of the evening.

Saskia the Seer

Otter and Raven walked along the well-worn dirt track to the feasting lodge. The lodge's entrance was adorned with tall totems on each side leading into the hall. The totems were beautifully carved and the detail intricate, each animal representing the clan's identity and family history. Laughing Bear was carved at the top of one of the totems, where under an eagle he sat in the form of a huge black bear holding two cubs with a salmon in its jaws. Carved under that was the wolf, strong and stable for the clan.

The totem on the other side was just as magnificent with the raven at the top then the beaver, frog and killer whale at the bottom. The carvers of this clan were truly exceptional craftsmen. Each totem told a story about the clan's ancestors and was usually carved from mature red or yellow cedar trees. The stories may be myth, or legend, or they may be a story from the life of a person represented on the pole.

Raven strode into the rustic feasting lodge, her heart aflutter with anticipation and her senses tantalised by the rich aromas that enveloped the room. The tables, adorned with a lavish spread of succulent meats, earthy roots, plump berries, crunchy nuts, wholesome seeds, golden honey and verdant greens, presented a feast fit for royalty. Her keen eyes quickly alighted upon the delicate watercress and velvety smoked salmon, her absolute favourites among the bountiful offerings.

As the group was guided to their seats, Raven found herself positioned closest to Laughing Bear, the esteemed patriarch of the community, who presided regally at the head of the long, polished wooden table. By his side sat his elegant wife, Ash, her dark obsidian hair cascading down her back like a river of night. Tied into a braid, a single white owl feather adorned her hair. Her eyes, an unusual shade of green, shimmered like the surface of the lake at dawn. With an alluring sense of calm, she watches everything in her presence, missing no detail.

As per tradition, the young children and revered elderly members of the clan were accorded the honour of being served first, their well-being and comfort held in high regard by all. The diligent women, who had dedicated the better part of the week to meticulously preparing the feast, approached with a heaping plate of delectable offerings, ensuring the guests' plates were filled with care and generosity.

Raven eagerly accepted her portion, her appetite whetted by the tantalising scents wafting from the spread before her. With each bite, she indulged in a symphony of flavours, relishing every morsel as if it were a precious gift. It was a meal that surpassed all expectations, a culinary delight among the company of loved ones.

After everyone had eaten their fill, the braves, who were of age, were led out and into one of the ceremony tents to begin their ritual. They all walked off in single file looking very much like a line of solider ants. All quiet and nervous looking, they knew what lay ahead. When the clan saw them again, the braves would have passed their initiation, and the chosen ones would become warriors and would be considered men.

After the satisfying meal, the trio was guided out of the bustling feasting lodge and into a secluded sweat lodge, where the air was heavy with reverence and mysticism. Inside, Grey Hawk, the esteemed medicine man of the tribe, sat serenely, his presence exuding wisdom and ancient knowledge, patiently awaiting their arrival. In the centre of the lodge, a crackling fire danced with vitality, casting flickering shadows and bathing the space in a warm, comforting glow.

Upon the earthen floor, intricate symbols of the crescent moon were delicately etched using sacred corn pollen, each line imbued with spiritual significance and ancestral wisdom. Ancient protection symbols adorned the walls of the lodge, their presence serving as a shield against malevolent forces, ensuring a safe and sacred space for the ritual to unfold.

The aromatic scent of burning sage permeated the air, as bunches of tied sage sticks hung from the sturdy lodge frame, releasing a fragrant smoke that swirled and enveloped the participants in its cleansing embrace.

Alongside Grey Hawk, three venerable elder men occupied the northern section of the lodge. To the south, three elder women sat with grace and poise, embodying a profound sense of nurturing and intuition. At the centre of this gathering, Saskia the Seer commanded a position of reverence and authority, her aura suffused with a quiet power that seemed to emanate from the very depths of her being.

In the dim flicker of firelight, the elders' weathered faces danced with shadows, revealing the intricate map of their lived experiences etched in the deep crevasses and lines that adorned their visages. These elders, the custodians of the clan's collective memory and spiritual heritage, bore witness to the passage of time with stoic grace, embodying a connection to the ancient rhythms of the earth and sky.

With a solemn gesture, Grey Hawk beckoned Raven to take her place before Saskia, positioning her at the epicentre of the ceremonial circle. Beside her, Otter and Silent Wolf were guided to sit in silent contemplation before the third elder man, their presence a testament to the unity and balance of the sacred circle. At the head of the fire, Grey Hawk's piercing gaze locked onto Raven, his eyes reflecting a depth of knowledge and insight that seemed to transcend the physical realm, drawing her into a realm of spiritual communion and transformation.

In his outstretched hand, Grey Hawk held a beaded medicine pouch adorned with intricate symbols and potent designs, each bead shimmering in the firelight like a constellation of stars against the night sky. As the beads swayed gently, casting prismatic reflections across the walls of the lodge, a sense of ancient magic and profound significance filled the space.

Grey Hawk held Raven firmly in his gaze, his fierce birdlike eyes like a vice. He untied the suede strip that secured the pouch's opening, which was adorned with a speckled hawk feather. Soft down fell from the top of the feather, and it looked so delicate yet in perfect condition, like new. Perhaps he had obtained it especially for this ritual

All Grey Hawk's ceremonial gifts held a profound significance to him, each one considered sacred in his eyes. He approached these treasured items with great reverence and care, handling them with a gentle touch that reflected the deep respect he held for his cultural heritage and traditions.

Motioning to Raven, Grey Hawk held open the pouch. She knew just by looking into his piercing gaze that he wanted her to add the magic mushrooms to the mix. Raven untied her own medicine pouch and selected a good amount of the fungi, dropping it into his bag.

Grey Hawk then presented his bag to Otter and Silent Wolf, who reverently added a handful of carefully selected herbs to the collection. Together, they honoured the sacred tradition with each thoughtful contribution, symbolising their unity and respect for the ceremonial process.

Once again, Raven detected the smell of rosemary, a popular choice of herb amongst their people, as it contained powerful healing qualities. A very important herb to consider when going into a dreaming ritual. One of Raven's small feathers was then added to the mix. Grey Hawk held the bag over the fire and started singing an ancient tune. He made circular motions over the fire with the bag, and they all rocked in a circular motion along with Grey Hawk's motions as they felt the haunting melody enter their minds.

Grey Hawk picked up an old and rather worn looking badger bone that he used to grind and mix his brews. He then emptied the contents of the pouch into a wooden bowl, along with the mushrooms, herbs of many varieties, and what looked like bear and wolf claws. He added some native bee honey, a few blue poppy flowers and a few handfuls of big ripe berries were the last to be added to the bowl. The brew was then mixed while Grey Hawk continued his chant. The elder women and men joined in the song, increasing its power.

Grey Hawk meticulously removed the claws from the brew before directing the trio to each drink a portion of its contents. The concoction tasted sweet, infused with the flavours of honey and berries, yet a potent, unpleasant pungency from the mushrooms lingered on the palate, challenging their senses with each sip. Despite the unpleasant taste, they understood the significance of the ritual and bravely embraced the experience, uniting in spirit and purpose.

After they had drunk their fill, he painted symbols of the crescent moon on their foreheads and protection symbols on their cheeks with the remaining mix.

They were then all instructed to lie down on the buffalo rugs. Raven would be able to connect with Silent Wolf and Otter in the dreaming ritual, and she felt comfort knowing they would be there to help guide her if she needed. As the elders continued to sing their song, she felt herself slipping into her dream, her head feeling light and slightly dizzy.

Raven was about to go deeper than she had ever gone before with the protection of the elders' presence. Saskia, the oldest elder woman, held great wisdom and was able to look inside her soul. She was a guide and seer for the clan, and she spoke in a soothing voice. She seemed to know all about Raven, and would be able to warn her if she were to stray from her path. This seer could alert her to any mischievous intentions and could guide Raven on her quest.

They trio listened to her slow, calm voice and went deeper within their trance. Raven fully relaxed her body and let the dreaming take over.

It was fast! She had entered the dark void once more. Instantly feeling fear take her over, the elder woman spoke gently and guided Raven to fly high, higher than she had ever flown before. 'Don't be frightened. I am here with you. You are not alone.'

Raven flapped her wings and flew hard with all her might; she gained speed and felt the cold air ruffling through and around her feathers. Raven flew on and heard a loud roaring sound. Over the tremendous noise, she only just managed to hear the seer as she sang in a slow and melodious tone. Raven pushed through the fear that was gripping her and flew on, where she thought she could sense something evil close by. Raven scanned down below and then behind her with her sharp eyesight, but she couldn't see anything.

She flew higher and higher, listening to the repetitive chant. Something was definitely near, perhaps well-hidden whatever it was, as it was so very black where she was. Spinning with fear, it felt like something was trying to push inside her mind. Raven fought against the feeling with every fibre of her being. There was an unfamiliar smell, and she could taste a strong metallic taste in the air. What was this? It hurt her throat to breathe. She screamed, and a guttural cry was all that escaped her throat. Raven didn't recognise the sound as belonging to her. Was there something there, or was it just her fear taking over?

Pushing against the evil presence that she felt, Raven concentrated, listening to the elder woman's voice. Just as she was about to lose all hope, Silent Wolf and Otter called out, 'Raven we're here! Fly to us!'

She could just hear them, their voices sounding so far down below, whereas she had flown to great heights. Raven sensed something was gaining on her, even if she couldn't see it, and she was terrified now. The elder woman continued on with her chant, louder now, and the whole group chanted repetitively together. Raven could smell a strong, pungent scent in the air all around her, but she could not see far for she was flying into a thick blanket of mist, which seemed to appear all of a sudden.

She heard a deep, low roar, and the sound of beating wings, only this sound was much greater than the sound her wings made when she flapped them. Raven was truly scared now, and the only thing she could think to do in her panic was fly as fast as she could. She had been training for this, so she listened to her inner voice and the chanting of the elders. Their song was loud, and the seer was leading the song, her voice reaching a crescendo. The power resonated through the darkness and the mist that engulfed her. Instinct kicked in and she pulled her wings in tight to her body, plummeting fast and sure of her flight. She flew down below the darkness until she could see clouds, great big coloured clouds that took on shapes of sharp teeth and claws.

Raven closed her eyes tightly, keeping her wings close to her body, and flew through the clawing clouds, down to the lightness of the forest. The moon was shining brightly in the sky, and the forest floor was illuminated by its brightness. As Raven landed, she transformed back into her human form once more. Otter and Silent Wolf were there waiting for her, just like they had told her. Silent Wolf had a fur in his hands as he approached Raven. She remained crouched down and hunched over, shielding her cold, naked body as best she could. Silent Wolf wrapped the large fur around her body, and she felt instant warmth as the softness encased her. It felt luxurious against her cold skin.

Raven felt great relief at seeing them both. 'I didn't think I was going to find you here. I was so frightened.' Her voice felt dry and raspy from the pungent taste on the wind, and that scream she had let out wouldn't have helped her throat either. Otter put his arrow back into the pack on his back and slung the bow over his shoulder. Silent Wolf looked at Raven, his shaggy grey hair hanging around his face. As his eyes held her in his gaze, she felt safe.

Looking around, up and behind her, she said, 'What was that chasing me? Did either of you see?'

They all looked up into the black night sky.

'Silent Wolf, I know you must have seen that? Its shadow was enormous, and I've never seen anything like it before.' Raven hesitated for a moment, listening, worried that whatever it was would return. 'I sensed magic and a feeling of dread, a dark evil.' She looked into his eyes, searching his expression.

'The seer will have the answers you seek, Raven.' His voice was calm and reassuring, while the seer was still singing her slow chant. 'We can return now. The elder woman would have seen whatever that was and felt its intention. She will know how to further guide you on your journey.'

Silent Wolf rubbed his fingers on the crescent moon shape on her forehead, following the outline.

'I will be seeing you, Raven,' he said. 'Look for me when the moon is high, and I will be with you in the forest, never far from you.'

Raven looked over at Otter, who was staring at her with the same confident look he always gave. She felt in control right there and then with their trust in her, and she knew she had the power to overcome this dark magic. She just had to trust her intuition and follow the advice of the seer.

'Listen to the elder woman, Raven, and she will guide you and Otter back home.' At that, Silent Wolf crouched down, and as he leaped forward, he transformed into his wolf form, a menacing yet beautiful big grey wolf. With his different coloured eyes, he looked up into the moonlit night, put his head back and let out a low, guttural howl. Oh, how she loved to hear him howl.

He leaped away, his great grey body loping through the forest until he disappeared from sight. Otter and Raven took each other by the hand and listened to the elder woman's voice.

'Come. Follow my voice and come home now.'

They followed her voice for what seemed a long time, back through the winding darkness of their minds' eye. She felt no fear this time, as Otter was still holding her hand. Then all of a sudden, she was coming to. Raven opened her eyes and saw the elder woman who had been guiding them. The seer was crouched over Raven, gently wiping away the potion that was on her forehead with a damp cloth.

'There, there,' she crooned, and gestured for Raven to sit up.

Otter and Silent Wolf were also waking up, and an elder man had been sitting near them through their dreaming. He also wiped away the crescent moon from their foreheads, and when they sat up they all looked at each other.

The seer's words struck a chord within Raven as she sat by the crackling fire. 'Your strength is undeniable, Raven,' she began in a hushed tone, her gaze fixed upon the flickering flames.

'I have peered into the heart of this malevolent magic,' her voice carried a weight of ancient knowledge.

'This darkness, it is familiar to us,' the seer continued, her words weaving a tale of a returning menace that haunted the very essence of their lands. 'The witch, and those before her, have been a relentless predator of our realm. Ivy has resurfaced. Her sights are set on you now, wielding powers of old to shape her ominous intent into a fiendish creature.'

Despite the lingering effects of the potent dreaming potion, Raven focused intently on the seer's revelations, her anticipation for guidance palpable.

'In my visions, I delved into the depths of the creature's being. A dragon,' Saskia revealed, her words laden with a sense of urgency. 'This dragon is merely a puppet to the blood witch's will, a sorceress whose unparalleled darkness now wanes and weakens with the passage of time's intricate web.'

In that moment, Raven comprehended the meaning behind her tormenting dreams. She nodded in understanding as Saskia's words transformed her fears into clarity and resolve.

'The witch, a cunning trickster draped in black magic, may deceive with her wiles, but do not succumb to her illusions, Raven. Prepare yourself for profound sacrifices. Your journey will lead you through the winding paths of the Zaltana Mountains, where you must bury your fears in the depths of the earth to shield your mind from the witch, Ivy's, taint.'

The mere mention of the blood witch and her draconic ally sent a chill coursing down Raven's spine.

'It will be tough, possibly one of the toughest challenges you will face. But it's here, Raven, that you will find the magic you require. Dig deep, you have yet to unlock all of your powers.' Saskia gazed intently into Raven's eyes, as though delving into the depths of her soul. A broad smile illuminated her kind face, brimming with encouragement and belief in Raven's untapped potential.

Raven's mouth fell open, a flicker of astonishment crossing her features. Saskia delicately lifted Raven's chin with two fingers, gently closing her agape mouth.

'Fear, my dear Raven, is the true adversary that threatens to consume your very essence,' Saskia imparted solemnly. 'Guard against its insidious grasp.'

'So, I have more powers? Do you see what they are?' Raven inquired with great curiosity, her eyes reflecting a mix of wonder and anticipation.

'I don't see what they are, little feather, only that you harbour an untapped power waiting to be unleashed,' Saskia spoke gently, placing her hand over her heart as she conveyed her belief.

With a tinge of hope in her voice, Raven enquired, 'I had hoped that Otter and Silent Wolf would accompany me on this journey?' Her expression beseeched the seer for reassurance, seeking solace in the wise woman's gaze.

'Indeed, Raven,' Saskia affirmed, her eyes kind yet resolute. 'The unity of your trio shall stand as an intimidating bastion against the old witch and her dark enchantments.'

The elder woman took Raven's face in her hands and looked deeply into her eyes. 'All will be as it should be.'

Raven felt so many emotions right there and then: fear, sadness, anger. Yes, that was it, anger most of all. She wanted to fly away and scream at the top of her lungs, 'Why? Why me! Why did I have to be born a shapeshifting *bird*! It's not fair.'

Raven swallowed hard and bit down on her lip, trying to contain her anger. She stared at the fire. She had just spent the last eight years training and learning how to harness her inner strength and magic to fulfil the prophecy. She would not be outsmarted by some old hag and her ridiculous dragon.

Raven sat tall, her voice firm and unwavering. 'I am Raven Shi-koba, the daughter of Little Wing and Silver Oak, carrying with me the ancient legacy of Mohawk magic. I refuse to cower before an old witch and her twisted incantations. No matter how desperately she tries to strip me of my power, she will ultimately fail. Of this, I am certain.'

Saskia's weathered face lit up with a smile, the lines of wisdom and experience etched into her features deepening as her lips stretched into a grin. She was heartened by Raven's resolute confidence and determination. Raven nodded, a newfound sense of purpose settling within her. She listened attentively to the elder woman, determined to uphold her strength as she had been taught. With the revelation of her latent power, Raven felt confident that her magic was strong enough to overcome Ivy. The knowledge of this additional power within her only fuelled her determination and resolve.

As Saskia gazed into the flickering flames of the fire, she cautioned Raven with a solemn tone. 'Beware the witch's noxious garden, for Ivy patiently awaits the blooming of her deadliest creation yet. Under the eerie glow of a blood moon, the devil's horn will unfurl its lethal petals. It only blooms once every decade, ensuring Ivy will be vigilant in harvesting its potent and deadly essence.

'You must destroy her garden and all of her noxious plants. She must not be allowed to wield its poison. I sense a shroud of darkness looming on the horizon,' Saskia's words trailed off, her expression grave and filled with foreboding.

Raven simply nodded with unwavering determination and acceptance. She knew she could do this; she would do this. Ivy would not dictate her fate nor the destiny of her people. With resolve burning in her heart, Raven was ready to confront the looming darkness and protect all that she held dear.

Removing her medicine bag from her waist, she opened it. The iridescent blue crystal shone with a beautiful blue light, and its illuminating glow covered her face and clothing in blue. She felt right there and then that this mission would be the most important thing that she would have to do in her life. Otter and Silent Wolf would go with her and would be there if she needed them, she reassured herself. They were both great warriors, so she knew she had the best chance at defeating the witch with them assisting her.

Raven looked at Otter and Silent Wolf, their faces also blue from the light of the crystal.

Otter smiled at her with his reassuring grin, having been quietly listening the whole time but not speaking so much as a whisper. Raven looked at the seer. Her face was glowing with blue lines, and her white hair was shining blue. She was as beautiful as she was wise and took Raven's face in her hands to kiss her on the forehead.

With that, the elder woman and Silent Wolf rose from their places and departed the sweat lodge. The fire had dwindled to smouldering embers, casting a dim glow in the quiet space.

Grey Hawk, with his penetrating gaze, gestured for Raven to stand. Otter rose alongside her, and Grey Hawk held open the flap of the lodge for them to exit.

They made their way back to Otter's camp, their bodies weary from the intense ritual.

'I'm heading to the warmth of my blankets,' Raven announced.

Otter, looking just as exhausted, nodded in agreement.

They slipped into the comforting embrace of their warm furs, covering themselves with only their faces exposed to the cool night air.

As the distant sounds of drumming and singing filled the background, Raven felt the weight of sleep descending upon her. For once, her mind was free from dreams as she succumbed to a peaceful slumber, wrapped in the tranquillity of the night.

Kasa 'Dressed in Furs'

Raven woke to the smell of a campfire burning and rolled over to look at where Otter slept. He had already risen before her, and she could hear him pottering around outside by the fire. She pushed off her fur, rubbed the sleep dust from her eyes, stretched her arms up high above her head and yawned. Otter opened the flap of his teepee and smiled his beautiful wide smile at her.

'Come on, sleepy head,' he laughed. 'I have a hot drink and some fresh smoked salmon for you when you're ready. When you can drag yourself out of those furs, that is.' His beautiful big grin showed off his perfect white teeth.

'I'm coming.' Raven got up and went out to the warmth of the fire, where the food was a welcoming sight and tasted even better. Otter had smoked the salmon and covered the fish with a lovely paste of herbs and honey. Manuka wood chips made a lovely smoky taste, and this was her favourite fish apart from trout, which her father used to catch when she was young.

They quickly ate, cleaned up and prepared to leave the camp, Raven fed and watered the horses. Silent Wolf had already left and advised Otter that he would meet up with them later in the day and to just follow the forest trail south.

Raven stared to the south, there they were, the Zaltana Mountains. They loomed in the distance like great ancient giants, their peaks shrouded in mist. The jagged silhouettes of the mountains cut a dark and ominous figure, their sheer cliffs and deep valleys hinting at the untold secrets hidden within their rocky embrace. A sense of foreboding washed over the land as the mountains stood sentinel, silent and unyielding, their presence a constant reminder of the power and majesty of the natural world.

They were busy securing their loads and checking that they had everything they needed when Laughing Bear and his wife Ashwiyaa, or Ash as she was called, appeared.

Ash smiled at Raven. 'It's so good to see you, Raven. I looked for you last night at the festival, but I understood when I didn't see you. It was explained to me that your ritual took a great toll on you physically.' She paused for a second, searching Raven's face. 'Did you find out what you seek?' she asked.

Raven was in awe of her, Ash's strong face was even more stunning than the last time she'd seen her. The warrioress seemed to grow more beautiful with age.

'Yes, the seer has given me much to think about, and I only hope I can do what needs to be done.'

She looked down at her feet to avoid Ash's eyes, as Raven didn't want the older woman to see the apprehension in her eyes.

Ash nodded. 'She has never given wrong council, to my knowledge, but I know this is a daunting mission for you. I see that you are almost ready to leave, but is there anything I can do to help?'

'We have everything under control, but your kind offer is truly appreciated,' Raven replied, her face radiant with her most confident smile, masking the uneasiness that gnawed at her insides like a hidden shadow.

Laughing Bear and Otter approached them, and Laughing Bear wrapped his giant bear arms around the three of them; they formed a circle and put their heads together.

Laughing Bear spoke a prayer, 'Great Spirit, hear me. Open your heart and help our friends on their journey. Let us all live in peace for as long as we all shall live.'

They stood together in silence for a minute, eyes closed and hearts full of gratitude and hope.

'Oh, Great Spirit, fill us with your love and light, give us the strength to understand and the eyes to see,' Raven said.

Otter approached the flickering flames and gently sprinkled a handful of dried herbs into the smouldering fire. As soon as the herbs made contact with the embers, they burst into a brilliant display of light and heat, releasing a rich and captivating aroma that enveloped them in a swirling cloud of fragrant smoke. He placed his palms up facing the sky, looked up and said, 'Great Father and Mother Spirit, help guide us and show us the correct path, watch over us and keep us from harm.'

Ash was holding a suede cloth, which she unwrapped and produced a large piece of tied sage stick. She held it up and showed it to Raven before wrapping it back up and placing the bundle in her hands. 'To keep away unwanted spirits,' she said.

'I look forward to us all meeting again soon and sharing a story around the great council fire,' Raven said, her voice filled with hope and a trace of uncertainty about the twists and turns her destiny might unfold before that cherished gathering.

Ash and Laughing Bear made a conscious effort to conceal their fears, striving to maintain a façade of positivity in the midst of the looming dangers surrounding Raven. Despite her best efforts, Ash found it challenging to mask the worry that grazed the depths of her emerald eyes. She fought back the tears threatening to spill over, determined to stay strong for their shared journey ahead.

Otter and Raven were all set. They had said their prayers and made their blessings to the Great Spirit, and had painted ancient protection symbols on both horses' rumps. Ochre had been used, and large circles were painted around their eyes to help them see better. The horses were dressed for battle and looked very fierce.

As they rode out of camp, several of the young braves, who had initiated to warriors the night before, rode out on their horses beside them. They were still painted and dressed up with their hunting gear, beaded breast plates adorning their proud, strong bodies. The warriors all had different war markings on their faces and horses, and they whooped and sang out war cries as they headed out for their first hunt alone. They were smiling and chanting, and it sounded as wonderful as they looked.

The new warriors waved goodbye as they veered off onto another track, so the fork in the trail was where they parted. Otter and Raven sat on horseback and watched them disappear into the dense forest. The air was cold and although the sun was dimly shining its way through the thick cloud, a light snow started to fall, which was unusually cold for autumn. Otter held out his hand to catch the very first snowflakes. The snowfall was only very light, but here it was, possibly soon to be a thick white blanket covering everything in sight.

'It has come early this season, so we had better make as much distance as we can before nightfall,' he said.

Raven nodded and pulled her soft fur hood up over her head. Her ears and cheeks felt the soft rabbit fur, and she thought of her mother, Little Wing.

They set off along the forest track heading south, following the winding pathway deeper and deeper into the forest. Raven loved listening to all the different sounds of the forest. It came alive as the morning light brightened, with numerous critters scampering about here and there, ducking in and out of the forest foliage. A little squirrel stuck its head out of a hole in a big redwood pine, its cheeks puffed out full and clearly stuffed with food. But it disappeared as quickly as it had appeared.

The snow was falling lightly, and soft white flakes fell around and on them; it really was such an amazing thing to watch, the very first snowflakes of the fall. The forest track was speckled with colour, and the snow that had lightly sprinkled the ground had all but melted already. The ferns and undergrowth were wet and shiny in the dappled sunlight that was flickering through the trees. It was a beautiful sight.

The horses ambled on, following the forest track. The snapping sound of branches breaking in the dense forest made Raven turn and look back. A red deer was looking back at her, and his big brown eyes met hers, then he stopped still like he was frozen. Maybe he thought if he didn't move, he wouldn't be seen. His large felt-covered antlers adorned his head like a giant crown, with ferns and strands of grass hanging off of them. As he stood there as still as a totem pole, he looked proud. What a majestic fellow.

Suddenly, he turned in the opposite direction, leaped with a single high jump and disappeared into the dense undergrowth. Otter and Raven continued and rode for a good part of the day, and all was quiet except for the sound of the horses thudding along the trail. Each hoof fall created a soft thud, punctuated by the occasional crunch of gravel and the gentle swish of loose dirt being displaced. As Raven listened to the rhythmic cadence of the horses' hooves resonating through the stillness of the forest, she felt herself gradually slipping into a trance-like state. The hypnotic melody of their steps seemed to weave a spell around her, drawing her deeper into a realm where time seemed to slow and the world around her faded into the background. Mesmerised by the harmonious symphony of nature and the gentle power of the horses in motion, she found herself lost in a moment of perfect peace and unity with the surrounding wilderness. The earthy rhythm of hoofbeats became a lullaby, soothing her senses and transporting her to a place where the boundaries between rider and horse, human and nature, blurred into a seamless tapestry of existence.

It was so peaceful that Raven almost nodded off. Her head snapped up suddenly as she heard a branch breaking to her left, the sound quickly bringing her back to reality.

Otter's urgent cry pierced the air, 'Look out, Raven!'

Her heart pounded in response to his warning, and before the full weight of his words could sink in, she was already leaping off Crow and seamlessly shapeshifting. A lethal arrow zipped past her, grazing her wing feather by a hair's breadth. With a grace born of instinct, Otter sprang into action, dismounting swiftly and returning fire with deadly precision, the air whistling as his arrows found their marks.

The war cries of the Mohican warriors reverberated through the forest, their painted faces and vibrant arrows a stark contrast to the shadows that cloaked Raven and Otter. As the skirmish unfolded, Otter's arrow found its target, a warrior's anguished cry rending the air before another charged at him, brandishing a spear with menacing intent. In a blur of motion, Otter reloaded his bow and unleashed another arrow, felling his assailant in a swift, lethal dance.

Raven's honed skills came to the fore, her movements swift and purposeful as she streaked towards Otter, her invisibility cloak enveloping them both in a shroud of protection. The warrior's cries of confusion abruptly ceased as Otter seemingly vanished before their disbelieving eyes. Superstition gripped the remaining men, their fearful gazes darting through the shadows in search of the unseen spectre that had outwitted them.

A loan warrior, emboldened by bravado, ventured closer to Otter's concealed position, oblivious to the impending danger. In a flash of steel, Otter's hunting knife sliced across the warrior's throat in a decisive, lethal stroke. The warrior crumpled to the ground; his life extinguished in a heartbeat. Bewilderment and dread gripped the remaining warriors as they beheld the inexplicable demise of their comrade, their minds awash with whispered tales of dark forces at play in the heart of the forest.

Suddenly, as if emerging from a nightmare, Silent Wolf materialised, his massive Dire Wolf form bursting forth from the dense canopy above. With a thunderous impact, he descended on an assailant and drove him into the forest floor. In a swift, savage motion, Silent Wolf's powerful jaws clamped down on the warrior's exposed neck, delivering a fatal blow with unyielding force.

The scene unfolded in a blur of ferocity and precision as Silent Wolf unleashed his primal fury upon the unsuspecting war party. His attacks were swift, his movements instinctual, as he swiftly dispatched each foe with ruthless efficiency, leaving a trail of chaos and carnage in his wake. The remaining Mohican warriors stood frozen in terror, their painted faces a mask of horror as they witnessed the unstoppable force that had descended upon them.

Silent Wolf's dominance was absolute, his prowess undeniable as he made quick work of the hapless warriors who dared to challenge him. With a final, chilling howl that echoed through the trees, he stood amidst the fallen, a fearsome guardian, his primal instincts and unwavering ferocity marking him as a force to be reckoned with. He stood amidst the aftermath of his brutal symphony, a lone sentinel in a sea of devastation, his once-grey coat now a tapestry of crimson hues as blood dripped from his shaggy fur.

Otter stood transfixed; his breath caught in his throat as he beheld the raw power that exuded from Silent Wolf. As the echoes of the battle faded into the forest's embrace, Raven swiftly shed her avian form, her human guise returning in a shimmer of magic. Sensing the chill of the aftermath, she reached for a thick fur skin, wrapping it around herself with a shiver, seeking solace in its protective warmth against the chill of the impending dusk.

Together they approached Silent Wolf, but before they could draw near, a primal rumble of sound pierced the air, reverberating through the clearing as Silent Wolf threw back his massive head, his jaws agape in a haunting howl that sent shivers down their spines.

In a breathtaking display of grace and power, Silent Wolf sprang high, his sinewy muscles coiled with latent energy as he leaped with agility, soaring above their heads with a feral elegance that defied gravity. His form silhouetted against the fading light, a spectral guardian retreating into the depths of the wilderness, leaving only the lingering echoes of his haunting cry.

Raven and Otter stood in the wake of his departure, their eyes wide with wonder and respect.

As they stood amidst the aftermath of the fierce battle, Raven's thoughts drifted to the mentor who had guided her on her path, his unparalleled strength and ferocity a revelation that had left her breathless. She had always known Silent Wolf to be mighty but witnessing his unleashed power had unveiled a new facet of his nature, one that commanded both respect and awe in equal measure.

The trio had stood united against the looming threat over Laughing Bear's village, this time. Nestled in the heart of the wilderness, its proximity to Lake Ontario making it a coveted prize in the eyes of their rivals.

The Mohicans, known for their fierce war parties and relentless pursuit of territory, had posed a recurring threat to the village, their ambitions fuelled by a desire for dominance and control.

In this fateful encounter, the warriors of the Mohican tribe had met their match, their plans thwarted by the unyielding determination and unwavering bravery of Silent Wolf, Raven and Otter.

Echoes of the battle still lingered in the air, a sombre reminder of the cost of their defiance, but amidst the fallen, a sense of triumph and relief washed over Raven and Otter, knowing that they had averted disaster and safeguarded the village from certain destruction.

As the last vestiges of daylight faded into the encroaching shadows of night, Raven and Otter shared a silent nod of understanding, their hearts heavy with the weight of the day's events. The threat may have been temporarily quelled, but they both knew that the spectre of war loomed on the horizon, a reminder of the ever-present dangers that lurked in the untamed wilderness.

'Where do you think he's gone?' Otter queried, as he quickly moved from warrior to warrior, collecting their weapons.

'He was covered in blood, so no doubt he's headed down to the lake. Can you imagine all that blood drying on his coat? Nasty,' she said, her lips pursed together in distaste.

'It'll be dark soon,' Otter remarked, looking back into the darkness of the looming forest. 'We should find a place to set up camp for the night, and fast. Maybe not here,' he added, looking at the carnage that lay before them.

They led the horses away, leaving the men where they lay, if more warriors came, they would see the bloodied mess, just as it had unfolded. Perhaps it would be enough to deter them from revenge, or maybe, it would be the fuel to light their fire. Either way, they stayed where they fell, a reminder of their defeat to all who followed in their wake.

No Man's Land

Quickly they found a place suitable to set up their shelter for the night. Two tall pines offered good cover and in no time they had a campfire burning while Otter had his tea boiling. Raven tended to the horses. The day had been mostly fine, as the snow had stopped falling early on in the morning and had since melted into the earth, leaving it slightly damp. The sun had been trying to push its way through the clouds all day.

Raven glanced over at Otter, and he was staring intently at her with a concerned look. 'Don't worry, he will be here soon. The night is only young,' he said, without even asking.

Otter knew she was worried that Silent Wolf hadn't returned yet. The young warrior and Raven held a special bond as they had been best friends since they were very young, and he had become her protector from the first day they had spoken to one another for the very first time.

When Raven was seven years old, the other girls in their camp didn't seem to like her very much. Silent Wolf and Raven were the only two in their clan who could shapeshift, and they were frightened of her magic, or so it was explained to Raven. She guessed they were jealous of her freedom, for Raven's teachings meant she was not in the group with the other children. She would instead spend her days one- on-one with Silent Wolf.

With the fire now burning nicely as she and Otter made camp, her belly full, Raven sipped on her tea and remembered her early days when she was just learning how to shapeshift. One day Raven had been sent out into the forest to collect herbs. Her mother had thought that it was high time she collected them on her own to help her learn which plant was which, and hopefully return without a basket full of weeds.

Raven had been busy investigating a bunch of what she thought was hemlock, but she wasn't quite sure as she was concentrating on the plant and not paying attention to her surroundings. Crouched down and staring intently at the plant, she fingered its leaves, which often helped her identify herbs from one another, especially if she couldn't detect the scent. Suddenly, she was surrounded by three girls from camp. Raven hadn't heard them come up behind her at all, and was quite taken by surprise.

Meda, the leader of this group, disliked Raven immensely. Raven could see the anger emanating from her, as her facial expressions said it all.

'Here she is,' Meda had said, with a seething tone. 'What are you doing, witch?'

The other two girls sniggered, their lips also curled up to show their hatred of her. Cheyenne usually just stood by behind Meda and didn't join in the taunting. Today, however, was not one of those oc-casions, and she joined in on the banter this time

Dakota, the third girl in the group, laughed and joined in on the ridicule. The three girls were the same age as Raven and inseparable at times, always together.

Before Raven even had time to get up from her crouched position, Meda grabbed her by the hair on top of her head and forcefully shoved Raven backwards, landing her in the pile of hemlock and squashing it flat.

'Get lost. Leave me alone,' Raven said.

'Or what, witch?' spat Meda. 'You think you're so special, don't you? Come on, why don't you use some of your special raven magic!' she screamed in her face. 'Or are you too much of a baby!'

Meda was so angry she was shaking with her rage. She was strong and quite scary if truth be told, even at that young age. The other girls followed her around like pack dogs. Raven couldn't understand why though, as she was nothing but a bully, tormenting those weaker than her.

From a very young age, Raven's mother had taught her that you never make fun of someone just because they may be different to you. 'We must learn to accept and love everyone as they are,' Little Wing would say.

Her mother would explain that a much better way to live was to help others if they needed it, especially the elderly and the not so fortunate. 'It's not unusual for people to fear what they don't understand,' she would reiterate to Raven, more times than she could remember.

'But I've never even used magic on them,' Raven had blurted out in anger. 'That's about to change though, don't you worry,' she'd added, spinning on her heal and marching out before shapeshifting and taking off at full speed, disappearing into the forest depths to cool off.

Raven had been sworn off using magic against her peers, and since her magic was only developing, and they were unsure of what her capabilities were, it seemed like a safer option for everyone, Raven included.

Looking into the hate that emanated from Meda's eyes, Raven held her growing temper and let the scene unfold.

Meda was shaking her fist in Raven's face, so she was waiting for the blow that was surely coming. Suddenly, there was a loud thud! Meda was hit, smack bang right on the back of the head with a fair-sized rock! She jumped back from Raven, spun around and yelled out, 'Owww!' while holding the back of her head and looking around her to see who had dealt the unexpected blow.

Looking down, she spied the rock. 'Who dared to throw that at me?' she fumed as she picked up the sizeable rock in front of her feet where it had landed.

Bringing her hand down from the back of her head, her eyes went dark with rage as she saw her hand was covered in a good amount of blood. She glared at Raven and spat, 'Was this you, witch?'

Raven just sat still, and smirked, happy that her tormentor was bleeding, and not by her hand, or magic.

The blood only enraged Meda more, and she turned again on Raven, bending over and grabbing her shirt and roughly dragging her onto her feet. 'You're going to pay, witch!' she seethed.

Meda brought her fist back and was about to strike Raven in the face, when thud! There was another whack to the back of her head. This time the force was harder, and even more blood gushed from her head. It was running down the back of her neck now and saturating her shirt. Meda almost fell over at this strike. She spun around, and all three girls backed away from Raven. They were searching the forest surrounds for the culprit, but not a sound could be heard.

Glaring at Cheyenne and Dakota, Meda spat vehemently, 'Get in there and see who it is!'

With that, they were off, running in the direction of the tree line bordering the forest. Meda continued staggering away from Raven, looking over her bloodied shoulder at her as she did. 'You'll keep, witch!'

And with that she turned and started to stagger in the opposite direction away from where Raven stood still in the same position. She listened and watched the forest for any movement or sound. Slowly and without sound, Raven's avenger appeared out of the shadows of the trees. Silent like a wolf, Otter approached her and held out his hand without even speaking to her. In his other hand he held his sling shot, and a bag was slung over his shoulder. He bent down and picked up the second rock that had hit its target and returned it to his bag.

Raven took Otter's outstretched hand, and he held hers for a second before he turned her around and brushed the dirt and leaves off her clothes.

'No harm done,' he said.

Raven felt ashamed for not defending herself, but she reasoned she had been just about to use her magic and simply disappear. No harm in vanishing, she'd thought, but then the young brave appeared. She knew she was different – okay, very different, but it didn't warrant that kind of treatment!

The boy held out his hand again, 'I'm Otter,' he said, formally introducing himself, as they had never officially met one another.

'Raven,' she replied.

Taking his other strong hand, he encased hers ever so gently with his. 'I know who you are,' he said, looking deeply into her eyes.

Raven immediately felt shy, and a warm feeling flushed her cheeks. He was so handsome, even at the age of nine, and she looked down at her feet. She had often admired him, only from a distance though. His shiny, long dark hair was braided with silver beads and feathers. Honey-coloured skin, much like hers only darker from being out in the sun all summer long, glowed with a golden hue. He had shaved the hair on both sides of his head that summer, leaving a strip of noticeably longer hair in the centre, which was braided on both sides closest to his ears. It was a popular style amongst the braves who were considered the best hunters. He looked both fierce and handsome for his age.

'Do you want to join me, Raven? he asked. 'I can teach you how to use the sling and other weapons too if you like?'

'Well, I don't really need to use weapons, being that I have magic.' Raven replied. 'But it would be nice to take a break from collecting herbs.'

Raven looked back at the squashed hemlock and decided she had collected enough herbs for her mother. The rest of that day, and many more days to follow, Raven spent learning how to use the sling. She was terrible of course and would need a great deal of practice. But this marked the first day of their friendship, and from that day onwards, they spent many days together learning the art of hunting. When Raven wasn't being taught the art of shapeshifting with Silent Wolf or making herb concoctions with her mother, that was.

There was always so much to do around camp, but Raven would make sure she quickly finished all of her lessons and chores so she could join Otter. He taught her everything he knew about hunting and fighting. Otter was very patient with her and never seemed to get frustrated when she didn't repeatedly hit the target, but was always just so chilled in his manner.

'And again,' he would say, over and over.

After a time, Raven became pretty good with the weapons. It helped keep her fit and strong, which was also a bonus as it helped immensely with her flying. As the years progressed, Raven became stronger and faster, and as her shapeshifting skills grew, she could just transform and fly away from the girls. It annoyed Meda and her gang immensely, Raven being able to fly away at will. Raven would shapeshift and use her invisibility cloak from time to time and simply vanish right before their eyes, she would caw loudly and fly down pecking the tops of their heads. They learned quickly not to mess with Raven after that. It could have gone a lot worse as well for the camp bullies. Raven had been very lenient indeed.

In Raven's spare time, which wasn't much, only two days of the week to herself when she wasn't training with Silent Wolf, Otter also showed her how to cure a skin. She started on small animals, rabbits mostly, before moving onto deer and buffalo. It was rewarding work when they finally finished and had a beautiful fur to show off.

Raven would often tell Otter all about her teachings with Silent Wolf. He was enthralled and soaked up everything she told him. One day when Raven was thirteen, she decided to take a well-deserved break from training. They found a lovely spot beside a creek, and the sun was full in the sky. It was a warm summer's day, and the forest was alive with birdsong. As they sat on the creek's edge, their feet soaking in the cool water, Otter said, 'It must be such a wonderful feeling of freedom to be able to fly. I wish I could join you and fly away with you one day.'

'I wish you could come with me too,' Raven replied. 'You know there are tales about the Great Spirit granting special wishes upon those thought to be worthy of such magic. Hunters like you, Otter. If we are lucky and this is truly what is in your heart, it may be granted one day.'

Otter had said nothing in reply, just watched the water. They had sat in silence and listened to the creek and the forest critters rustling about. Raven had so many wonderful memories of their time together when they were young.

Bringing her out of her reverie was Silent Wolf stalking out of the trees and into sight. And what a sight he was. His huge muscular wolf body was remarkable. His eyes searched all around him before he crouched down and returned to his human form, quickly grabbing a fur and wrapping it around himself.

Raven jumped up from the campfire and embraced him. He smelled wet and musty. Silent Wolf sat down beside the fire and rubbed his hands together, warming them.

Without breaking his gaze away from the fire, he asked, 'Have you had anymore visions, Raven?'

'No,' she answered truthfully.

'They will come,' he said, as he slowly got up from the fire and scanned the forest with his sharp eyes. Then he rubbed both eyes with the balls of his fists and yawned. With that, Raven had the sudden urge to yawn as well.

Otter let out a laugh. 'Come on, you two ancient ones. Time to rest your weary bones, I think.'

As they all settled into the shelter for the night, Raven listened to their breathing for a while, until she drifted off into slumber. It was not long before she was dreaming, but it was different this time. This time she was not in the dark, but inside a great storm instead. It was so white; the snow was deep, and walking was slow and laborious. She could not see far in front of her for the wind and snow blew fiercely.

Raven stood quite still and listened around her for something other than the storm. She called out to Otter and Silent Wolf, but there was no reply. Hearing a screech, she looked above her to see a great owl sitting on a tree branch high above. It was staring down at her with large yellow eyes, and she knew that this owl was a messenger sent to help guide her through the storm.

Suddenly, Raven woke up and sat bolt upright. 'A storm is coming,' she cried.

Otter and Silent Wolf both sat up simultaneously.

'What, Raven?' asked Silent Wolf.

'I had a vision. We are going to come into a great storm, but an owl will show us the way. I think we will be separated as I couldn't find either of you two.'

'See, your visions are strong. They will help to keep you safe,' encouraged Silent Wolf, before lying back down again.

Otter nodded in agreement, but his eyes were clouded with worry. Raven laid back down and pulled her fur up around her, just her nose, eyes and forehead poked out. Her heart was still racing, so she took a few deep breaths to calm herself. She slipped back into sleep and slept deeply, with no more dreaming that night.

The Blood Witch

Deep in the heart of the Zaltana Mountains was the blood witch's fortress. Rarely was her name spoken aloud, for it was believed that speaking her name gave her, a necromancer, more power. She was feared far and wide for she was no ordinary witch but a blood witch. On the night of her birth, her mother and grandmother had brought her into the world under the glowing red light of a blood moon. Upon seeing the baby, they were elated with joy when seeing the dark red birth mark in the shape of a poison ivy leaf adorning the babe's cheek.

'Ivy,' her mother had bellowed proudly as she'd held the baby high above her. The baby's naked little body, still covered in blood, was bathed in the blood-red light from the moon, absorbing its power. Having been marked with the poison ivy leaf, she would be considered one of the most powerful blood witches of all time. She not only carried the blood-red ivy mark, but she had also been born into a long line of blood witches before her.

And so it came to be, just as the prophecy foretold. As she grew up, Ivy was well-schooled in the art of being a powerful blood witch. She gained a reputation over the years, living up to her name, for her nature was equally, if not nastier, than the poison ivy leaf that marked her. Ivy was a natural; conjuring spells and killing came easily for her, and her mother passed on all the wickedness that she could to her daughter.

Shrouded by ancient trees and mist, lay Ivy's fortress, a foreboding structure of dark stone and twisted iron. It was adorned with sinister symbols that seem to pulse with an eerie crimson glow, casting long shadows that danced in the moonlight, hinting at the forbidden secrets and powerful magic that resided within its hidden walls.

It was as if it was alive and breathing, spewing its stench out into the clean air around it and fouling the air with its poisons, with every puff that escaped its chimney. Around the back of her fortress, the old witch potted about in her garden, picking the deadliest flowers for her concoctions under the light of a full moon.

Ivy grew many deadly and potent flowers, which she used to make her dreaded spells with. Deadly nightshade, wolfsbane, hawkweed, hemlock, mugwort, nettle, thornapple, yew, rosemary, thyme and lavender. Her most prized poison amongst them though, grew alone in all its glory – the devil's horn – beautiful, yet deadly in its disguise. This rare and most precious flower only bloomed once every ten years in the dead of winter and under the glowing light of a blood moon. A magical blue light radiated from within its little petaled horns. Its sap was a thick blue-black pus, almost purple in colour and most deadly. Ivy patiently awaited its arrival.

Angel trumpet trees grew in several areas around her fortress, close to the edge of the woods, the pungent scent of their flowers blowing on the wind into her hut. The flowers ranged in colour from white to a rich apricot and deep-veined purples. The purple flowers were double- or triple-layered petals within the trumpets, most unique to the region, and they were as deadly as they were stunning. Ivy picked and used these toxic flowers in many of her incantations, and around her hut walls and on her work bench she painted binding symbols and runes with the potent paste she made. These symbols acted as protection for her and her familiars.

In the back of the fortress, Ivy had a large, old stone fireplace built into the wall. Its stones had been taken from the old ruins of the

Sacred Sisters Circle. These were ancient stones, chosen because of the magical properties that had once been cast upon them within their sacred temple, where they'd once stood, so many years ago. Now only fragments of the rock remained.

Witches from all over the world had claimed the pieces to keep in their sacrificial circles. Ivy's stone fireplace was well built. A long, thick cast iron plate sat on top above the stones. Its two heavy well-constructed doors of thick fireproof glass were encased in iron frames and locked securely with a heavy iron and wood handle. To one side of the top plate, she had a big black cauldron, suspended over it with cast iron rods upon which the cauldron hung.

With age weighing heavy upon her, Ivy, once a formidable visage, was now marked by time's relentless passage. She hungered for the vitality and untapped power of Raven's magic. Her eyes lit with a desperate longing as she schemed to siphon the girl's essence, seeking to rejuvenate her own form and reclaim the potent magic of her youth.

Hanging from the roof of her hut were many bones and feathers of various kinds that she had kept as decoration mostly, but also as a reminder of her kills. Human vertebrae hung from cords of sinew along with peacock feathers, their ocular eyes forever watching. To the right of the fire, pushed up against the stone wall, Ivy had her sturdy wooden table, where laid out were all sorts of potions, lotions, ointments and such things that a old witch might use. Crystals, twine, sinew and bloated eyes lay strewn about amongst other items on her untidy workbench. As much as the table was in disarray, she did have an order of sorts, with each chaotic pile of spell books, twisted herbs, and shimmering crystals holding a place known only to her, a mysterious arrangement that whispered of arcane knowledge and hidden power waiting to be unleashed.

Next to Ivy's magnificent workbench stood an old, gnarled oak tree, the fortress built around its ancient trunk, preserving its majestic presence within the heart of the structure. The roof gracefully curved around the tree's towering branches, leaving them exposed to the sky, a testament to the enduring power of nature amidst human creation.

The oak's knotted branches were cloaked in a lush blanket of dark green moss, adding an air of mystique and timelessness to its welcomed monstrosity, its twisted and tortured shape commanding reverence and awe in its grandeur.

At the top of the branches of the tree were two of Ivy's favourite familiars, her cat Luna, and snake Silas. Silas coiled his long bright yellow and white patterned body around the knotted branches, his smooth skin glistening in the candlelight, giving the appearance that he was wet. With his poor eyesight, he watched Ivy silently go about her business. Every now and then he would stick his forked tongue out and taste the air, searching for a scent. Luna sat above the serpent on the highest branch of the tree, observing all with her slitted green eyes. At night, her eyes became luminous great orbs, similar to the moon, and she had the ability to see into the future. Not much passed the cat without her seeing, and the feline would relish whispering in Ivy's ear of looming danger.

Luna was able to forecast the weather; when she scampered and cavorted, wind was on its way; when she washed her ears, rain was coming; when she sat with her back to the fire, they awaited frost and storms.

Ivy's most trusted familiar was an elegant feline of deepest obsidian, her coat devoid of any hint of white, a sleek embodiment of darkness and mystery. Her fur, black as midnight itself, was velvety soft and shimmered like liquid onyx under the enchanting glow of moonlit nights. Ever devoted to Ivy, Luna found solace in the witch's presence, eagerly awaiting the opportunity to join her on exhilarating flights astride the broomstick, their silhouettes dancing against the silvered sky.

A skilled huntress in her own right, Luna often accompanied Ivy on her forays into the wild, her keen senses honed to track and capture prey for their shared craft. With a silent grace, she would present her mistress with offerings of mice and rabbits, gifts of the hunt destined for Ivy's alchemical creations, further cementing their symbolic bond in the world of magic and nature.

Apart from Ivy's familiars, the witch lived alone, getting all the comfort she needed from them. This way, she was able to fully concentrate on her spells and bindings, which were versatile tools in her mystical arsenal. Serving her in weaving protective shields, calling upon dark spirits, unveiling the veils of the future, shaping reality itself, enforcing cosmic order and bringing forth the unseen into the realm of the known.

Ivy had waited a long time for Raven to come of age and for her powers to fully develop into the powerful magic that it now was. Killing her and stealing her power was going to be hard, but her conniving mother and grandmother had spent many moons casting and teaching her binding spells to prepare for the arrival of the devil's horn, the sacred flower that would soon be her greatest ally.

Ten years earlier, the flower had been destroyed, its powerful blue light diminished and lost to her. She seethed when she remembered the night, but it was best not to think of such things as the sadness was too great. Usually, blood witches like her did not weep, but she had wept that night. And she wept now, tears of blood dripping from her eyes. The pain was almost sweet, and she licked the blood from her gnarled fingers as she wiped it from her cheeks, tasting a strong combination of metal and salt.

In the distance, a night bird joined her, and they wailed a shrill cry, mourning the loss together. Ivy vowed to never make the same mistake twice and guarded her garden of poisons like her life depended on it. Well, it really did depend on it, for she now knew that Raven, in her dream, had escaped her greatest familiar creation, the dragon, so Ivy needed the powerful devil's horn more than ever.

Deep below the ground in a cold, dank cavern, she kept her creation: the dragon. She had created it from every dark and onerous spell she could summon. It was fashioned in the form of a great serpent, its head much larger, sharp teeth protruding from its maw. Its body was covered in large, thick scales, which would make it hard to penetrate, so it was the perfect armour. Its eyes were a deep blood-red colour that glowed like orbs in its skull. Ivy had made this beast as large as she possibly could, so his wing bones sat on broad shoulders that were supported by powerful muscles. He would need to be strong to fly great heights.

She had covered his neck and stomach with a jewelled breastplate, for both his protection and adornment, and his saliva was sticky and had adhesive properties. The large scales were pentagonal and shaped like teardrops, with two long sides and two shorter ones. He could make his scales stand on end whenever he liked, and preened over them often.

Ivy revelled in the manifestation of her creation, bestowing upon the fiery beast the name Valcor. She felt sheer and utter delight as she beheld his majestic form, finding him to be a breathtaking sight that stirred a deep sense of beauty within her. With sinister pleasure, she delighted in observing Valcor's menacing presence as he stalked Raven in the depths of her dreams, savouring each torment he inflicted before she eventually become the instrument of her capture.

After Dark

As she moved about her kitchen, Ivy's dress hung off her slight frame. Lard, dried blood and guts stained a good part of it, but it had once been very beautiful, handed down from her mother. It was made of black velvet and red lace, and the sleeves ballooned out. Sections of now-filthy lace bordered the cuffs and bottom of the dress, which was old and tattered just like her.

Ivy's hair was matted together underneath, and long dreadlocks now fell around her face, tied tightly. She had braided strands of coloured twine into the hair, which was also entwined with beads and gemstones of various colour. Bloodstone was one of her favourite stones, and she had collected many over the years, crystals too. Silver medallions that had been passed down from her great grandmother still shone brightly from her dishevelled hair.

Her eyes were black, like obsidian, and they had once shone brightly, but were now dimmed with age. Her eyesight was not so powerful anymore. Luckily for her, her familiars kept guard for her. On her head, she wore an old black and well-worn velvet hat; its tall peak stood stiff and was dull now with age. It was adorned with various dried poisonous flowers from her garden, along with other charms she had collected over the years: crystals, gems, bones, hair all twined together and stitched on with the sinew of animals she ate. Few parts of the animals she killed went to waste in her lair.

During solstices, Ivy would exchange her well-worn hat for a pair of huge stag horns that she had fashioned into a head dress. They gleamed under the moonlight, and coloured feathers hung from the horns, which she kept well-oiled with the fat she had rendered down from her kills.

Talismans hung from them and spilled down onto the sides of her face, acting like jewellery. She felt powerful when she wore this.

Ivy, a master of enchantments, wove numerous spells to conceal the true extent of her age, a veil of magic carefully crafted to mask the passage of time that had etched its marks upon her weathered visage. Despite her once formidable powers, even she could not bear to gaze upon her own reflection, her obsidian eyes reflecting a longing for the youthful façade she so meticulously maintained through her arcane arts.

Preserving a youthful appearance was not merely a vanity for Ivy, but a strategic necessity in the perilous world of magic, where appearances could deceive, and power dynamics often hinged on the perception of strength and vitality. Maintaining a façade of youth allowed her to command respect, instil fear and wield influence without the burden of age casting doubt upon her authority in the mystical realms she navigated.

In the corner, next to her bed, her trusty broom stood. It had served her well and she kept it in mint condition. Not only did the sacred stick hold powers that were bound from the magic of her ancestors, the magical energy that transported them partly came from an ointment, also thickly smeared over her body. This potent mixture contained the most potent herbs from her garden – monkshood, henbane, deadly nightshade, mandrake and hemlock – blended with other extracts in a base of lard, and the fat of her enemies. This was preferred as it held more power, and she was able to spirit herself across entire countries in the twinkling of an eye.

Ivy had led a mean and violent life in her prime. In her twenties and thirties, she often travelled in animal form for convenience. But it entailed risk to do so, as animals were vulnerable to the weapons of hunters and to the teeth and claws of stronger beasts, and she was never able to stay in animal form for very long either. This was a huge risk, for her magic would often wear off and she would find herself in the most obscure and dangerous position, narrowly avoiding death on many occasions.

The cruelty of the witch was seen nowhere as clearly as in the rugged islands off the Scottish Coast and in the Highlands, where the mountain winds moaned and wuthered all year long. In this bleak land, Ivy loved to hunt. The cries of wheeling curlews carried far, and the belling of stags in autumn echoed loudly across the slopes. The summers were short and unpredictable; the winters long and dark, just how Ivy preferred. She chose not to reside there and kept this land to hunt deer and the rugged men, who were born hardy and dour. Their hatred and fear of her was remarkable, and she returned the enmity in full measure

In her youth, Ivy revelled in the thrill of the hunt, cultivating a taste for the rich essence of European blood that fuelled her dark powers. However, as the years advanced and her once-potent magic began to wane, a palpable sense of fear crept into her heart, knowing that the hunters, relentless in their pursuit of the rumoured blood witch, were now actively scouring the lands, their eyes keen and their resolve unwavering in their quest to bring her to justice.

Ivy had grown tired and impatient at times as she aged, just waiting, for it had been a long wait. Sixteen years in fact. But the long wait was soon to be over. She knew that Raven's magic was indeed strong, and that she travelled in the company of a medicine man, who could also take the form of a wolf, and some other long-haired lad.

But she would soon deal with them with the help of Valcor. Ivy had been unable to control him during her last dreaming spell, but she wasn't entirely sure what had gone wrong on this occasion. Maybe she hadn't practiced enough with him; he was, after all, a very new creation, and she couldn't muster him to breathe fire in the dream so he had failed, allowing Raven to slip through his great claws.

Their next encounter, however, would be in the flesh, and the girl would not be so lucky next time around. Ivy threw back her long-matted dreadlocks from around her face and shoulders and let out a deep guttural cry at the thought of finally devouring Raven's blood and soul, absorbing her power and her shapeshifting magic.

Ivy longed to be able to shift at will and stay that way if she so desired. Her magic lacked this power, and although she could make deadly spells and cast fear upon those who looked into her obsidian eyes, she could not change herself for lengthy periods. Her spell and guise would soon wear off and she would once again be the old haggard woman.

Once Ivy devoured Raven and drank her blood, the witch would inherit her magic, making her the most powerful blood witch that had ever lived. She would finally be able to shapeshift at will and live an eternal life. Her age would disappear, and she would remain a beautiful, strong witch. Her wrinkled body would once again be youthful, and her hair would once again return to its former glory and be a thick lustrous black colour. But this time it would shine with the blue-black colour that Raven possessed. She intended to keep Raven's skull and add it alongside her other human skulls, a trophy of her greatest achievement.

She had seen Raven's fear through Valcor's eyes and felt her desperation lingering like a lost soul in the darkness that night. It was this fear that she was counting on to be Raven's downfall. Once she truly opened her eyes and saw the beast in all his devastating glory, the girl would be like wax in her hands. She would melt like molten liquid under his enormous power and feel the burning heat of his fire on her feathers, scorching her. Ivy laughed her evil laugh at the thought of snuffing out her existence.

Ivy would be busy this evening, for she had been conjuring a spell over her cauldron for many nights, adding poisons and festering items to its mix. This potion had to be strong, so she required the aid of her old spell book on this cold autumn evening. For many years she had spent reading its stained parchment pages. The deep red leather cover was inscribed with the same five-pointed star as her necklace. Around the edges of the cover, the same vines and leaves were etched that were also on the wooden box beneath her bench. She turned the pages of the spell book until she came to the Storm Demon spell. In one hand she held the spell book, in the other hand she held her silver amulet of the five-pointed star, which was tied with a thick braided black cord hanging around her neck.

Ivy rubbed the star between her fingers as she spoke the words of her spell. Staring intently at the pot of bubbling pus, yellow and green and putrid in its colour now, the potion slowly reduced in volume, thickening as it did. The bloodstone ring on the middle finger of her right hand flickered and shone flecks of a bright red colour in the firelight.

Ivy stirred her pot some more until she was happy with its viscous consistency, for she was conjuring one of her most powerful spells yet. She had sent her owl, Moonshadow, to spy upon Raven many times, and the owl had warned her that Raven was in fact heading towards her, accompanied by her trusted friends. *No bother*, thought the witch to herself. She would enjoy being her menacing self and bringing as much fear and desperation to the young girl as she could.

This game of cat and mouse she would eventually have to stop playing though, and then she would kill them all. Ivy would take immense joy in finally catching the girl, stripping the skin from her bones, and sucking the marrow from within. She smacked her lips together in anticipation of the flavour. She used to hunt on the humans that populated the surrounding forests once upon a time. It was, however, becoming increasingly dangerous for her to prey on them as they had populated the earth like rabbits. Once there were few; now there were many. The warriors, once oblivious to her presence or dismissive of the legends, now viewed her with suspicion and fear, banding together to protect their community from the perceived evil that loomed in their midst. Each hunt became a perilous gamble, with the warriors closing in and the stakes rising higher, threatening to unravel the fragile balance of power that Ivy had long held in the secluded wilderness.

The thought of the taste of human blood once again after so long absent from her diet sent shivers of pure delight down her spine. The soft regrown hair on the nape of her neck stood up amongst the goose bumps that presented themselves in excitement. Ivy rubbed at the back of her neck and flattened the hairs back down, wiping away beads of sweat as she did so. It was hot in her fortress now, and thick white vapours swirled in a circular cloud-shaped form above the cauldron.

'Ah yes, the storm is brewing nicely.'

Ivy made for one of her windows on the opposite side of her kitchen and pushed the heavy wooden frame open wide to allow some of the cool night air in. The vapours above the cauldron continued to swirl, and the cool night air mixed in with the cloud as it swirled faster now. The cloud grew and darkened as the brew below bubbled and boiled.

As she looked around her gardens and forest borders, Luna joined her and jumped up onto the windowsill. She too spied into the night with her large green eyes, her pupils fully dilated and on point. No movement stirred, all was cold and still.

'Right, let's get down to business then,' Ivy said as she patted her familiar. 'That's enough of this cold air! Let's see the clever little Raven escape this storm! I will plant the seed in her dreams tonight so she will think all will be well.'

And with that, as quickly as she opened the heavy window, she pulled it firmly shut and secured it with a solid steel latch. Returning to her fire and cauldron, she stirred the mix once more. The vapours continued to swirl above, and the brewing storm thickened and expanded considerably in size.

Luna returned once more to her post on the old tree branch, while Silas maintained his position, as though his lifeless body was stuffed. His eyes were pinned on the witch, and one would not be so foolish as to think him dead except for the fact that his tongue occasionally licked the air.

The spell was now complete.

Ivy closed her weary eyes and sleep came quickly for the old, worn-out blood witch. She would need to sleep well tonight, for this night she would invade Raven's dreams once again, only in the form of a friendly wise old owl this time. Very cunning indeed.

The Storm

Raven awoke early. Otter and Silent Wolf were still soundly asleep, and she could hear their deep breaths, almost in unison. Lying where she was for a little while, Raven listened to the morning forest as the cold wind rustled the trees around their shelter, the sound of an early winter fast approaching. Otter was still wrapped up tightly in his fur. Raven got up and crept quietly out into the fresh morning. The air was misty, and a dense fog hung in the air.

Crow looked up from his patch of grass at her and gave a soft neigh. Raven looked around the forest boundary of the clearing, which was all quiet. This was strange as usually the forest would be alive with birds greeting the dawn, but the only sound was the tall trees rubbing together in the wind. It sounded like they were speaking, and she listened to see if they were trying to tell her something, a message perhaps.

She got a fire going and pretty soon the crackling of the dry branches filled the morning air with smoke that was carried up and away into the treetops. Raven rubbed her frigid hands together in front of the fire to warm them before getting their meal underway. They had hung their food from a tree opposite the camp just in case of the odd bear that hadn't gone into hibernation yet, but nothing had bothered them or their food, which was a blessing.

Otter must have smelled the food cooking as he poked his head out of the shelter, still wrapped in his fur, and joined her. They ate in silence, listening for sounds in the forest.

'It's unusually quiet,' Raven said. 'We should hurry and pack up quickly. I fear it's the quiet before the storm, if my vision is correct, and I think a storm will soon be upon us.'

Otter gulped down his drink and nodded. They finished their food and hastened to pack up the supplies. Raven stomped on the remainders of the fire embers until all that remained was the scorched earth and blackened ash. Silent Wolf emerged from the shelter and looked around at the gusty wind.

Raven hurried and fed the horses before they raced to mount them and make their way out of the clearing.

Silent Wolf crouched down and leaped into his wolf form. He loped alongside as they quickened their pace as much as they could while pulling their heavy loads. The wind continued to pick up speed quickly and was gusting all around them now. The snow was falling heavier and faster as well, and together the combination of wind and snow made the visibility quite hard to see ahead. This storm had come upon them quicker than expected.

Raven shielded the weather from her face and held a cupped hand over the top of her eyes to try and see better. She squinted into the distance as they continued on, but it was getting almost impossible to see very far ahead at all.

The trio scanned the forest the best they could, looking for any cover that may offer shelter from the storm.

Suddenly there was a loud crack in the sky, like thunder only much more deafening. It cracked with such force that Crow reared up and Raven fell backwards, landing hard on the ground beneath her. Crow took off at great speed and disappeared out of sight into the blizzard, which was blowing and howling from all directions around them. Raven had never known Crow to be jittery or easily scared before, but then again, they had never been faced with a storm of that magnitude either. They were travelling into unknown territory as well.

Otter called out to her to stay put as he turned his horse Spirit around and took off after Crow, disappearing almost as quickly into a sheet of whiteness. Raven stood still, looking in dismay at the severity of the storm, the worst she had ever seen. Silent Wolf stared up at her before he scoured the surrounds, looking all around them for what may be coming.

'Go after them,' Raven shouted over the roaring wind.

Silent Wolf leaped off in the direction they had gone. Raven was now alone, and the wind continued to blow harder. The snow was coming in on an angle and felt like tiny needles piercing the skin that was exposed on her face and hands. She looked around trying to see anything other than the blanket of white around her. Hearing a screech above her, she glanced up, trying to see through the sheet-like snow that was hammering down. There above her a large, beautiful owl circled. She instantly knew that this was the owl she had seen in her dream the previous night, and it did seem like the owl was trying to communicate with her.

It screeched loudly as it flew above her, and Raven followed her instincts, which were to listen to her dream and follow the owl. Raven was sure it would lead her to safe shelter. The owl flew down low towards her, and if she had reached up high above her head, she could have touched it. As it flew ahead of her, Raven looked around and saw no sign of Otter or Silent Wolf, which was just as her dream had been. Raven was alone, so she decided to follow the owl. It circled a few times as it waited for her to catch up, and Raven ploughed through the thick snow as fast as she could.

The wind was howling and blowing her backwards, making each step challenging. Raven watched where the owl was flying and could faintly make out trees and a set of big rocks in the distance, which looked like a cave. There would be shelter there, she felt sure of it. The owl would lead her to safety, she had seen it, and her visions were rarely wrong. Just as Raven was about to continue on, she heard a loud screech from above. Squinting her eyes to protect them from the needles of snow, which felt like it was hitting from all directions now, she witnessed the owl falling from the sky with an arrow straight through it. Its piercing cry filled the sky above her, and the great bird plummeted down, landing on the snow not far from where she stood. Dead.

'Noooo!' Raven yelled above the screaming wind.

She tried to run over to the bird as fast as she could in the thick snow, but each step was so deep. Looking behind her, Raven saw Otter and Silent Wolf approaching with Crow. Otter had shot the owl, his arrow had met its mark, and it was swift, instant death for the bird. Almost as quickly as the storm had started, it stopped. They all stood there together looking at the great owl lying on the white snow, red blood splattered the ground where it fell.

'I can't believe it,' Raven said, full of sorrow. 'But I saw it in a dream that the owl saved us from the storm.'

'This was no ordinary storm,' Silent Wolf said. 'The witch tricked you, Raven. Saskia warned of her tricks, and this was one of them.'

'I believed it to be true. I feel so stupid!' she said.

Raven looked down at the poor owl that had lost its life and felt sorry for it. It was just an innocent pawn in the witch's game. It had been the most incredible looking large snowy owl, but its large yellow eyes were closed now. Raven bent down and rubbed its soft milky white feathers. She picked it up from the bloodied snow and held it in her hands, saying a prayer to help guide its journey to the spirit realm.

Otter came over and joined her, and Raven could tell that he didn't like having to do what he did, but Silent Wolf had told him of the witch's familiar and that it was doing her bidding. He pulled out his arrow from the blood-soaked bird and wiped it clean before returning it to the quiver slung over his shoulder.

'The witch is powerful, Raven. It's not your fault, as your dreams have always been your guide. I would have believed it too, had it been my vision,' Otter said, trying to make her feel better about the situation. 'The owl was just one of her tricks. But she is going to have to do better than that. Silent Wolf told me to shoot, or I would not have known.'

'Now that the storm had subsided somewhat, we should look for shelter to work out our next move,' Raven said, boiling with anger inside that the witch had so easily tricked her.

She walked over and took Crow's reigns, rubbing him on his nose and whispering to him. 'That was loud, huh! It's okay, boy,' she said, as she continued to rub him. 'We'll find a good spot to rest.' She pointed to their south, where there was heavy forest.

Raven mounted Crow, and Silent Wolf took him by the reigns this time and walked along beside them. They plodded on through the fallen snow, slowly and with caution, all on high alert now for they knew that the witch was aware of their position.

'We are going to have to put our heads together and think about our way forward if we are to outsmart the witch,' Silent Wolf said.

Raven looked at Otter, who nodded, and she agreed as well. As they continued deeper into the wooded forest, the snow dissipated and became less dense. The large pine trees growing closely together had sheltered the forest floor, so it was much easier to walk now. They found a light trail and followed it deeper into the mountains. Finally, the wind stopped blowing as fiercely. A light howling sound blew around them and rustled the treetops every now and then, almost like it was speaking to them, warning them to turn back. The snow had stopped falling for the time being.

They came to a quiet, secluded part of the woods. It was well sheltered, and they would be able to rest there and discuss their plan. They found a fairly dry spot to place a few furs down, and all sat closely together, listening intently before anyone dared to utter a word.

When Raven thought that it was safe to do so, she spoke. 'So how are we going to defeat this witch?' She didn't even like talking about her, as she was afraid of giving her more power than she already had. The seer had warned her to not speak her name for she grew more powerful this way.

Silent Wolf answered, his voice almost a whisper. 'She will have familiars that will assist her and warn her, and they will be hard to get past, but if we work together, we have a better chance at beating her. She won't be able to watch the three of us at once, and she will be distracted with you, Raven. Taking out her familiars first will be just as important as taking her down. She is powerful, but she is old, so hopefully we will have that to our advantage. Otter, you are the best shot with your bow and arrow. Raven, you will have to taunt the witch into chasing you, as she will not be able to resist when she sees you. If you lead her back to us, we will be waiting, and hopefully we will be able to take care of her, and her dragon.'

Otter nodded, no words needed.

'Well, I for one, won't be fooled so easily again,' Raven said. 'Obviously, I can't rely on my dreams anymore, she has made sure of that.'

'Just be aware that everything will not be not as it seems from here on in,' said Silent Wolf.

Raven nodded in acceptance and stilled her mind; it was racing with many different thoughts.

'Is it safe to make a small fire so we can brew a tea at least?' asked Otter.

Silent Wolf nodded, and they both got up and went about looking for dry sticks and pine needles to burn.

Raven sat still, legs crossed, eyes closed, focusing on quieting her mind, slowing her heartbeat, surrounding herself and their area with white light. She was going to have to do this nightly from now on to help shield them from the witch's spying eyes. When she opened her eyes and refocused her gaze, Otter and Silent Wolf had a small but well-lit fire going with minimal smoke, which was desirable now, as they had to be extra careful if they were to stay hidden.

It was only going to get harder from here, the deeper they went into the mountains. The night was getting dark quickly as they were already so deep in the forest, so the light disappeared fast. Otter quickly had one of his tea brews bubbling over the fire in a small metal pot, which was well worn and blackened from the flames. He passed them each a cup of steaming hot tea, and the mint and honey hit Raven's senses before the cup even reached her lips. Lovely, as per usual.

They all sat quietly sipping their drinks and listening to the forest for any sounds. The flames blew around the fire, changing direction with the wind. The warmth of the fire was welcoming, and they realised that they were going to have to stay there for the night.

'It will be dark soon,' Otter said.

'I'll take a look around and make sure no one has followed us,' said Silent Wolf. He got up and crouched down then leapt into the air and changed into a wolf. Taking big strides, he made his way along the track they had come in on. Suddenly, he veered off the track and headed up into the dense forest, following the ridge line until he disappeared out of sight.

'I'll get our shelter up for the night,' Otter said as he finished off his drink.

He got up and didn't waste any time unpacking their supplies and laying everything out on the ground. Raven got up and assisted him, and pretty soon they had their camp sorted, furs all warm and dry for the cold night that was soon to follow. Otter heated them some food and they were enjoying their meal, when no sooner had her mentor disappeared, he reappeared again. Silent Wolf's large body loped back into sight, his shaggy grey fur wet from the snow. He dropped a large snow hare down in front of the fire and shook the remaining water from his coat before he changed back into his human skin.

Silent Wolf picked up his fur and wrapped it around his wet body before he plonked himself down in front of the fire. 'I thought you might like fresh rabbit tonight,' he said, licking his lips and rubbing his face dry with his fur.

Otter snatched up the rabbit and took it over to a fallen log where he quickly skinned and gutted it. He returned with the meat and threw it into a pan over the fire. As soon as their meal was cooked and they were all warm again, they extinguished the fire as they didn't want to take the chance of being found. They were getting too close to risk it.

A distant owl called out in the night, and Raven lay listening with her sharp hearing. Apart from the hooting owl, all was quiet. For now...

Murder on the Mind

Meanwhile back in Ivy's fortress, she sat up and screamed out in pain, holding her chest as she felt the arrow piercing her feathered friend. Luna jumped up from her spot and came to Ivy's side, looking at her sorceress with worry for she could see that something was wrong.

Ivy threw back her covers and got out of bed before stomping her way over to the fire. In a rage, she opened her fireplace doors with force and threw small twigs onto the glowing embers, blowing into the base of the fire to reignite the flames once more. The dry sticks caught fire at once and started to burn, so she picked up her wooden spoon that was lying on the hearth of the fireplace and stirred the thick muck once more.

'Clever wolf,' she seethed.

Ivy had loved the owl; well, what she thought she knew as love, and she relied on the owl to spy for her. She knew not to use a crow again, because the humans had grown suspicious of crows. Now here on this very night, her beautiful Moonshadow had been killed. Once again, the pain was so great. She sobbed over the cauldron, and tears of blood dripped down into the sludge that now remained in the pot. Returning to her work bench, she found a few items to add to her potion.

'An eye of newt, poison ivy, yes, yes,' she muttered to herself. 'What else?'

She pushed aside bits and pieces that were of no use and dug deep into a toad-skin bag that lay at the rear of the table.

'Ah, yes,' she said, wiping the tears away with her fingers.

Licking her fingers clean from the blood that covered them, she dug out a small glass vial from the bag. The vial contained the saliva from her toads, and it would come in handy and keep her well hidden. Invisible for a time anyway, long enough to pierce the young hunter's heart, just like he had so cruelly done to her owl. She was going to need all the help she could get. Ivy had underestimated the wolf; he was going to be more of a problem than she first thought.

She placed the vial into her charm bag that was tied to her belt around her waist.

'This will do nicely.'

Luna joined Ivy and rubbed herself on her legs to show her approval.

'I'm going to head out and catch a feast for my winged friend. I want him strong and well fed for flying. Are you coming?' she asked.

Luna did not need to be asked twice. Ivy held out her hand and with a shrill, blood-curdling cry, called out her command. The broom shot up to attention and hovered in front of her. She leaped onto the broom with a single jump, Luna joining her and sitting in front of her, wrapping her long black tail around the broomstick in a vice-like grip.

Ivy issued a command once more, and with the wave of her hand the heavy front door was thrust open. They shot out at great speed and flew up high into the night sky. The chilly night air blew around them and whisked past their faces. Throwing back her head and sniffing the air, Ivy pushed down on her broom, and they started heading down towards the tops of the trees. Within no time at all, she had picked up the scent of a herd of deer. The frightened animals scampered to their feet as she flew overhead, then shot off in panic in all directions into the heavy woodlands.

However, the witch was swift, and she homed in on the biggest male stag, who due to his heavy antlers, was not as fast as the others in his escape. Ivy swooped down upon the unsuspecting animal and landed on his back, swiftly grabbing him by his large antlers and pulling his head back hard. She plunged her knife deep into his neck and slit his throat neatly from one side of his neck to the other with her razor-sharp knife. She had done this many times and was very skilled indeed.

The stag fell to his knees as he slid to the forest floor, leaving a trail of bloodied snow behind him. Ivy quickly tied the stag's legs together and secured the rope into a tight knot with the wave of her hand. The pair mounted the broom once more, and in the blink of an eye, they were back home. Her broom did all the arduous work as it brought the stag to Valcor's door. Ivy waved her hand again, and the stag dropped to the ground with a heavy thud. Valcor was quick to appear, his blood-red eyes glowing in the night. Opening his huge mouth, acid and salvia dripped from his jaws, and he spat a blot of hot fire onto the stag. The smell of burnt hair filled the air around them, Valcor picked up the smouldering heap of meat between his sharp teeth and threw it up into the air before catching it between its massive jaws, crunching bones and gulping it down.

He stood and looked at Ivy for a minute before turning and making his way back into the darkness of his cave. Ivy closed the heavy iron door behind him and secured it once again.

'Now,' she said, looking at Luna, 'let's sort out this murdering monster that travels with Raven. Nobody kills my familiars except for me!'

Luna shot her a look and cringed.

'Not you, my furry friend,' she said as she rubbed the top of Luna's head affectionately.

The familiar relaxed as she followed her back inside. With the wave of her hand, Ivy's candles burst into flame throughout as they entered, lighting the dark space. Ivy had a plan. She selected several jars and took out a good handful of some fresh dried flowers that littered her work bench.

'Yes, yes,' she muttered, 'fresh is best.' She selected the most poisonous flowers she had on hand for this evil concoction: angel's trumpet, nightshade and hemlock.

Adding the flowers to a wooden bowl, she grinded the contents to a fine powder, then added this to her cauldron. The mix was so strong now that the powder sizzled and hissed instantly, disintegrating into the yellow-green slop. She dug into one of her toad-skin bags and presented a vial of what looked like white sap. After adding this to her potion, her spell was almost complete. One last ingredient was all that was needed, and as she spoke her incantation over the bubbling pot, she took her razor-sharp knife that was tucked into her dress belt and neatly cut along the length of her palm. As the blood gushed, Ivy tightened her fist into a ball, so a decent amount of blood dropped into the cauldron. As it pooled on top of the mixture, she winced with the pain of the cut and uttered some words to bind the spell.'

Ivy continued to stir the contents of her poisonous brew until her blood was well mixed in. She retrieved her ladle and scooped out a vial-full of the nasty concoction. A thick consistency it was, perfectly potent. Shuffling over to the corner, where her spider, Eve, sat, spinning her web, she said, 'You are needed on this night, my fiendish friend.'

Eve came forward as Ivy held out the vial, looking up with her many eyes and opening her mouth, her sharp needle-like fangs exposed. Ivy poured several drops from the vial onto the spider's fangs, which looked like sharp little syringes sucking up the poison. She then held her two front hairy legs up and allowed a couple of drops to coat the hairs as well. Eve rubbed her legs over her hairy body before looking at the witch and awaiting her command.

'Broom,' Ivy called out in her husky voice, and the broom sped to her side. 'Eve will ride you tonight. Take her to Raven's camp, where she will be in the company of a nasty wolf. Beware this hairy creature for he is sneaky, but I am sure you are sneakier and will be undetected.

Poison the long-haired warrior who travels with her, and he will meet his demise.' She cackled at the thought of how sick he would become before his last breath was taken.

Eve instantly obeyed, and with a single leap, jumped onto the broom. With the wave of Ivy's hand and a few words, a finding spell was spoken, and the broom and the spider took off out into the cold winter night.

The Spider and the Toad

The broomstick flew silently high above the clouds in the night sky, keeping well hidden up so high. Eve hid amongst the bristles at the back of the broomstick, gripping her hairy legs around the bristles tightly. She flew into the night and arrived at her destination in the early hours of the morning, reaching the camp of the unsuspecting sleepers. As quietly as if it were not there at all the broomstick hovered over the shelter, allowing the spider to spin a long, thin web so she could lower herself onto the top of the shelter.

Eve scurried across the top and squeezed her way inside. She lurked there assessing the situation and watching with her many eyes. Seeing no movement as they were all deeply sleeping, she determined it was safe. Spinning another web, she lowered herself onto Otter's furs. Crawling over the furs ever so silently to his exposed face, she made her way onto Otter's face, one leg at a time, so as not to wake him. Eve rubbed her hairy leg over a spot on Otter's cheek, depositing a small amount of the poisonous sap to his face. This would act as an anaesthetic so he would not feel the sharp sting of her needle-like fangs.

Waiting a few seconds for the sap to do its job, she sank her fangs gently into Otter's face, spewing the poisonous venom deep into his cheek. Her work was done. As quickly and quietly as she came, she left, making her way back to her web that was floating gently in the air above Otter. Latching onto her hanging web, she raced up and out of the shelter. The broom was hovering, waiting for her return, and as soon as the spider crawled back safely into its bristles, it sped off into the frosty night once more.

They flew all morning before they arrived back home once again. With a tap on the door from the broom, Ivy waved her hand to open it. After flying in, they hovered in front of her. With another wave of her gnarled fingers, the heavy door slammed shut again.

'Success, I take it?' Raising her eyebrows, Ivy looked up at her spider as she crawled out of the broom's bristles. Eve stood up on her back legs, holding her two hairy front legs up in the air, a sign that all went as planned.

Ivy puffed on her pipe and scoffed a gruff laugh. 'Good work, my hairy little friend,' she said before the broom returned the spider to her web.

***

Raven woke to the unfamiliar sound of Otter's rapid and shallow breathing. Was he dreaming? Silent Wolf also woke up, and they sat up at the same time, both looking over at Otter. He was sweating heavily and had pushed his fur off. Raven and Silent Wolf immediately went to his side.

'What's happening to him?' Raven asked.

Silent Wolf looked closely at Otter's face. He could see a red mark where the spider had bitten him, so examined him closely. 'Otter,' Silent Wolf said, 'can you hear me?'

No reply.

Otter was shivering and started murmuring, making no sense with his words. He sounded delusional.

'He has been poisoned,' Silent Wolf determined. 'See the mark here on his cheek?'

It was indeed red and swollen in one spot.

'Poisoned,' Raven whispered. 'But how?'

'The witch is crafty, and she would be furious, no doubt at her owl's demise. I should have been more vigilant and been on watch last night. I don't know exactly how she did it, but she has somehow achieved her malintent.' Silent Wolf picked up Otter's furs and shook them. Nothing. 'She is as sneaky as she is deadly with her attacks. We must act quickly, or I fear he may not survive this. Hurry, we need to get his body heat down as he's burning up.'

Otter was sweating and shivering at the same time, shaking with each laboured breath. He did not look good. The colour was gone from his face, and he was pale and hot to the touch.

'I will try and suck the poison out,' Silent Wolf said, 'but I think it's already too late. Give me your knife, Raven.'

She quickly retrieved her knife from her pack, and Silent Wolf made a small nick across the bite mark on Otter's cheek, then squeezed around the cut. A yellowish-white pus oozed out of it, he kept squeezing and wiping until only blood ran freely from the wound.

'We will gather some river rocks and make a small fire to create steam. I can then add the sacred herbs to help break his fever.'

They worked as fast as they could, but they were a bit of a distance from the nearest river. Loading both horses with bags of rocks, they raced against time and got to work digging out a hole to place the fire in. On top of the fire, Silent Wolf found some fallen wet maple and pine tree branches. They were hardwood, so would be harder to burn, allowing the rocks to heat without the wood burning away. In a very short time, he had heated the rocks and took them into the shelter.

Otter's breathing continued to be laboured, and Raven was very concerned for her friend. He had been a part of her life for many years now, and she couldn't and didn't want to imagine what life would be like without him. She was grateful that Silent Wolf had taught her early in his teachings about the importance of herbs and their healing qualities.

'This is a time where the blue crystal will serve its purpose,' Silent Wolf said.

Raven presented him with the crystal he had first given her, its shining blue light emanating out of the bag as soon as it was opened. The sheer brilliance of the beautiful, radiant light alone filled her with hope that Otter would be saved. Silent Wolf picked up the crystal between his fingers and held it up towards the light. Looking through the crystal, he spoke healing words. Placing it on a rock, he took out a knife, and using the bone handle, he gently broke off a small piece of the crystal. He delicately ground the broken crystal piece between two rocks until it was a fine powder, then added the powder to his herb mix and rubbed a small amount into the now very red and angry-looking wound on Otter's cheek.

The rest of the mix he added to the hot rocks, which he then poured a small amount of water over. This created a beautiful bluish steam that quickly filled the small shelter. The herbs smelled lovely, and the luminescent light that shone brightly from the crystal was still present through the steam. They could feel the healing qualities it possessed as they breathed it in.

Raven held Otter's hand and prayed. Silent Wolf continued to stoke the fire and create steam, and for most of the day he stayed by Otter's side. Raven only left to bring Silent Wolf a drink, as the sweating effect also meant he lost a lot of fluid. Apart from Silent Wolf's low and melodic chanting, they did not speak, just focused all their attention on healing their friend.

It was late into the evening before they saw any change in Otter's breathing. His fever finally broke late that night, and he started coughing. It sounded wet, but that was the first sign that he was perhaps going to be okay. They sat him up and gave him small sips of water, but Otter started retching. Raven grabbed the pot of water off Silent Wolf and tossed the water out the shelter flap door, quickly returning under his mouth to catch the sickness that flowed. He vomited long into the night. It seemed like it was never going to end, and each time he was sick, Silent Wolf would give Otter a drink of the herbs he had mixed. He hoped that the healing potion would remove the toxic poison from Otter's system. The vomiting was what was needed, and as awful as it was, this was good.

'He is out of the woods,' Silent Wolf whispered. 'The worst of it is over, now he just needs to rest and recover. We will need to be on guard from now on, and we can take turns doing this. One will stay awake through the night, always watching, as Ivy will be enraged when she discovers that her plan was not successful.'

Raven nodded, and although she was relieved that Otter seemed to be over the worst of it, she also had a feeling of dread. This had been a close call. Ivy had almost had her revenge, delivering an evil blow. Raven sat close to Otter and continued to hold his hand. His breathing had almost returned to normal, but was still a bit shallow. Silent Wolf reassured her that this was good, it wasn't racing anymore, and slow and steady was good. He was healing, sleeping and recovering from his ordeal.

They sat quietly through what felt like an eternal night, listening and watching Otter, just in case he took a turn for the worse again and his symptoms changed. It was in the wee early hours of the next morning that Otter coughed. Raven grabbed the pot thinking that he was going to be sick again. He looked at the pot and pushed it away from his face, looking up at her with weary red eyes. Strands of his long black hair were plastered to his face, and she gently brushed the hair away from his eyes.

'That was rough,' he whispered feebly.

'Just lie down, the worst of it is over,' she reassured.

He took a few deep breaths in and out before closing his eyes, and was sleeping once again.

'I will keep watch, if you want to rest now,' Raven said.

Silent Wolf nodded and returned to his fur. He fell asleep instantly, worn out also. Raven couldn't sleep even if she wanted to, for she couldn't believe how close they had come to losing Otter. It had been a very narrow escape indeed, and it angered her. She was also worried about sleeping. Her dreams were constant now, mostly terrifying or deceiving in some way, shape or form. Raven wanted to avoid sleep, and what better way to do so than to keep watch. Nothing would get past her now, of that she was certain.

Raven headed out into the cold night air. Crouching down low onto the cold earth beneath her, she sprang into the air and changed into her raven form. Flapping her wings hard, she flew high up into the top of a huge pine tree – its thick branches would offer a comfortable perch for the night.

Raven would be able to see far with her sharp binocular eyesight and hear a great distance away having super-sensitive hearing. She ruffled her feathers to puff up her down, which would offer warmth in the cold, and settled in for the night. It felt so good to be in her true form again. Raven would be ready if Ivy decided to attack again. *Bring it on*, she thought to herself, so angry that she was ready to take her on now. As Raven sat quietly alone on a branch and listened to the night settle in around her, she reflected on Ivy and all her nastiness, and no matter how much Ivy loathed her, Raven felt a twinge of sorrow deep within her for the sorceress. To live a life like hers, full of hate, must be such a sorrowful thing. Raven filled her entire being with a strong feeling of love, surrounding herself within a cocoon of it and encasing herself and her friends within its circle of safety. She continued to send a loving light as far as she could, for in the end, love would ultimately save them all, she thought.

✳✳✳

Ivy was having a restless night, watching through her dreams and waiting for Otter's heart to stop beating. She was fuming with rage upon waking from her dreamlike state. Luna avoided her in case she received a kick in her anger. Silas was coiled around the tree, as still as ever, watching the sorceress through slitted eyes in all her fury.

'Clever wolf,' she spat venomously. 'We will wait, and you will come.'

She had not thought that the wolf had the knowledge let alone the know-how to combat her toad's poison. 'That man has indeed come a long way over the years,' she seethed through her stained yellow teeth. Some of her teeth had long rotted and fallen out, but she paid no heed as she preferred the blood and marrow and fat of her victims anyway – soft, and juicy, less chewing required.

It would soon be time to unleash Valcor, her greatest creation yet.

Dark Bloom

Raven was perched quietly, looking out into the early morning light. The night had been cold, and she ruffled her feathers to remove the light snow that had settled over her bird form throughout the night. The weather had settled down considerably and all was quiet except for the birdsong of those waking to greet the dawn. Their sounds filled the still morning air, and it gave her a settled feeling that all was well for the time being. She scanned the forest as far as her spectacular sight could see.

It was such a beautiful part of the country. The forest was thick and lush, covered in white snow now, but she could imagine it on a perfect summer's day. Raven sat for a while longer, appreciating the quiet. It had been a long night, but all her memories had kept her company, for she had many that she liked to reflect on, especially about her parents and their early days together.

Silent Wolf had taken over their teachings when her parents passed, so their bond was extraordinarily strong. Raven flew down from the tall treetops and returned to her human form once more as she landed near their shelter entrance. She grabbed her fur and wrapped it around herself, feeling the softness of it on her cool naked body. She swiftly changed, pulling on her warm boots. Lifting the shelter flap, she poked her head in. Otter was still sleeping, and Silent Wolf was waking up, rubbing his eyes and peering at her, asking without speech if all was quiet on the home front. She nodded without uttering a word. He clambered out from underneath his fur and staggered out, still looking tired.

They had only just sat down together when suddenly, Otter stuck his head through the flap and gave them both a wide grin. His cheek had a small cut visible, but the angry redness that was there had all but disappeared.

'How are you feeling, Otter?' asked Silent Wolf. 'Up to breaking camp? I feel we should get a move on if you are up to it. Ivy has had one attack on you, and I can't imagine it being the last.'

Otter nodded and agreed. 'I feel a bit weak, but I'll manage,' he said.

Silent Wolf and Raven packed up while Otter rested to regain his strength. They would press on and cover as much ground as they could, needing to hurry if they were going to catch the next blood moon.

The trio discussed their plan.

Raven believed it would be the most significant challenge she had ever encountered. She knew she would need to delve deep within herself to confront her fears. The task was far from easy, as Ivy, a malevolent old hag, had a dragon as her ally. Raven would now have to confront this creature not only in her dreams but in reality. Mentally preparing for the fight of her life, Raven pushed her fears to the back of her mind.

Once they had packed up, they covered their tracks like they always did, brushing the blackened earth with a pine branch. The ash scattered as Raven swept the branch backwards and forwards over the area, then she threw enough snow over it to hide any sign of them ever being there. Raven and Otter mounted the horses while Silent Wolf shapeshifted and ran alongside Raven as he preferred to do.

They continued on in silence, Otter looking back over his shoulder at her from time to time, checking on her. He still did not look quite right yet, the colour in his face was still slightly off. Normally, he would have flushed cheeks in this cold weather, but his pallor was pale compared to his usual honey skin tone. As they rode further into the darkness of the deep mountain, the more the forest looked like something out of a magical dream. The stories were starting to live up to their reputation. The forest was so dense now that most of the forest floor was free from snow, and the treetops overlapped each other looking like huge dark green blankets. The treetops were covered in snow, and moss covered the knotted roots that protruded the earth. Mushrooms popped their tiny heads out in bunches looking for light.

They travelled day after day, deeper and deeper into the forest. Silent Wolf would run off at night and hunt, often returning with some fresh kill for them to cook up. Every night they took turns to guard the camp, looking and listening long through the night for any sounds or sight of the witch. Nothing. It was quiet, night after night, making them wonder just what the witch was up to and why she had gone quiet suddenly.

It was cold, and even Raven's fur-lined boots did little to protect her against the icy weather, her toes felt like they were frozen solid, most uncomfortable. They travelled as fast as they possibly could, but it was slow going in some areas, and Raven felt like they were never going to find Ivy's fortress. They now were deep in the heart of the remote Zaltana Mountains and could feel the energy around them changing. It was like a dark cloud was hanging over them all, so they knew they were getting closer, and the blood moon would be upon them very soon.

After making good ground, they stopped in a clearing to set up camp. All of a sudden, the forest lit up around them. Raven looked behind her and saw a great swarm of glowing lights heading towards them. She instantly knew they had reached the firefly glade the seer had told them about. The tiny fireflies flew around them, converging together around the top of Raven's head. Their bodies produced bright lights that flashed and twinkled, synchronising together as the mass lit up the darkening sky around them.

The trio sat there in amazement, watching as more and more joined in numbers. Within a few minutes it looked like hundreds if not thousands of the tiny bugs had arrived and were flying together in a circular motion above and around Raven. It was like they were dancing as waves of luminous lights flashed in unison together, swirling, twisting and turning, flying in circular motion then changing their direction and swarming off and up into the night sky. It was a magical sight, and they had never seen anything like it in their lives.

'We are to follow them,' Raven said.

No sooner had Raven spoken than the little fireflies started flying off together in their thousands through the glade. The sky was now so bright from their lights that it appeared to be day. They all followed and listened to the bugs' tiny wings beating together with a droning sound that made a chorus of music. It was amazing.

They eventually came to the edge of the large glade, exactly where they were supposed to be.

As they followed the fireflies' light once more, they came to a lake, which was mostly frozen over now. The trio was nervous about crossing the lake, but they trusted the seer, so they gingerly followed the bugs, being extra careful with the horses and their loads. They all walked single file, and once one had reached the edge, the next person would cross, until they were all safely across. The fireflies converged together in their masses and hovered in the night sky waiting for the group to cross the lake.

The deeper they were led into the forest, the trail disappearing, Raven wondered how far had they actually travelled in distance. They had been away for three full moons, and the next moon would be the blood moon. The forest was very thick now, and following the fireflies was becoming difficult. All of a sudden, they flew back towards Raven and gathered about her in a swarm, then flew over and around her. When they were all together, once again in unison they flew to a large nearby tree. Landing on the trunk and branches, they illuminated the tree, and it looked spectacular and incredible all at the same time.

Beyond the tree, Raven could see a thick wall of vines, which looked impenetrable. She looked at it in amazement for a second or two before she realised what she was looking at. It stood in front of them not far from the tree the fireflies had landed on, and had to be the work of the blood witch, as it definitely had a magical element to it. She could feel it. Raven knew then that they were not far away from her lair now. She had built this incredible fortress of a wall to keep everyone out and inevitably keep herself safe from hunters.

Raven jumped down off Crow. Silent Wolf and Otter were still looking at the fireflies like they couldn't pull their eyes away.

She coughed, breaking their gaze. 'I think we should think about making a shelter before the light vanishes and we are in complete darkness.'

Otter agreed. No sooner did she have the fire going when the fireflies started to depart the forest. In one large group they flew towards Raven, and lit up the sky around her. She felt truly blessed and raised her arms up high above her head to say thank you. They formed a long line as they flew away, back the way they had come, towards the lake. The forest glowed with a beautiful green hue the farther away they were. It was mesmerising. The trio sat around the fire, discussing the magic of what they had just witnessed.

'Well, I don't mean to change the topic, but how are we going to get through that?' Raven said, pointing at the great wall of vines.

Silent Wolf peered into the night at it. It was hard to see the enormity of the wall fully as they didn't want to risk the flames for long, being so close in the witch's territory now.

'I will take watch tonight while you two rest, and we will figure it out tomorrow,' Silent Wolf said.

They drank and ate quickly then extinguished the fire and slid into their furs. Silent Wolf sat outside the entrance of their shelter curled up in his great wolf form. No one was going to sneak up on them tonight. Raven felt safe with him on guard, and was so tired.

Otter asked if she was alright.

'Me?' she asked. 'It should be me asking you if you are okay?'

He chuckled. 'I'm okay,' he said.

'I was so frightened, Otter, that I might lose you. I have never seen you that sick before.' She hesitated before adding. 'It reminded me of when my parents were sick, as your breathing was the same.'

'I must admit, I was a bit worried myself. But thanks to you and Silent Wolf, I live to fight another day, and I have every intention of killing that witch, before she kills me, or worse, us.'

Sleep came over Raven fast, and she fell asleep before Otter this time. No dreaming tonight, for a change. When she opened her eyes again it was morning. It was early, as she always woke early, no matter how tired she was. It had always been this way, and was the bird in her, she guessed.

Crawling out of her fur, she slipped past Otter, quietly leaving the warmth of the shelter. Silent Wolf was still sitting there, his impressive body guarding the doorway.

'Good morning,' she said as she rubbed him between his ears.

He licked her hand, and his tongue felt rough on her smooth skin. Raven laughed and wrapped her arms around his neck. Jumping up and onto his back, she leaned down and hugged his huge body. His fur was so soft and warm and felt so lovely on her cheek. She buried her face deep in his thick winter coat and breathed deeply. His scent was primal, with a blend of earthy musk and untamed wilderness, and she loved him with her whole being. He just stood there, allowing her to hug him. Raven thought he too felt the present threat that they were all about to face soon.

Raven jumped off Silent Wolf's back, feeling satisfied and ready to tackle any danger that Ivy could throw at them. She only hoped that Otter was feeling up to it as well. Silent Wolf was always ready; she didn't need to worry about him. Disappearing into the shelter, he shapeshifted back into his human form, got dressed and reappeared to join Raven. Otter strode out, looking much improved.

'You're looking a lot better this morning,' Raven said, giving him a relieved smile. She didn't want him to see an ounce of worry or fear on her face. They just had to get on with this and push forward.

'I'm feeling a lot better,' he replied as he joined them by the fire.

They all looked at the great wall of vines that lay before them.

Silent Wolf approached the wall and stood peering into it as best he could. 'Raven, there is no going through this wall. It's no ordinary vine, its poison ivy, so touching it is not wise. You can fly, but then only you can get above the wall, as the seer predicted. This is where you must continue on alone.'

She investigated the dense wall of poisonous vines, and looking at it closely, she could see the leaves were covered in tiny hairs.

Raven knew that the wall was too high for any mere mortal to climb, as the poison ivy and thorns on the twisted vines made sure of that.

'The day is not getting any younger, so we may as well get this over with,' Raven said, looking at Otter with the most confident look she could give.

Otter obviously saw straight through Raven's façade and came up behind her and hugged her tightly, wrapping his strong, muscular arms easily around her small waist. 'It's no time to start doubting yourself now.'

Silent Wolf placed his hand on her shoulder and said, 'Once you get over the wall, it won't take you long to find Ivy's lair. Once you do, wait and hide and watch her, as she will no doubt be waiting to harvest her precious flower. This is where you will have to use your smarts and taunt her with your presence. She will try everything to capture you, for it's your magic she ultimately wants. She will give chase, I'm sure of it. Remember, she has the dragon to do her bidding, and she will unleash it, so be sure to fly fast. You must avoid it, and fly back to us, Raven. We will be waiting. Together, all three of us can destroy her and her beast, and once they are taken care of, we can concentrate on destroying the flower once and for all. Let her pick it first, then that's when you show yourself. She will think that all her plans have come to pass when she sees you under the light of the blood moon.'

Raven nodded then turned around and faced Otter, gazing up into his beautiful brown eyes. He looked down and kissed her lightly on the top of her forehead.

'I love you, Raven. Be strong.' He stroked her cheek gently with his large hand.

'I love you too.' She looked deep into his eyes, as it felt like it could possibly be the last time she would get to look at him again.

He pulled her to him even harder, then went to his pack and pulled out two large knives. He also grabbed his bow and arrows then slung his quiver over his shoulder and back. He slid a knife into his boot with just the bone handle sticking out. Silent Wolf and Raven watched him prepare himself. He looked up at them both and said, 'One can't be too careful, now, can one?'

Raven slightly snickered before scrutinising Otter's arrows with a little amusement and determination. 'I believe I can imbue your arrows with magic,' she mused thoughtfully. 'Ivy's dragon will require more than just ordinary arrows to defeat. It's a daunting foe.'

'It's worth a try, I guess?' Otter replied, his voice sounding a little uncertain. 'I mean, as long as you don't destroy them in the process that is.' Otter gave Raven a side-long glance, his grin slid off his face as quickly as it appeared.

'Have a little faith, Otter, I'm sure I can manage it,' she said, trying to sound confident.

'But if you can do it, why haven't you done it before now?' he questioned, trying not to sound too harsh, as he handed her his quiver. His trepidation, however, was warranted as she had never done anything like it before.

Raven just sighed deeply through her nose ignoring his comment. With unwavering concentration, Raven tapped into her magical abilities. In an instant, a dazzling brilliance enveloped her, radiating outward in a cascade of light. The arrows shimmered with an enchanting, otherworldly glow, now infused with mystical power.

Otter's eyes widened in astonishment as his quiver gleamed with a radiant golden light emanating from the enchanted arrows. A wide grin illuminated his handsome face as he eagerly rubbed his hands together with exhilaration in anticipation of wielding these newfound magical arrows.

Silent Wolf couldn't keep the smile from his face either, feeling most proud of his protégé's progress and newfound strength. Together they stood ready to face the looming challenge with resolve and unity.

'Let's get this done and finally vanquish the wretched hag,' Raven declared, her voice laced with steely determination as she mustered all the confidence within her.

***

Meanwhile Ivy too gathered her arsenal of weapons, her familiars. She knew the blood moon would soon be upon them, this very night in fact. Flitting around her table, she gathered all the heinous poisons she had. The devil's horn would bloom this night and finally her long wait would soon be over. Ten long years had passed.

Everything was in order.

It was going to be a night full of torture and pain, and Luna was looking forward to this as much as Ivy, for the wait had been long indeed.

This was the night she needed to kill them all and consume their blood, especially Raven's and the wolf's, for they held the most power. She sneered to herself as she thought about snuffing out their miserable lives, and the thought of Raven's blood sent shivers of delight down her body.

The Blood Moon

Raven finished saying her goodbyes to both Otter and Silent Wolf. Shapeshifting into her raven form, she flew up high and disappeared out of sight. The well-constructed wall continued up, so she flew high above the clouds, flapping her wings hard.

Finally, she could see the top of the wall. Raven wanted to land there to spy below, but wary she was of its hairy poisonous leaves. She flapped her wings and hovered carefully above the vine's branches, seeing a clear spot amongst the leaves where a bare branch sat. As she landed, it was difficult to avoid the immense number of sharp thorns that were protruding from all angles, but she managed to avoid the poisonous hairs that were covering the ivy leaves.

Raven scanned as far as she could over the other side of the wall, but she could barely see the forest below she was that high. She knew there would still be a way to fly, as there was no way Ivy would have the wall directly near her fortress. Jumping off the wall, she took flight once again.

Raven was fast and fit; she had been preparing and training for this very night her entire life. It felt exhilarating and free to be high up in the sky once more. Only one of them would be victorious in the end: the witch or her. Destiny would choose her future.

Raven felt apprehensive going it alone, but she reassured herself as she flew, because Ivy had to make a dragon to help her, so how strong was she really? She was old too, Raven reasoned, encouraging herself to push forward. She had to keep her fears at bay, push them to the very back of her mind, hide them there, for she couldn't risk exposing herself by being scared and fretful. No, Ivy would not sense her coming, and she pulled up an invisible veil of light around herself as she was flying. This would help guard her from Ivy and her familiars' spying eyes.

Raven flew lower so that she could search for the lair, so she pulled her wings in tightly to her body and plummeted towards the forest trees below. Just as she was about to reach the trees, she opened her wings and soared above the treetops, gliding on the updraft.

Raven landed on a pine tree branch and searched the dark, dense forest for any signs of life. She knew she had to go deeper still, where it would be the darkest part of the forest, before she would find Ivy's fortress. Raven flew on feeling quite confident that she would stay well hidden with her black feathers, especially flying from tree to tree and blending in with the thick canopy. She used her magic and closed her eyes, harnessing her mind's eye and searching all around her. Raven held on tight to the thought of the veil of light around her, so she would not be easily found.

Not much farther along, Raven reached the forest's edge, where she beheld Ivy's fortress looming ahead, a sight of dark magnificence. The structure was enveloped in a crimson aura, hinting at a potent protective enchantment. Heavy smoke rose from the towering stone chimney, casting a shadow against the late afternoon sky. Isolated in its clearing, the fortress exuded a noxious odour that Raven recognised instantly from her previous encounters during the dreaming ceremony, a scent so repugnant it made her shudder. Simply horrid.

Raven spied quietly from the canopy of the trees where she could see Ivy's lethal garden. She could see many poisonous plants with twisted vines bearing crimson blossoms that seemed to pulse with a mysterious otherworldly energy. The garden exuded a heady, intoxicating scent, a blend of sweet yet metallic notes that hung heavy in the air, mingling with the earthy undertones of damp soil and the faint whisper of ancient spells woven into the very fabric of the plants.

Raven stood vigilant, and her pulse quickened with anticipation as she meticulously replayed the scenario in her mind, each detail crystallising into a strategic masterpiece. Silent Wolf's cunning plan lingered in her thoughts like a well-crafted weapon awaiting its moment of deployment. With unwavering focus, Raven knew that Ivy would pursue her without hesitation, unwittingly following the trail straight to Otter and Silent Wolf. The night held the promise of Ivy's downfall, a resolution that Raven was determined to see through to its final, decisive end.

With each member of the trio possessing unique abilities, Raven held steadfast confidence in their collective strength to confront the ageing witch. Her only imperative was to outmanoeuvre the dragon, trusting that their well-honed skills would pave the way for success.

As the cold night slipped in around her, so too did the blood moon appear. There she was, grand Mother Moon! Bright and beautiful, glowing red. Ivy suddenly appeared at her front door, Silas wrapped tightly around her neck like a shawl, protecting her from the frigid night air. Luna walked alongside her, keen to see the devil's horn finally bloom after so many long years of waiting.

Ivy's laugh echoed through the night, a chilling symphony of dark delight. Her eyes gleamed with an eerie light as she continued to gaze at the moon, a twisted grin spreading across her pale, moonlit face, revelling in the power and magic that coursed through the night sky.

Raven remained still, watching the old woman make her way into her garden. As soon as she reached the rickety gate that surrounded her sacred flower, she paused and looked up right towards where Raven was sitting in the tree. Raven couldn't tell if she was looking at her or just searching, but Raven felt her heart stop beating.

Luna looked in her direction also, and Ivy put her head back and sniffed deeply into the night air in Raven's direction.

She knew Ivy hadn't seen her, or she would have given chase, that's for sure. The blood moon shone its ruby red colour down upon the earth, and suddenly right before Raven's eyes, the devil's horn flower started to bloom and open under the glowing red light. Unfurling its velvety petals, the flower revealed a mesmerising blue hue. The air filled with a scent both intoxicating and sinister, a seductive blend of floral sweetness laced with a hint of dark, smoky undertones.

Ivy's deep-crevassed face lit up, and she smiled from ear to ear. Without hesitating, she grabbed her pouch from around her waist belt, opened it and produced a small glass vial. She pulled out the cork plug, and from one of her dress pockets, pulled out a pair of razor-sharp snips and forceps. Cutting through the bottom of the stem, Ivy quickly turned the flower upside down to contain the sap that flowed from within.

A sticky blue sap flowed out of the stem and into her little glass vial. She replaced the cork plug in the vial and stored it back in her pouch, which was still hanging off her belt, then secured it to the top of her pouch.

Ivy placed the flower, which was still glowing, into a wooden bowl that had been placed at the garden gate, ready for this very occasion.

This was the time. It was now or never. As the witch turned towards her hut, Raven shook herself lightly and readied herself.

Raven skilfully lifted her invisibility veil, allowing Ivy to swiftly detect her presence. The desired outcome unfolded as Ivy and Luna turned their gaze towards her simultaneously. With a piercing caw that echoed through the night, Raven gracefully ascended from the branch and soared directly towards them.

***

Ivy's shriek pierced the air. 'There she is! How did she elude me?'

As Raven closed in on them, Luna leaped into the air, claws outstretched, narrowly missing Raven's sleek feathers. With expert precision, Raven veered to the right, evading the feline's attack.

Cawing defiantly, Raven seemed to taunt them, challenging them to give chase.

Enraged, Ivy thrust her gnarled fingers forward, attempting to strike Raven with her magic. But Raven was too quick, deftly manoeuvring with lightning speed, darting from side to side with agility and grace, staying just out of Ivy's reach. The tense dance between predator and prey intensified as Raven showcased her unmatched skill and agility.

Ivy seethed with rage as Raven deftly slipped away, her furious screams reverberating through the surrounding woods. Raven couldn't help but chuckle softly, deliberately slowing her pace to goad Ivy into giving chase.

With a determined glint in her eye, Ivy sprinted as fast as her legs could carry her, intent on securing her precious flower in a safe location. She swore that this time, Raven would not slip through her fingers. Frantically scanning the forest for any sign of the wolf and hunter that were Raven's companions, Ivy found nothing but the eerie silence of the night. Despite the strangeness of their absence, Ivy overwhelming desire to claim Raven's magic blinded her to the potential danger that lurked in the shadows. Her single-minded pursuit of power fuelled her every step.

Screaming a command at her broom, it responded instantly, hovering obediently in front of Ivy. Luna wasted no time and leaped onto the broom beside her mistress, ready for the impending chase. Silas, coiled securely around Ivy's neck, exuded an aura of cold indifference, a trait that Ivy found oddly comforting. With a decisive gesture, Ivy directed the broom to take off, propelling them into the blood-red sky. As they soared higher, Ivy's hand motioned stiffly, and Valcor's solid door swung open with a resounding creak. The magnificent beast wasted no time, spreading his colossal wings and launching himself into the air with powerful strokes.

Ivy sped after her creation, issuing rapid-fire commands for Valcor to track down and capture Raven. As the hunt began, the night air crackled with tension and anticipation, setting the stage for a thrilling pursuit through the glowing red skies.

There Will Be Blood

Valcor's pursuit was relentless, his massive form cutting through the air with alarming speed. Yet, Raven, fuelled by adrenaline and instinct, managed to stay one step ahead of the monstrous creature. A deafening scream ripped through the sky, causing it to split open with a thunderous crack, intensifying the sense of imminent danger.

'Don't be scared, don't be scared,' Raven repeated to herself like a mantra, desperately trying to suppress the rising tide of fear threatening to overwhelm her. Valcor's roars echoed once more, signalling his increasing velocity as Ivy trailed closely behind, her determination palpable in the night air.

Raven's heart pounded in her chest as she deftly dodged and darted, narrowly evading the scorching flames that erupted from Valcor's gaping maw. The once serene forest now lay in ruins, consumed by the searing inferno unleashed by the relentless pursuer.

Descending swiftly, Raven plunged into the dense canopy, expertly navigating through the labyrinth of trees with breathtaking speed. Valcor's massive form struggled to follow her into the canopy, but he continued to rain down destruction with his fiery inferno. The chase had escalated into a heart-pounding race for survival, with Raven's every move crucial in evading the relentless onslaught of destruction behind her. Raven pushed herself to the limits of her speed and agility, darting through the forest with determination. Her keen eyes scanned the surroundings, aided by the eerie glow of the blood moon casting a spectral light upon the landscape. She knew that she had to ascend above the dense canopy to confront the imposing wall of vines that stood in her path, a daunting obstacle that required her to expose herself to the fiery onslaught of the pursuing beast.

Meanwhile, Ivy's frantic commands echoed through the night, urging Valcor to greater speeds as he unleashed another ear-splitting roar. The thunderous flapping of his wings reverberated through the air, signalling that his pursuit was closing in on Raven.

With a surge of adrenaline, Raven ascended above the treetops, her heart hammering in her chest as she beheld the looming shadow of the dragon's massive form hovering high above her. A chill of dread gripped her as the tops of the trees erupted in flames, painting the night sky with a menacing glow. The race against time and the fiery wrath of Valcor had escalated into a heart-stopping battle for survival, with Raven's every move crucial in evading the danger that threatened to engulf her.

The billowing flames licked closer and closer to Raven, urging her to push past her limits as she flew faster than she ever had before. The frigid night air clawed at her throat as she ascended higher, determined to conquer the seemingly impenetrable wall of vines that loomed before her. Just as she neared the pinnacle of the night sky, a searing inferno painted the night sky with its fierce glow.

The scorching heat surged towards her, enveloping Raven in a blazing wave of fire. She instinctively turned away, but not before feeling the intense heat singe her tail feathers and legs. A guttural scream of anguish tore from her throat, a thick metallic taste flooded her senses as pain surged through her being. Through sheer willpower and grit, Raven pressed on, pushing through the agonising torment as she soared over the wall's crest. The biting cold air tore through her charred feathers like fiery blades. The night air echoed with her cries of pain as Raven forged ahead, her resilience tested to its very limits.

The beast unleashed a thunderous roar fuelled by the witch's fury, its enormous form hurtling through the night with flames erupting in its wake, painting the sky with cascades of scorching fire. Valcor's fiery breath resembled molten lava, a searing force that clashed with the icy chill of the air. Despite his proximity, the dragon's flames fell just short of consuming Raven entirely, a narrow escape that spurred her on.

Raven instinctively wrapped her wings tightly around herself, forming a protective shield akin to a cocoon, safeguarding her vital organs beneath the canopy of her feathers. Hurtling towards the ground like a speeding arrow homing in on its mark, she accelerated, driven by a fierce determination to outpace her fiery pursuer.

With Valcor closing in, Raven stole a moment to glance back, locking eyes with the beast's monstrous red orbs that blazed like infernos within his skull. The intense gaze of those fiery eyes bore into her, seeking to instil fear and uncertainty. Refusing to yield an ounce of her resolve, Raven steeled herself against the creature's malevolent gaze, knowing that fear was the dragon's sustenance, a weakness she could not afford to show.

Raven sped towards the ground where Otter and Silent Wolf stood poised for action. Otter, his golden arrow drawn taut, awaited the perfect moment to release his shot. In a swift and calculated manoeuvre, Raven abruptly pulled up, and executed a rapid change in direction, deftly outmanoeuvring Valcor and leaving the fiery beast momentarily exposed, just as they had planned.

Due to his massive size, Valcor struggled to adjust his trajectory swiftly enough, his jaws gaping wide as he prepared to unleash another blistering blast of fire. A primal cry reverberated through the night, signalling the dragon's impending attack. Sensing the opportune moment, Otter released his arrow with precision and skill.

As the golden arrow sliced through the air, it hummed with a faint, mystical energy, leaving a trail of sparkling stardust in its wake. It met its mark and went straight into the dragon's wide-open jaws, disappearing into the blood-red maw. A perfect shot. The arrow tore through the roof of the beast's cavernous maw, fatally piercing through its scaly armour and delving deep into the creature's brain. A guttural roar echoed through the air as Valcor let out a shrill cry of pain and rage, his massive body writhing in agony.

But Otter was not one to hesitate in the face of danger. With a swift and practiced motion, he notched another golden arrow, his eyes fixed on the wounded beast before him. The tension in the air was palpable as he took aim, his focus unyielding as he released the arrow.

His second shot flew true, and the arrow found its mark with deadly precision, hitting the creature squarely in its fiery red eye, a fatal blow that sealed the dragon's fate. With a deafening roar that shook the very ground beneath them, Valcor plummeted from the sky, his scaly form hurtling towards the earth below.

The ground trembled as the dragon crashed down with a thunderous impact, his once mighty wings now limp and lifeless. The beast lay motionless, fatally wounded and defeated.

***

Ivy's anguished scream of rage echoed through the frosty night as she felt the fatal blows delivered to Valcor. His lifeless body was sprawled on the unforgiving snow. Her heart pounded in her chest, fury boiling within her veins at the sight of the majestic dragon, his armoured scales now stained with crimson, two gleaming golden arrows cruelly piercing his snake-like head.

The blood witch's mind raced with thoughts of vengeance as she clenched her fists, her eyes ablaze with a fierce determination. To-night, the hunter and Silent Wolf would pay for this heinous act before she would seek out Raven. Ivy knew deep in her core that Raven wouldn't stray far from her companions in their darkest hour; the bond between them was unbreakable. All hope was not yet lost.

With a steely resolve, Ivy's grip tightened around the precious flower's sap she carried. Swift as the wind, she flew after Otter.

Raven streaked ahead of her companions, her body ablaze with searing pain from the burns inflicted upon her. Resolve etched on her face, she soared towards the sheltering embrace of the dense forest canopy. As she reached the protective haven of the trees, she summoned her magic, weaving a potent spell that cast a shimmering veil of invisibility around them, concealing their presence. Within the magical cocoon of secrecy, Raven and her companions found respite, hidden from Ivy's wrathful gaze.

Frustration and fury seethed within Ivy as she frantically scanned the surroundings, her senses keen but thwarted by the mystical barrier that shielded the fugitives from sight.

Ivy's disbelief mounted as she realised that all three had vanished into thin air before her very eyes, slipping away like shadows in the night. Her hands clenched into fists, her jaw set in a grim line as she muttered curses under her breath, a storm of emotions swirling within her. The canny trio had eluded her grasp, leaving Ivy fuming with a mixture of anger and bewilderment at their strange disappearance.

Silent Wolf's eyes gleamed with a primal ferocity as he lay waiting, his muscles coiled like springs as Ivy's enraged approach drew nearer. With a swift and savage lunge, he leaped towards her, jaws snapping with deadly intent. His sharp fangs sank into Ivy's flowing dress, tearing the fabric and sinking deep into her flesh, crushing bone with a sickening crunch. Ivy's piercing scream of agony shot out into the night as she felt the searing pain shoot through her body.

As the blood witch tumbled from her broom, crashing to the ground with a bone-rattling impact, the world spun around her in a haze of torment. Desperation etched on her face, she summoned the remnants of her waning strength, her hands weaving intricate patterns in the air in a bid to unleash her magic against her assailant.

Silent Wolf's relentless assault had left Ivy's leg gruesomely mangled, blood staining the pristine white snow beneath her. Luna, ever loyal, darted towards her mistress, a protective instinct guiding her. But before she could reach Ivy's side, Otter's arrow flew true, finding its mark in Ivy's shoulder, the barbed tip piercing through her flesh and pinning the snake to her chest.

Silas, the snake familiar, twisted and writhed in pain as Ivy's screams of torment filled the frigid air. Otter, unrelenting in his precision, swiftly notched another enchanted arrow, his movements fluid. With deadly accuracy, he released the arrow, striking Ivy's abdomen with unerring aim, a surge of unparalleled pain coursing through her shattered form.

The once indomitable blood witch now lay broken and bloodied, her breath ragged, her body a canvas of agony. A darkened blood moon loomed overhead, casting an ominous glow upon the macabre scene unfolding in the snow-covered clearing.

As Ivy spat a blackened ichor onto the pristine white canvas, the chilling realisation dawned upon her – this night would perhaps witness a blood moon offering, a sacrifice to the relentless march of fate.

Realising the imminent threat to her life, Ivy's mind raced with urgency as she made a split-second decision to flee to the safety of her fortress. With Raven now aware of her hideout, time was of the essence, and Ivy knew she had to act swiftly to outmanoeuvre her relentless pursuers.

Through gritted teeth, Ivy issued a commanding hiss to her broom. Responding to her call, the enchanted broom swooped in with Luna by her side, and her loyal snake guardian poised for any unseen danger. In a blur of motion, the broom whisked Ivy off the ground, lifting her to safety just as Silent Wolf made a final desperate lunge, his menacing fangs narrowly missing her jugular by mere inches.

As they ascended into the ink-black sky, the night enveloped them in its shroud of crimson light.

Silent Wolf's frustrated growls echoed through the night as Ivy vanished from his reach, the wind carrying her away under the ominous gaze of the celestial sentinel.

With her fortress looming in the distance, Ivy knew that the night held more trials and tribulations yet to come. The pursuit was far from over, and the blood witch steeled herself for the challenges that lay ahead, her heart heavy with the weight of impending conflict under the watchful eye of the blood-red moon. Her only consolation was knowing that she still had the devils horn flower, and if she could survive this night, vengeance would be hers. All hope was not yet lost to her.

***

Raven's tense muscles gradually uncoiled as a fleeting sense of relief washed over her, her weary body aching with exhaustion and pain. However, the respite was short-lived as the gravity of the situation loomed large in her mind. The night was far from over; the hunt for Ivy had just begun, and with the blood witch wounded, she presented a vulnerable target ripe for the taking. This was the opportune moment to bring an end to Ivy's reign of darkness once and for all.

With decisive resolve, Raven removed her cloak of invisibility, as she glided to her companions' side. Their awestruck gazes were fixed upon the fallen form of the magnificent armoured dragon, a sight so extraordinary and awe-inspiring that it left them speechless, their minds struggling to comprehend the sheer magnificence before them.

As they stood in silent reverence, a sense of wonder and curiosity enveloped them, mingling with the urgency of the task in hand.

Raven's fingers trembled as she reached for a fur, wrapping it tightly around her shivering form, seeking solace from the biting cold that gnawed at her burnt skin. Each step she took sent a jolt of searing pain through her blistered feet and legs, the icy chill of the snow offering a strange but welcome reprieve amidst the agony. With a wince, she reflected on the brush with death, her voice steady but strained as she spoke, masking the pain that threatened to overwhelm her.

'That was too close,' Raven exhaled, her breath forming mist in the frigid air. 'I feared I might journey to the spirit realm to join my parents sooner than expected.' She fought to maintain her composure, a flicker of vulnerability betraying the façade of strength she presented.

Otter, ever the pillar of support, draped an arm around Raven's quivering shoulders, his voice filled with genuine admiration. 'You were extraordinary, as I always knew you would be,' he murmured, his words a balm to her weary soul.

Their collective gaze turned towards the fallen creature sprawled before them. As they stood in a moment of stunned disbelief, the once impenetrable barrier of vines and thorns that had shielded Ivy's domain began to crumble, disintegrating into ethereal ash that danced on the wind before vanishing into oblivion.

A shared realisation dawned upon them, reflected in the widening of Raven's eyes. This was a tangible sign of Ivy's weakened state. The shattered remnants of the protective wall bore testament to the blood witch's vulnerability, her power waning in the face of defeat. The question lingered unspoken but palpable in the air: What purpose would be served by allowing Ivy to live, to rise once more and resume her persistent pursuit of Raven?

In that fleeting moment of decision, a silent understanding passed between them. They had journeyed far and faced insurmountable odds to confront Ivy, and the time for mercy had waned. The fate of the blood witch now hung in the balance, a pivotal moment in their quest for redemption.

The once vibrant forest lay in desolation, scarred by the fiery wrath of the dragon. Charred remains of once towering trees stood as solemn guards amidst the devastation, their blackened husks a haunting reminder of the destructive power that had swept through the woodland. Blackened trails snaked through the ashen landscape; a stark path of destruction left in the dragon's wake.

Otter retrieved his golden arrows from the blood-drenched scales of the fallen beast, each shaft gleaming dully in the cold light as he meticulously cleaned them in the snow, before returning them to his quiver. With a reverent touch, he plucked a tooth from the great monster's maw, a tangible memento of his triumph over the mighty adversary, a trophy to mark his greatest kill.

Running his fingers over the iridescent scales that once adorned the dragon's large form, Otter scrutinised every intricate detail, marvelling at the creature's majestic but now lifeless beauty. Yet, just as with the enchanted wall that had shielded Ivy's fortress, the dragon began to disintegrate before their eyes, its corporeal form melting into a noxious pile of acidic sludge that seeped into the earth.

The dragon's existence was unveiled: the fearsome creature was but a façade, a creation born of potions and poisons woven together by a malevolent spell. The awe-inspiring beast that had instilled fear in Raven's dreams was nothing more than a macabre illusion, a hollow shell of magic and malice.

Otter unwrapped his suede cloth that he had wrapped the beast's fangs in to see if they were still there, or had they too decayed? But the fangs were as they were, giant-sized and sharp. The trio weren't sure why they had remained when the rest of the beast had disintegrated. Perhaps because Otter had removed them before it started breaking down? It was a question they would ponder over for many years to come around the campfire, they imagined.

Silent Wolf retrieved a salve from Raven's rabbit skin bag, which she kept all her ointments and herbs in. He got her to lie down while he rubbed the ointment all over the back of her lower legs and feet. The cream instantly felt soothing on her hot burnt skin. Thank goodness for the snow also, for that saved her from the fiery pain.

'Raven, you know where she lives, so we will follow you. You can fly, and I will carry Otter for we will be fastest that way.'

Otter shot a glance at Silent Wolf as he had never ridden on him before, so this would be a first. It was something he had always secretly wanted to do but had never asked or spoken about. Finally, after all these years, he would fulfil a deep desire to ride on the Dire Wolf. They all held hands for a minute and brought their heads together.

'The dragon is dead, and the witch is greatly wounded and weak, so we strike now,' Silent Wolf said, before shapeshifting into his wolf form.

Otter then grabbed a handful of Silent Wolf's shaggy fur around his neck and leaped up and onto his back. He held tightly as Silent Wolf raced off towards the witch's fortress. Raven was still in pain from her burns, but she jumped up as high as she could regardless and shapeshifted once again into her bird form. She could feel how hard each change was beginning to be and realised that it wouldn't be long now, and she wouldn't be able to change back. Raven tried not to think about it as she caught up to Silent Wolf and Otter. She flew above them but just above their heads. He ran at great speeds, so she flew faster to stay just a little ahead of them both.

They continued under the light of the blood moon that was still shining brightly in the sky, illuminating the snow with a red hue. It was quite beautiful and equally haunting to see. Had this been under different circumstances, she would have enjoyed seeing this rare event. For many clans this night, there would be a special occasion marking the coming of the blood moon. There would be ceremonies held for days marking the event, for her people believed that the blood moon represented a time of change and cleansing. Although the moon looked angry in its shade of burnt red, it actually brought about positive change within the clans, and harvesting and planting would be carried out as soon as their celebrations came to an end. Clans from all over would converge together and have great powwows. They would dress in their colourful outfits, headdresses proudly displayed as they danced and sang around the campfire, giving thanks to the Great Spirit for Mother Moon shining her red light down upon them, feeding the earth and their souls with her magic.

Raven thought about this as she flew and wished she was also celebrating at her camp with her loved ones. She loved watching all the dancers tirelessly singing and chanting to the drumming beats. Raven was looking forward to ending this witch once and for all and returning home. As they continued deeper and deeper into the dark woods towards her fortress, Raven wondered if they would indeed reach her in time, or would she have escaped as wounded as she was? They would find out soon enough.

The Cut Runs Deep

Ivy only just made it back to her fortress deep in the forest. Her door barely opened with the wave of her wand, so weak she now was. Once inside, she didn't have the strength with her magic to light all her candles, and only a couple sprang to light with a little flame shining from them. She fell hard to the stone floor off her broom, writhing with pain and sobbing over the death of her beast. Blood ran down her face, yet she didn't wipe it away this time, just allowed it to flow as it fell to the ground. It had taken her a long time to create Valcor. And now he was gone, just like that, with two deadly arrows from that long-haired fool. Two gleaming magical arrows.

'I underestimated them all.' She spat out blood.

Luna came to her side and licked the blood from her face, trying to pacify her mistress. Ivy knew she had to work fast as she was bleeding a lot. Two golden arrows protruded from her old body, so she needed to remove these first to stop the blood flow.

Ivy crawled over to her fire where the embers were still glowing red in the bottom of the firepit. Opening the great glass doors, she stuck a cast iron poker into the bottom. Once heated, it would help to seal the wounds once the arrows were removed. She first held up her snake's head, for he too had died after the arrow had pinned him to her chest. She bawled not only with the pain of the warrior's arrows, but for the loss of two of her beloved familiars on this night.

The lifeless body of the snake hung off her neck. She should not have brought him; it was foolish of her to underestimate them. Ivy continued to cry as she gripped the first arrow tightly between her hands, encasing it fully and pulling it with all her might. Silas dropped into her lap as she freed him from her chest, and blood gushed out of the open wound. Ivy grabbed the iron poker that glowed bright red from the heat of the embers. It was ready. She took a deep breath and held the hot poker to the open wound on her chest, screaming aloud, guttural cry with the pain. The wound sizzled, and she smelled her flesh burning as the poker cauterised it. The blood stopped flowing, but Ivy felt extremely weak, and she still had another arrow to remove and her mauled leg to deal with.

It was almost too much, but she wouldn't give up, not yet. She still had the flower, and if she could sort herself out before the return of the hunters, she may still have a chance of escape. Ivy returned the poker to the heat of the embers once more and waited for it to heat up again. She picked up her beloved snake and cried tears of blood that flowed down her wrinkled face. She would later place her snake in the great tree where he'd loved to sit so much, coiling his great body around the ancient tree branches. He would feed and nourish the tree with his body, offering it sustenance for all the years it had offered shelter to him. The tree had been his home, and he would eventually return to the earth once more as his blood and bone would continue to sustain the tree.

Ivy held him close to her body, hugging him and feeling the smooth, cold scales for the last time. She would mourn him for many years along with all the other familiars she had lost over time. The blood witch readied herself to pull out the second arrow. She carefully and lovingly placed the snake's great body beside her now and took several deep breaths before pulling the embedded arrow out of her abdomen.

The pain sent a shooting wave through her as it came out, and blood poured from the wound. Ivy screamed and passed out, falling backwards and lying next to her snake on the hard stone floor. Minutes later she came to, her cat licking her face, cleaning the tears of blood away. The stones were covered in her and the snake's blood, as the wound on her right side slowly oozed blood still. Ivy gathered herself together and worked quickly, grabbing the boiling hot poker from the embers and shoving it into her open wound. She screamed again, in pain. She thought she may die. This was not good. Weakness seeped in, and she knew she was in grave danger. She needed to stop the bleeding, retrieve her flower and escape before the hunters were upon her. For surely, they would give chase now that she was unable to hold her magic and retain the poisonous wall.

Ivy was lucky her broom was fast, or she may not have made it back. Still, her broom was only fast while she was well, and since she was so wounded, it was unable to fly without her spells and incantations. If she made it out of this, it would be nothing short of a miracle, but Ivy had at least managed to cauterise the wounds and stop the bleeding. Now she had to deal with her torn leg. Looking down at her leg, a great gash from where the wolf's teeth had torn into her flesh was slowing trickling blood out of the wound, which was deep and to the bone.

Working fast, she covered the wound on her leg, filling the gash with herbs to help stop the bleeding and wrapping a cloth around her leg, covering it fully.

Luna sat next to the fire, watching Ivy. Ivy couldn't stand it if her beloved familiar met her death on this night also. 'Go to the window, my friend, and watch for them, for they are surely on their way.'

Ivy was compromised, and she knew it. It was dangerous to remain here. As weak as she felt, she knew she could not stop and rest, for to do so would mean certain death. Ivy waved her hand and muttered a command under her breath. The window did not open, only shook a little. She was indeed injured a great deal. Her magic was waning, getting weaker as she succumbed to the wounds.

Ivy quickly retrieved the flower. Removing it from the bowl, she wrapped it in a piece of leather cloth securing it tightly so that the tiny needles covering the stem would not stick through the leather wrap. That was the last thing she needed, to be stabbed by one or more of those needles, as it would mean certain death, and a rough death it would be.

She raced against time, for it was not on her side tonight. Grabbing a few of her favourite poisonous blends, she stuffed as much as she could into a toad-skin pouch to keep them dry. She placed this into another bag that she would carry over her back. Moving as quickly as she could, Ivy grabbed as many items as possible that she could before her defeated departure. The burning heat of the wounds throbbed as if they had their own heartbeat as she packed her ancient spell book. She couldn't forget that! It was most sacred to her. Ivy suddenly realised that she would need her flying ointment this night. Retrieving the tallow, she peered into the almost empty jar. There was only enough to cover her face and maybe her forearms, so she used all of it, quickly smearing the fatty balm into her wrinkly face and forearms, which would have to suffice. It certainly wouldn't whisk her to the other side of continent, but it would aid her speed in her initial escape. That was all that really mattered right now.

Tears of blood welled up in her eyes as it ran down her face and over the top of her once beautiful dress.

Eve was in the centre of her beautifully weaved web. 'I'm sorry, my friend. I have failed, and we must depart at once.'

She held out her hand in front of her spider. Jumping onto it, Eve ran up the length of Ivy's arm and hid amongst her dreadlocked hair. She had no time to say a spell, but hastily called her trusty broom. It hovered in front of her, but Ivy was too weak to jump up. She spread her legs and pulled her dress up so that the broom could easily fly between her legs and lift her up. Luna leaped onto the front of the broom where she usually sat.

Too weak to command the door open with her hand, Ivy leaned over as far as she could to reach the door handle. The pain seared her with fiery heat as she stretched the wound on her side. Moaning, Ivy unlatched the door and muttered a command under her weak breath, with a feeble flick of her hand. The broom sped through the door into the night.

The blood moon was now at its fullest in the sky, shining its bright red light down upon her. Suddenly, an arrow whizzed past Ivy's face, narrowly missing her. She pulled up on her broom handle and they sped off as fast as she could muster. That had been a very close call. The warrior had almost ended her life on this night. She let out a weak scream as she fled into the blood-red night sky. Ivy had always thought that the great wolf and Raven would be her greatest threats, but how wrong she had been to underestimate the three of them together.

After narrowly escaping, Ivy knew exactly where she would find cover. She had planned for this, even though she never actually thought she would ever need to flee. Fifteen years earlier, Ivy had spied upon a young witch one night when she was hunting in England, and this would be her safest bet, deep in the forested English countryside she would hide, recover and plot her revenge. For if Raven thought that this was over, she knew nothing of Ivy and her longing to consume the girl's blood and magic. This was far from over.

Ivy crouched over the front of the broom, resting as she gave its coordinates. She had escaped the fatal shot from Otter's arrow and would have her revenge on the three of them, for all three must die now.

The blood moon waned and faded as the night passed them by. Ivy's wounds were so severe she barely made it to the English countryside. The wrappings that covered her wounds were wet and saturated with blood. She had not had the time to take anything for the pain, needing to flee in such haste. But she had escaped with her precious flower and two of her familiars, so everything was not totally lost to her.

Flying above the treetops, she kept well out of sight. She knew where the young witch lived, well maybe not so young anymore, perhaps in her early thirties, Ivy thought, but still much younger than herself. Ivy hoped she would not turn her away for she was far too wounded to fly any farther. The pain was excruciating, so much so, that the flight seemed much longer than she had ever remembered. Ivy looked down over the forest, noted a landmark and gave her broom the instruction to fly down to the forest floor.

Luna stayed close to Ivy's side as she held her wounds and doubled over, hobbling and using the broom like a crutch to hold onto for support. After making her way along the forest track for a while, Ivy came to a large rock wall of boulders, hidden neatly off the side of the well-worn track to the left. Vines and hedgerow mostly covered the rocks, so it was hard to see if you didn't know it was there. To the naked eye, you wouldn't see the narrow crevasse that led through the rocks, where deeper within that was a cave. Ivy had come here many years ago now. She had been hunting humans and had seen a young witch flying through the night sky. The young girl appeared no more than fifteen years old at most, and she was so busy sobbing that she didn't even notice Ivy trailing behind. Ivy was intrigued and decided to follow her and see where she was going. It was then that she discovered the secret entrance to her hideout.

She hadn't alerted the young witch to her spying eye, but had kept quiet and left again, thinking to herself maybe one day, one never knew if they ever need somewhere to flee. It was always a good idea to have a backup plan in case you needed it. She was glad she did now. Ivy made her way through the narrow rock formation of boulders and passed through the cold cave. The ceiling of the cave was covered in glow worms, and their little bodies lit the way quite well for her.

Continuing as best she could, Ivy stopped every now and again and doubled over in pain. Every time she stopped to try and focus ahead, the pain would come in waves like a hot stabbing knife, through her side and chest. Her leg was throbbing with every step she took, and it was excruciatingly painful. In the distance she could finally make out a dim light ahead, so she pushed on, slowly, her breathing becoming shallower and more difficult, like the air was closing in on her.

As she came out to the other side, she saw a welcoming sight. A stone house stood before her, looking much like a castle but smaller in size. It was still grand though. She could see in the fast-approaching morning light that the walls of the house were covered in moss and a creeping rose vine. She could imagine it in full bloom in the spring and summer months, when it would look incredible. A herb garden was off to the right. It reminded Ivy of her own place, and a pang of pain stabbed her in the side.

It was cold here also, but the weather was nowhere near as severe. Ivy was glad, yet she needed the warmth of a fire to soothe her cold, old bones. She staggered to the young witch's garden path, almost tripping, and made her way, each step agony now. Ivy wiped the blood from her eyes and face with the back of her dress sleeve. She didn't want to alert the young witch that she was in fact a blood witch, for she would finish her off for sure if she knew the present danger that she faced.

Ivy knocked on the large wooden door. The heavy door opened carefully, just enough to look through at the unexpected visitor. A red-headed woman spied through the smallest crack, her emerald-green eyes searching Ivy's face. Ivy could not utter a word, for her pain was so great, and beads of sweat covered her brow, so very weak she now was. The shocked woman looked her over, her gaze landing on the blood-soaked cloth in several places.

'I fear, I need your help, for I am mortally wounded,' was all that Ivy could whisper.

With that, she dropped to the ground, her trusty broom falling with her. Ivy could go no further, and if this was her fate, so be it, she thought to herself as she lay there at the mercy of this stranger's feet. Collapsed in a bloody pile of putrid mess, she lay completely still. Luna meowed a long and sad cry, looking up at the stranger before her, begging with her beautiful green eyes.

***

The young woman looked the cat over, seeming to ponder the possible dangers of letting a stranger in, but seeing the wounds and the age of the old woman, she thought to herself that she posed no threat.

'Don't worry, I will help her, but I just need to get her inside by the warm fire,' she said, trying to comfort the sad-looking cat that accompanied the old woman. The younger woman was known in these parts as Freya, and she was a white witch. Calling to her broom, it hovered above Ivy while Freya lifted up Ivy's arm. Freya spoke in a tongue the cat had not heard before, and the broom slid under Ivy's arm and together they assisted her inside. Freya made her as comfortable as she could on a big sofa, which was close to her stone fireplace. It was covered in animal furs and velvet covered cushions and appeared to look very cosy.

Her fire blazed brightly, filling her house with warmth. Flanking her fireplace stood two imposing stone gargoyles, their eyes vigilant as they surveyed the living room. They were simultaneously beautiful and terrifying.

Freya went to work, collecting several items she would need to clean Ivy's wounds.

 Carefully unwrapping Ivy's bandages, she examined the wounds closely, sniffing them before finding the herbs she needed. She could smell the burned flesh and looked into the old woman's face, wondering what had happened to such an old soul. Ivy was pale and still passed out, so Freya worked quickly before she came to, dressing the wounds with a pre-made poultice of healing herbs. She carefully cleaned the wounds from all the congealed blood and herbs that Ivy had packed them with before smearing a thick layer of healing ointment on each open wound.

'She will be okay, and she is lucky to have come here to me, as some folks in these parts are not so helpful,' she said, pacifying the fearful-looking cat.

Freya stoked her fire with more wood to keep it well burning through the night. She wiped Ivy's brow with a damp cloth every now and again, wiping the beads of sweat that were appearing, a sign that the injured woman was feverish. Every so often, Ivy would let out a little moan, her wrinkled face screwing up in pain as the sounds escaped her parched lips. Freya wiped Ivy's lips with the wet cloth also, trying to keep them from totally drying and cracking.

As Freya continued to wipe Ivy's face with a cool, damp cloth, she took note of the red-shaped ivy leaf that was on her cheek. It was an odd birthmark for sure, but she thought nothing more of it. Freya continued to care for and watch over Ivy before she was satisfied that there was nothing more she could do now, except wait. She made herself comfortable with a hot drink and sat watching Ivy, waiting for her to wake. She knew nothing about her, so sat and waited until she woke, just to be safe.

Beauty in the Sorrow

Back at Ivy's fortress, Raven, Silent Wolf and Otter looked around in case she had any other unsuspecting familiars still lurking. All was quiet. Raven and Silent Wolf changed back into their human skins, both grabbing a fur from Otter's pack and wrapping it around themselves. Otter was disappointed that his third arrow had missed its mark. It was unlike him to miss, after all.

'Don't worry, Otter. This is far from over. She has the flower, so she will be back to seek her revenge and try to steal my magic, I know it,' Raven said.

They all gingerly walked in single file into Ivy's abode. The reek of blood and fat hit Raven like a punch to the face. Never had she smelt anything so putrid and overwhelming to her senses before. Her face screwed up in disgust.

After finding no trace of the devil's horn flower, they knew what had to be done. 'There is no way this stone fortress will burn, but we must destroy her poisonous garden. She must not be able to return and find anything else to use against us,' Silent Wolf said.

Otter and Raven nodded and looked around at all the horrible bits and pieces Ivy had collected over the years. Various bowls of poisonous flowers were dried and surprisingly kept in a sort of order amongst the disarray on her bench.

'All of this should be destroyed as well,' Otter remarked, pointing to the noxious display.

They carried armfuls, dumping everything they planned to destroy, out to her toxic garden.

Silent Wolf searched her workbench, seeing it was congested with many items. Before he even saw it, he smelled it: a big, blackened pot filled with a putrid-smelling substance. As he examined the pot closer, he realised the yellowish looking liquid was fat. He didn't need to sniff it to know what it was, as the odour hung like a thick blanket in the air, pungent and revolting.

'This will burn nicely,' he said as he carried the pot, holding the handle out and away from his body. He found the iron poker Ivy had used to cauterise her wounds still on the ground where she had dropped it before she escaped. He picked it up and examined the end of it closely, sniffing it and smelling her burnt flesh. He could also see some of her skin remained stuck to the end of the iron.

'Ivy has used this to help stop the bleeding of her wounds,' he said, as he held the iron poker up in the air for them to see.

Otter and Raven looked over at Silent Wolf, and Raven thought how painful that must have been, burning your own flesh. She still felt the burn from the dragon's fiery breath on the back of her legs and feet. So, Ivy and Raven had both suffered similar wounds from the attack. She wondered if the seer had seen any of what had played out between them.

Silent Wolf continued to look around her macabre home, at the grotesque candle arborer, where large deer antlers tied together with misshapen melted candles had long melted and dripped and splashed all over the floor and surrounding area where it sat. The giant oak tree was something to behold, as he could tell that the tree was ancient. It was a living organism that he held sacred in his circle of life.

He placed his palm flat on the moss-covered tree trunk, closed his eyes and listened within. Silent Wolf concentrated his thoughts and centred his mind's eye, feeling the vibration of the tree as its life pulsated within. He opened his eyes and looked up into the tops of the branches, spotting the dead snake coiled around a branch, his final resting place. At least this witch cared about something, so it seemed.

They were done looking around Ivy's home. It had an imposing, sinister energy about it, the witch's energy, and he didn't want to be in there any longer than he needed to. He found some cloth that he wrapped around the end of the iron poker then used it to deposit the cauldron fat on the lethal garden, and all the selected poisons from her home, using the remaining fat to cover the gate that surrounded the plot for her sacred flower. He smeared the tree trunks and all that he could until there was nothing left of the putrid cauldron lard. If Ivy ever returned here, there would be nothing left of her garden. Another blow to her. They all stood at a distance and watched as the flames took hold and engulfed everything, until there was nothing but ash. They all exhaled a sigh of relief as the garden, along with the devil's horn, was destroyed.

'Thank the Great Spirit' Raven smiled despite the pain she was in, feeling happy that at least this part of their journey was complete.

Silent Wolf recommended that it was best to find shelter for the rest of the night. The early hours of the morning would soon be upon them, and they needed to rest before making the long track back home again. Raven could not wait to be out of the forest, and once they were in more open woodland the ground would not be so wet. All was quiet in the surrounding forest the following morning, and Raven was glad, as she did not want any more surprises. As they made their way out of thick of the forest, Raven's mind wandered to Ivy. She would remember everything about the night of the blood moon, the event being etched into her memory for many years to come after how utterly terrifying it was. Raven was so glad that Otter was such a skilled marksman, and that Silent Wolf was such a ferocious and formidable friend to have on her side.

Raven thought about Ivy's escape, and that it would be quite amazing if she did indeed survive. Raven wondered where she went and in what state she was. Did she still live, or were the wounds she received too great for her weathered, old body? Ivy had been a powerful witch though, and a blood witch at that, exceedingly rare, or so it was told. The seer had told Raven that blood witches were rare due to the intricate and forbidden nature of their craft, as they draw power from the life force within blood, making them immensely powerful as they harness the essence of life itself in their magical workings.

They rode on, only stopping occasionally to have a drink of cool water as refreshment. Raven and Otter did not speak at all, both lost in their own trail of thoughts no doubt after their ordeal. There had been no sound from Silent Wolf either, before he disappeared into the forest again.

As the day pressed on, Otter called out, 'Raven.'

Raven pulled Crow to a stop and without dismounting, turned and looked in Otter's direction.

'We should probably stop here and make camp for the night. It's getting late in the day.'

She nodded, glad to be stopping for the day as her burns were starting to really ache.

It would be dark soon, but where was Silent Wolf? Raven worried when he disappeared for so long, but he always returned unharmed and usually well fed.

After they'd set up camp and finished their meals, Otter took Raven's hand in his and held it tightly.

'How are your feet and legs feeling?' he asked with a little worry in his voice. 'Should I put more salve on for you?'

'Probably not a bad idea.'

Raven walked gingerly over to the shelter, throwing her fur on top of the other furs, and removed her boots with a lot of trouble. Her feet were swollen; she knew it as her boots felt like they were stuck in place. Lying on her stomach, she waited for Otter to bring the cream. He tenderly unwrapped the cloth from around her feet and lower legs, exposing blistered skin, red and angry. Raven could tell he almost didn't want to touch her skin, but he knew it had to be done.

Otter carefully lathered the salve on, trying not to rub it too hard. Not a sound escaped her, even though the heat coming off her burns was intense.

'I'm so sorry, Raven,' he said.

'It's not your fault. I wasn't fast enough.'

'You were fast enough. You're here to tell the tale, somewhat burnt, yes, but alive, and that's all that matters.' Otter got clean cloths and carefully wrapped her feet and legs again.

'Thank you, it feels much better.'

Otter hugged Raven as she sat up, embracing her in his strong arms. She felt safe and secure in his arms and didn't want this feeling to end, or him to let go. Hugging Otter back, they just stayed that way, enjoying each other's embrace.

'Should we go back out to the fire?' Otter asked.

'I guess, if you want to?'

She wasn't sure that she wanted to. It was warm in Otter's arms, and he was so protective. Raven buried her face in the nape of his neck and sniffed deeply, smelling his scent. A warmth spread over her, along with feelings she hadn't experienced before. She felt embarrassed yet excited all at the same time.

'I guess Silent Wolf will be here before long, so maybe we should go back to the fire?' Otter said.

Raven thought that maybe Otter was feeling the same way that she was. They shared a love for one another, but up until now, for Raven anyway, it had only been a close friendship. But now there was something more there, a deeper feeling.

Otter built the fire up with more wood, then wrapped his fur around Raven's shoulders, fussing over her lovingly. He looked her in her eyes and kissed her on the cheek.

Raven felt a warm flush come over her face. *What is this?* she thought to herself. She wasn't sure, but she liked the feeling and gazed at Otter like she had never looked at him before. He returned the look, a look of love and longing.

He kissed Raven on the back of her neck and got up, removing himself from her scent and warmth. She smiled at him, her beautiful face radiating love. Raven studied his masculine, yet handsome face. She wanted to get up and go over, embrace him in her arms and kiss his full, soft lips. She knew he moved away from her because he was feeling the same things she was, she could sense it. It emanated from him, as his smell was different, stronger to her, and her body was responding with some intense feelings.

Otter threw on various sticks, keeping himself busy, pushing logs around, doing anything than looking at Raven directly. He seemed to need the distraction.

***

Silent Wolf suddenly came into focus and stood staring at them both, the fur around his mouth covered in blood. He had obviously caught something. He shook and shapeshifted back into his human skin, grabbing Otter's fur and wrapping it around himself. Otter wet a cloth and handed it to him so Silent Wolf could wash the blood from his face.

Silent Wolf looked at Otter, then at Raven, picking up a scent on the air with his keen senses. He also picked up something else from them both, something that he hadn't before. He watched them closely and knew their love was growing and their bond deepening.

Otter and Raven's eyes met across the fire, and they shared a look between them. Silent Wolf pretended not to see, and shuffled in his fur, adjusting it around his shoulders and uncomfortable with the new situation. He hoped that they kept their feelings to themselves for the time being, as they did not need the distraction, not now. Everything was way too uncertain, what with the blood witch still out there. He knew she was injured but could feel that she wasn't dead.

'How about a story?' Otter offered.

'Maybe another night? As much as I love your stories, Otter, I am still a bit spent. The hunt today has done me in.'

Raven yawned. 'I think I need to lie down too. My legs are quite sore.'

'Time to turn in then. I guess we don't need to be on guard to-night?' Otter said.

Silent Wolf shook his head, and together he and Raven made their way to the shelter.

'Otter changed my dressings and applied more ointment earlier,' Raven said, when he asked her how her burns were.

'That should tide you over. See you in the morning then,' he replied, feeling his way over to his furs and climbing under to settle in for the night.

Good night, Otter,' Raven whispered.

'Good night, Raven,' he whispered back.

Silent Wolf was quiet, saying nothing.

Raven tried desperately to sleep, she drifted off, but the pain in her legs and feet kept her awake somewhat, and she tossed and turned. Her feet were throbbing, and her legs were hot, so she threw off the fur from her legs, just keeping the top of her body covered. It was not until the early hours of the morning when she finally succumbed to sleep.

***

Otter woke first, and Silent Wolf came out next.

'Organised as per usual, I see,' said Silent Wolf.

'It's not like Raven to sleep in,' Otter said when she didn't appear behind Silent Wolf. 'I'm going to check on her.'

He pulled open the shelter flap door and peered inside. Raven stirred and groaned.

'My feet and legs are throbbing,' she grimaced.

'What can I do?' he asked.

Silent Wolf joined him and looked Raven over. He could see in the dim morning light that she was feverish from her wounds. 'Get me some cool water and a cloth,' he said.

Otter raced out, worried that he did not realise how serious Raven's burns were when he was dressing them. He was kicking himself now. Returning, Silent Wolf had already unwrapped her wounds and was inspecting them. They did not look great, but he could help her if he found the right herbs to bring down her fever and pain.

'Raven, where is your herb bag?' Silent Wolf asked.

'They're all gone. We used them when Otter was poisoned. I was going to go out this morning and find more herbs for myself, but…' her words trailed off.

She was exhausted. The blisters on her feet and lower legs were weeping and oozing pus, and now looked infected. Silent Wolf cleaned her wounds with cool, clean water and let them air dry before rubbing more salve on them. He wrapped them in clean cloth before heading out of the shelter, gesturing Otter to follow.

'Keep wiping her brow with the cool water. I'll head out and find the herbs we need to help with the pain and fever as quickly as possible.'

With that, Silent Wolf shapeshifted and raced off and out of sight into the forest.

Otter sat by Raven, wiping her brow with the cool cloth and holding her hand. He thought that this was as good a time as any to tell her one of his stories. It was called The Bird and the Brave. Otter left out a good amount of the story, mostly focusing on the part he really wanted her to hear.

'The bird and the brave's undying love for one another allowed the brave to transform into a bird also, for he had shown great strength and courage in the face of death. And so, it was told, the brave had been granted a wish from the Great Spirit, and his one and only wish was to become a raven and join his love in flight. As the brave was about to change into his raven form, he asked, "But what if I fall?" To the brave's question, he heard a reply, "Oh, darling, but what if you fly?"

'The brave was transformed, and his brown-black feathers glistened in the summer sun. He stretched out his wings and flapped them, testing his new limbs. The brave heard whispering on the wind, and it told him that "fortune favours the brave, you have escaped the cage. You have wings, now fly." Together they flew, they carolled and sang, and their songs were happy songs. The two ravens rose and dived upon the ground like clear drops of morning dew, higher and higher, their beautiful strong wings taking them to new heights. They climbed the thermal updrafts together, weaving their way far upward above the puffy white clouds until a great peace washed over them.'

Otter wished with all his heart that his story was true. That one day, he would do just that and join his beautiful raven in flight.

'Maybe if I pray to the Great Spirit, it will be granted,' he whispered in Raven's ear.

Raven slept now, so he was not sure if she'd heard him or his story at all, but he felt good to tell it anyway, even if it was just a small part of the story. Otter continued to wipe away the beads of sweat that formed on her brow. She had sat with him while he was ill; now he sat with her, praying to the Great Spirit to heal her and take her pain away.

Otter watched over Raven through the day and continued to care for her as best he could, waiting patiently for Silent Wolf to return. He had managed to heal Otter, so he was sure he would find the right herbs to help her. Silent Wolf returned later in the morning with several different herbs: a large piece of aloe, some calendula, gotu kola and feverfew. Otter was starting to know his herbs. Raven had taught him how to identify many different plants over the years. She used to collect a variety every week, and Otter would join her, watching with interest how and when she harvested them.

Silent Wolf quickly ground the herbs to a paste and added it to the salve that they already had. He cleaned and redressed Raven's burns then made tea out of some of the calendula and feverfew, which he cooled before giving it to Raven to sip on.

'She'll be okay,' Silent Wolf said, after several hours had passed. 'Her fever has broken, so she just needs to sleep now and recover.'

Otter sat silently, staring at the fire, thinking about everything that had happened so far, and everything that was going to happen, the uncertainty of it all. Nothing was guaranteed, except for two things: his love for Raven – and their need to end this miserable witch's life.

The snow had ceased falling, but it was still cold, and the trails would be slippery and wet as the snow started to melt. They would have to be careful as the trails could be treacherous this time of year. Rocks gave way as ice and water melted, and exposed knotted tree roots were super slippery. They would have to watch their step and guide the horses carefully. The clouds started to dissipate, giving way to patches of blue sky, and the sun was now shining patchwork patterns through the canopy of the trees. Flickering light burst its way down between knotted branches, offering a tiny taste of what was to come in the following months, a tiny tease of spring.

***

Raven tossed and turned on top of her furs in the shelter. She slept deeply, but now she dreamed. She was flying, and it was dark at first, like it usually was, but this time she was not afraid. It was silent, and there were no sounds except for the beating of her wings on the wind. The cool air surrounded her feathers, and she felt free. This was pure bliss, and she didn't have the desire to call out for she wasn't lost. She was flying free and felt this path had purpose. It was dark except for the stars shining brightly in the night sky, tiny little sparkles filling the space around her. The sight was beautiful. Raven glided on the breeze, no flapping required, and sheer and utter happiness filled her bird body as she continued to glide through the starry void. Suddenly, rainbows of colour engulfed her. It was incredible, and she had never seen anything like this before in her dreams. A feeling of love surged through her, and she twirled and twisted around the colours, almost as if she was dancing.

What was this place? Where was she? Wherever she was, this was magical, and she did not want to wake from the feeling of love. It was exhilarating and exciting. The colours intensified and glowed brilliantly all around her, vast in their glorious waves. She felt she could lose herself here, and not wake up, just stay in this feeling and remain forever. She had no pain here, knew no sadness, just sheer and utter love was all she felt.

As beautiful as it was though, she was alone. If only Otter could be here to experience this with her, the magic, how incredible it would be. Silent Wolf too, she thought, as she danced in the glorious magic of coloured light. The colours danced in waves of bright then dull, bright then dull, like someone was turning them off and on, or like they were following the beat of a drum, bright, dull, bright, dull.

Then as suddenly as they came, they were gone. Raven knew that this was the most magical dream she had ever experienced. It was over for now, but if it had meaning, the seer would be able to guide her and have answers. As Raven started to wake from her dream, she flapped her wings to land on the forest floor. As her claws touched the cold, hard ground, she woke. Looking around at the forest, it was so exceptionally beautiful. What a wonderful world, so full of magic and possibilities.

Raven looked up into the top of the shelter. She felt okay; actually, better than okay. There was hardly any pain in her feet and legs, but how was this possible? Some mystical magic that she could not explain, that was for sure. She felt incredibly grateful for it, as somehow the experience she'd just had had somehow helped her heal, she knew it.

Getting up, she made her way out of the shelter and over to Otter and Silent Wolf sitting by the fire, sipping tea, and talking quietly between themselves. They both looked up at Raven with the most astonished looks on their faces.

'Raven,' Otter stammered. 'You're up!' His tone sounded amazed, as did the look on his face.

They both jumped up, and Otter took her arm and led her over to his fur, where she sat down. She was even able to cross her legs. Otter's eyes widened in astonishment, and he looked at Silent Wolf.

'Can you believe what you're seeing?' he asked him.

Silent Wolf stared long and hard at Raven. 'Something is different,' he said, without breaking his gaze.

'Yes,' replied Raven. 'I had a of vision.'

Otter handed her a cup of warm tea, and she sipped it as she retold her dream. Silent Wolf and Otter sat and listened without uttering a single word. They were as stunned as she was. When Raven had finished retelling her tale of magic, Silent Wolf agreed that she'd had some divine intervention and help.

'How fortunate, and blessed,' he said, joining both hands together and giving his thanks to the Great Spirit.

Otter asked Raven if she had heard his story while she was recovering from her fever. Raven said she'd heard his voice, that it was soothing to her, but that she could not make sense of what was said. Just bits and pieces, as she'd floated in and out of consciousness, far away in magical lands of her own. She thanked Otter for sitting by her side and telling her a story, and that she would look forward to hearing it again by the fireside one night.

She also thanked Silent Wolf for collecting healing herbs for her and looking after her so well. Raven looked up into the sky at the white clouds, soft and puffy, grey and white, mixed amongst the blue patches. She remembered the rainbow colours so vividly as they'd danced around her head and would never forget it for as long as she lived. They all sat in silence, enjoying the warmth of the fire, the hot tea and the good company of each other. It felt like this was going to be a good day, she could just feel it in her soul.

The Beast Inside

Ivy the blood witch gradually came to, her trusty cat Luna sitting by her side, watching with her lovely green eyes. She meowed at her companion, greeting her with affection. Ivy stirred, her wounds still sore as she moved, fuelling her hate and anger at the warrior for his deadly arrows.

Ivy eased herself up, guarding the wound on her side and looking around the house she was in. *Not bad*, she thought to herself, although it was a bit too clean and tidy for her liking. She preferred the darkness of her fortress in the woods. Ivy's abode had emanated power, something she did not feel here. The fireplace she was in front of was beautiful indeed, with the gargoyles looking ominously down at her with their dark eyes and sharp jaws, handsome winged creatures carved in stone. She would enjoy taking this house for her own.

Freya's home contained many things that Ivy's had not. Her stone table was neatly organised with jars and bowls of all sizes, much like Ivy's, only tidy. There were no dripping candles, everything had a place, so it seemed. This witch was ridiculously organised, so much so, it made Ivy feel sick to her stomach.

Now, where was the stranger? Ivy scanned the house, but there was no sight of her. Luna meowed and rubbed herself against Ivy, looking over at the window and door.

'Ah,' whispered Ivy, 'out in her garden, is she? That's good, it gives me time to snoop, and do what I do best.' Ivy rolled to her left side and managed to push herself up, feeling a little better than when she arrived. She hobbled over to the table, dragging her injured leg behind her, and sorted through Freya's belongings: spices, herbs, flowers, feathers, crystals and bones. On a shelf above the table, Ivy spied dusty scrolls and antique charts gleaming with gold leaf and bound in satiny leather. Obviously, there were some rare ones as they were chained in place.

Feathery goose and crow quills, and jars of oak bark were steeped in water for the making of ink. Scattered amongst the books were various lenses and prisms, a type of unusual-shaped glass for watching eclipses. There was also a gleaming brass compass, alidades, quadrants and an ancient-looking astrolabe for observing the heavens.

Ivy had seen her grandmother carry and use an astrolabe, for she had been skilled in astronomy. Ivy often used to play with it when she was young, but this item had been sacred to her grandmother, so it was buried along with her and her other most treasured items. As Ivy spied Freya's collection, she thought to herself that they did both possess some items that were similar. For amongst her items, she had a tidy collection of assorted bones, skeletons of birds and other small animals, which were displayed on her table and bookshelf along with other various flasks, bell jars and crucibles of a practising alchemist.

Indeed, Ivy would have to be wary and careful in how she went about stealing the witch's magic. If this stranger knew that Ivy was indeed a blood witch, it would change everything. Best to let her think her a defenceless old witch who posed no threat. Ivy limped back over to the sofa in front of the fire and gingerly sat down, keeping her right side as straight as possible. The pain in her leg throbbed just from walking that short distance.

'Damn that wolf,' she fumed, but then calmed herself.

She didn't want to alert Freya when she came back, so she would have to be on her best behaviour. It would be a good disguise, she thought, as it allowed her to fool her opponent and come off as just old and powerless.

The wooden door opened with a creak, and Freya came in quietly so as not to wake the wounded witch. But the old woman was sitting up, sort of, lying on her side anyway, awake, and looking at the fire. Freya came to her side.

'I'm known as Freya in these parts,' she said, holding out her hand to Ivy.

Ivy looked at her hand for a minute, and thought it best not be rude, even though she didn't want to shake Freya's hand. She took her hand ever so gently and tried to appear as feeble as she could.

'Ivy,' she croaked.

Freya, seeing she was feeble and weak still, went to her fire. She had a cauldron suspended over it, and bubbling away was a lovely-smelling chicken broth. Freya grew her own vegetables, so had added some carrots and potato, along with some greens. She scooped out a ladleful and handed Ivy a small bowl. Ivy smelled the broth to make sure it wasn't something sinister. She just couldn't help herself from being suspicious as this was her nature.

Realising what she was doing appeared rude, Ivy said, 'Lovely, you seem quite the cook? Thank you for taking us in, it is very appreciated, but we will be out of your hair as soon as I am able to fly.'

'No hurry,' Freya replied. 'I haven't had a visitor, let alone one not from these parts, for so long. I look forward to the company and hearing all about your story.'

Freya smiled at Ivy and sat down beside her on the rug in front of the fire, looking like she was ready, right there and then for the story.

Ivy thought fast. 'It's not much of a story,' she whispered as she slurped away at the broth.

It wasn't too bad tasting, much better than anything she had ever made, and the greasy chicken fat slid down her parched throat and soothed it. Ivy couldn't help but think about snuffing out Freya and she almost let out a little snicker but managed to stop herself in time. She didn't want her malevolent nature to show.

Freya got herself a bowl of the broth also and joined Ivy, eating so politely. It was sickening, Ivy thought, how pretty she was. Ivy watched her as she ate, her pale skin soft and wrinkle free, and Freya's beautiful emerald-green eyes looked back at her. Freya's hair was the most gorgeous colour of red, and the soft locks glistened in the firelight with hues of orange and red. Her Scottish accent also sounded very posh! *Oh, it'd be delightful to see her pristine floor stained with her blood.*

When they'd finished eating, Ivy watched as Freya washed up. Her slim body looked fit and healthy, and her clothes were neat and tidy, no stains to be seen. Ivy looked down at her own dress; it was horrid, so stained in blood. What must Freya think of her. Even though it didn't bother Ivy to be covered in blood; she actually liked it, the smell of it, reminding her of her kills, the sweet taste of the warm blood as it gushed in her mouth. How she would enjoy draining this beautiful woman's blood from her body. But for now, Ivy knew she couldn't stay like this, in her filth, in Freya's company. If she did, it would in fact give away her guise, and Freya would soon work out who and what she was: an evil blood witch from an ancient bloodline, so powerful in her youth.

Freya returned to Ivy's side and decided this was as good a time as any to question the old woman.

'What on earth has done this to you?' asked Freya, as she examined the deep tears on Ivy's leg.

'A stag's antler.' Ivy visibly blanched. 'He almost had me too,' she added. 'It was a silly accident; one I won't make again. Luckily, I had my broom, so I could escape.'

Ivy could tell that Freya wondered if a stag's antler could do so much damage. It probably looked more like teeth wounds to her, but she was too polite to say anything.

'Ivy, I have a lovely bathroom outside, behind my house. Can I run you a hot bath and get you cleaned up before I dress your other wounds?'

'I guess I do need to bathe and change,' she replied, looking down at her filthy dress.

Freya raced off to get the bath ready for her guest. Her bathroom was indeed very beautiful, as she had lovely green and purple vines growing inside on the wall. Green and orange-coloured glass bottles were built into the wall on the far side of the room, and when the sun shone through it was pretty like stained glass. Stained glass was one of her talents.

She added essential oil of lavender and rose, along with some dried rose petals to the bathwater, to give the old woman a lovely smell. With the soothing properties of the lavender, she would have Ivy feeling much better in no time. Placing several candles around the bath's edge and on top of the windowsill, the flame would shine through the glass bottles and look very pleasing. Happy with her setup, she returned to help Ivy.

'It's all ready for you,' said Freya.

She got under Ivy's left side and assisted her to stand. Ivy, in a great deal of pain, hunched over and put her weight onto Freya's arm. Ivy limped, grimacing with each step.

As they entered the bathroom, Ivy's senses filled with the fragrances of the oils and soaps that Freya stored within the room. They weren't really her cup of blood, but she pretended to enjoy the smell. Freya helped Ivy remove her dirty and blood-sodden clothing before assisting her into the bath. Ivy grimaced, as the hot water stung her wounds, and she would have preferred not to bathe. However, she kept her true feelings to herself, and sat quite still in the steaming hot bath.

'Would you like me to do anything with your hair?' Freya asked.

Ivy almost choked out her reply. 'My hair remains as it is.'

'Should I at least run some water over it, so that the bath oils will give it a nice scent?' asked Freya.

'I would rather you didn't. I mean, no thank you, dear.'

Freya looked at the two wounds the arrows had made and asked Ivy about them. Ivy knew that all witches around the world were hunted by hateful humans, so this was as good a story as any to give the younger woman.

'A hunter who has been trying to capture me for many years almost had his pleasure and shot me with two of his arrows. I was just lucky enough to escape and tend to my wounds before finding my way here.'

As Freya washed Ivy's back, she asked ever so gently, 'And just how did you come to find my place?'

'I was flying in your lands one night, as I often like to do. It was here that I saw you in the dark of night, flying on your broom, so I decided to follow you. I'm so glad I did. I thought you looked very kind and beautiful, and right I was.'

Freya brought over a big, fluffy towel and assisted Ivy to climb out of the bath, wrapping the large towel around her and covering Ivy's wrinkled body. At least she was clean and didn't have a pungent odour anymore. Then she assisted Ivy back inside her house and sat her near the fire.

'I will just go and get you something fresh to wear, as I'm not sure your old dress can be saved,' she said, looking at Ivy's reaction to this comment.

Ivy felt a pang of sadness and wanted to let the tears flow, but she wouldn't. She couldn't or be exposed she would.

She held back the tears and swallowed hard. 'It's very dear to me, but I understand there is probably no coming back from the damage it has endured. Although, I wish for the dress to stay as it is, and with me, for I cannot bear to part with it just yet.'

Ivy remembered the flower and glass vial still hidden well within the dress pocket, which she couldn't risk Freya finding if she were to wash the garment and try and repair it. Ivy would keep a very watchful eye on her old dress until she could retrieve the items and hide them safely.

Freya had many old velvet dresses herself that she had collected and others she had made herself. She was sure she would find her something, as equally if not more beautiful than her old, tattered dress.

Leaving Ivy's side, she disappeared up a spiral staircase to the upper level of her house, where her bedroom and closet were. Her closet was jam-packed full of lovely dresses and skirts of all kinds of fabrics. Freya could see that Ivy's dress had indeed been beautiful in its day. Antique for sure, its style outdated now, but still most lovely. Freya searched through her assortment of clothes and found some nice under garments that Ivy may like, a black singlet made from brushed cotton, soft to the touch.

Deep in the back of her cupboard she found the perfect dress. It was old, but Freya had restored it to near-new again. It was in mint condition, like everything in Freya's house, and a deep velvet blue-black colour, trimmed with lighter blue lace on the sleeves and neckline. It gathered at the waist, giving the dress a timeless, elegant look. Freya observed that Ivy's stature closely mirrored her own – tall and slender, although a bit more stooped and malnourished – leading her to believe that her garments would suit Ivy well. If anything, they might be slightly oversized, given Ivy's thinner frame. Nevertheless, Freya was confident that any adjustments required could easily be made.

Freya returned to Ivy, who was sitting patiently waiting for her, still wrapped in her wet towel. Freya held up the dress in front of her, and Ivy's eyes widened. This was indeed most unexpected – the dress was stunning. Ivy let out a little gasp as she reached out to feel it.

Ivy ran her wrinkled hand over the front of the dress, feeling the soft and luxurious fabric. 'This is most generous,' said Ivy.

'I'm only happy to help, and above all, is it to your liking?' replied Freya.

'To my liking?' Ivy said, 'I love it. It is the most glamorous dress I have ever seen. Where on earth did you come across it?'

'Let's just say that I acquired it for a job I did for one of the old town's folks. Having no money, and knowing my love of sewing, they offered this dress as payment. It needed some tender loving care, but I was more than happy with this arrangement.'

Ivy nodded, understanding and appreciating this strange witch just a little bit now, for she did not expect her to produce anything of such value, let alone gift it to her like she just did. This was something that Ivy would never do, for she was a taker, not a giver like Freya. Ivy almost felt bad at what she was secretly planning; almost, but not really. For it was not in Ivy's nature to feel anything other than hatred and contempt for anyone she met. The only people she had ever cared for were long gone now. Now she only cared for herself and her will to live, and to be the strongest and most powerful witch of all time.

Eternal youth, power and her two familiars that were left were all she cared about now, as her dark master had abandoned her years ago. Ivy would not allow this new witch to seep her way into her emotions. She didn't want to like her or care for her. So, she pushed the emotions of sheer and utter delight down into the core of her body, hiding them there.

'What sort of job did you do to be paid so handsomely with this dress?' Ivy continued feeling the glorious texture of the velvet between her gnarled fingers.

'I healed a sick child that a mother could not help any further. She had tried everything she knew, and fearing her child's death, the woman sought help where she never thought she would ever seek it: from the help of a witch. My healing abilities and magic have been spoken of throughout the town for many years, and many fear me. But the desperate kind, like this woman, so desperate was she to help her child that she put her fears aside and came deep into the forest late one night in search of me. She was in luck this particular night for I just happened to be out collecting mushrooms and herbs, when she stumbled across my path. She begged and cried for my help, and I couldn't refuse her, for she had shown great courage this night in her quest for her child's life.

'I went with her to her home hidden under the cover of night and assessed her child, who was her frightfully ill, and racked with fever. I retrieved what I needed, then returned to the woman's home and healed her child.'

Freya continued to prattle on, regardless of Ivy's obvious boredom and before long, Ivy found her mind drifting off, Freya's words dripping with exquisite tedium, and she wished she would just shut up.

Ivys sat deep in thought and watched the fire, the flames dancing around the hearth, the light casting shadows around the house and the ever-present gargoyles watching down over her like they were alive and knew her deepest, darkest thoughts. Ivy shivered.

Freya mistook her shiver for being cold. 'I have just the thing,' she said, as she retrieved a fur blanket and placed it over Ivy's legs.

Her caring nature sickened Ivy but smile she did. Freya disappeared again up her spiral staircase. Ivy was glad, as she could relax and stop being so nice. It was annoying. Just when Ivy thought she could sit and think, Freya returned as quickly as she had left. She produced a woollen knitted scarf, similar in colour to the blue-black dress. Could this get any better, as once she had devoured Raven's magic, her hair would return to its former glory and also have the beautiful colour that Raven possessed in her feathers: blue-black.

It was meant to be, thought Ivy, everything that had happened that had led her here was supposed to happen. The colour of the dress and now the scarf made her certain of it.

Ivy smiled her best smile. She really was happy that Freya had produced not one but two quality products for her to keep. Freya wrapped up Ivy's dreads and covered the top part of her head. It looked much better than the pile of dirty locks that was presently Ivy's hair.

Freya would work on this later, once the old woman warmed to her affections. Freya could tell that the old witch was not used to being shown any sort of affection, maybe not for a long time anyway. She would change all that, for what was life without some love and friendship in it?

Lady Evil

Ivy woke to the sounds of Freya stoking the fire and adding more wood, igniting it out of its dormant state, once again. Ivy pretended that she was still sleeping and watched the young witch through slitted eyes. Ivy was starting to crave blood; she needed it if she were to recover quickly; otherwise, she would be stuck here for a lot longer than she wished. She also needed to extract the sap from the stem of the flower. This was most important otherwise its potency would be lost. Keeping her eyes shut tightly, she thought of a devious plan to get rid of Freya for the day.

Freya went about her daily routine and using her mortar and pestle, selected the herbs she required, and she ground them, but only slightly, just enough to release the aroma. Freya was making quite the noise now, there was no way Ivy could lay there any longer, for the sound of her banging and tapping her tea pot and herbs annoyed Ivy to no end.

She sat up and glanced over at Freya, glaring a hateful look her way. But she quickly changed it to a half-crooked smile, a poor attempt without doubt.

'Oh, I'm so sorry Ivy, did I wake you?'

She had to be kidding, thought Ivy. 'Oh no bother,' Ivy replied in her nicest voice.

'Would you like a cup of tea? I have made a fresh pot.'

Ivy thought about it. 'What sort of tea have you made?' she asked.

'One of my favourites, rose, peppermint and honey,' Freya answered with a friendly smile.

Ivy should have guessed; this witch seemed to have a thing for roses. Ivy, being quite thirsty, said as politely as possible, 'That would be just lovely, dear,' but she felt sick to her stomach, and it wasn't from her wounds. Being so nice was just hideous to her.

Freya made her tea, she stirred and stirred it, Ivy thought she may very well stir the bottom out of the cup she stirred it so much. 'There' she said, 'Perfect' as she handed Ivy a cup. Ivy blew it, sniffed it and sipped it ever so cautiously, as if the contents may end her life. Ivy decided it was not so bad, not really what she liked, but it would do, she would have to put up with it for a while longer. She sipped the tea slowly, in no hurry to finish the sweet rose-scented brew.

She thought about a plan to be rid Freya for a while. 'I wonder, my dear,' Ivy croaked, trying to sound as feeble as possible. 'Would you do an old woman a good deed and fetch me a rabbit for Luna to eat?'

Freya looked at the old woman's face and was a little surprised at her request. 'A rabbit?' Freya stammered. 'We mostly live on the wild game around my little cottage, and Luna would be most appreciative as well.'

Ivy patted her cat, who was sitting attentively at her side. Luna meowed as if to agree with her mistress. Freya looked at the cat and had to admit that she felt sorry for the pair, and she felt obliged to offer her services so she agreed.

'I will head out very soon then before the sun comes up or I will not find any, they will be well hidden within the safety of their burrows.'

Ivy knew this, and her plan had worked perfectly. Freya finished her tea and grabbed her broom. She told Ivy she would be back as soon as she could and to make herself at home while she was gone.

Ivy had every intention of it, she almost chuckled at how easy it was to get rid of her. She held in her devious laugh and continued patting Luna. Ivy waited a few minutes to make sure Freya was well and truly out of sight, just in case she came back. She couldn't think of any reason other than to catch her out, but perhaps that was just Ivy's suspicious nature playing at hand.

With no sound of Freya returning, she made her way to Freya's bench, the pain in her wounds aching, but she pushed the pain away as she needed to focus on the job. It didn't take her long to find the items she needed. A small-handled sharp knife, this would do nicely to cut the stem with. She remembered she still had a pair of small scissors in her dress pocket, and could hold the stem with these, avoiding the fine needles that covered it. Her soiled dress was stuffed under the blankets on the sofa. As quickly as she could, she made for the table. She needed to hurry, not knowing when Freya would return, and pulled out the flower that was safely wrapped up in the leather cloth. Carefully she unrolled it open, laying the cloth flat so she could inspect it. The flower was still glowing.

A devious sneer spread across her face.

Ivy hurried, her movements a careful balance of speed and caution. The urgency felt foreign to her, a stark contrast to her usual meticulous pace. Her old, gnarled fingers flew over the task, deftly completing it before she paused to wipe the sweat from her brow. Inspecting the table, her dull eyes scanning every detail, she quickly cleaned the knife, wiping the blade free of any sap. She placed it back in its exact spot, ensuring everything was just as it had been. With everything in order, she moved as swiftly as her wounded leg would allow, clutching the poison and dress. Reaching the sofa, she stuffed them deep beneath the cushions, hiding them once again from sight.

Ivy sighed deeply through her nose, realising she still had to get rid of the flower. Picking it up ever so carefully with the scissors, she limped towards the door. Her leg ached, and her desire to sit was rapidly growing. She peered out, and there was no sign of Freya so the coast was clear. Making her way outside, she followed the pathway to the garden and dropped the flower. Squatting down proved harder than she thought, and she bit down on her lip, grimacing in pain. Using the scissors, she frantically dug a hole big enough to conceal her secret, covering it over and hiding any signs of the earth being disturbed.

As she stood up, her eyes scanned the garden for any lingering evidence of her actions. Her heart pounded in her chest, each beat echoing the urgency of her situation. The garden, with its vibrant blooms and lush greenery, seemed to mock her with its serenity. She brushed off her hands, dirt clinging to her fingers, and took a moment to steady her breath.

And not a moment too soon, and as if scripted by fate, Freya emerged from the lush green hedgerow at the end of the pathway. A rabbit, trussed by its feet, dangled over her shoulder as she made her way towards Ivy, her expression betraying a hint of astonishment at discovering her there, bathed in the soft glow of the morning sun.

'Is everything alright, Ivy?' Freya inquired, a touch of concern colouring her voice.

Ivy paused for a moment, contemplating, before responding swiftly. 'I simply fancied a stroll to stretch my legs, and the allure of exploring your beautiful garden beckoned. Besides, since you've graciously spared me the task of capturing a rabbit, I felt it only fair to dispatch it for my feline companion.'

A sense of relief flooded over Freya, grateful to be spared the grisly chore of the kill.

Ivy's eyes sparkled with a mischievous glint before darting downward, evading Freya's inquisitive gaze.

'Well, if you're absolutely certain you're up for it?' Freya responded, a genuine note of concern lacing her voice as she observed the pallor of Ivy's complexion, tinged with a grey hue, and pondered how long she had been exposed to the brisk elements.

'I'm more than willing to assist, my dear,' Ivy cooed, her tone as smooth as silk, exuding an air of innocence that belied her cunning intentions, secretly pleased that her scheme was unfolding according to plan.

Freya handed the rabbit to Ivy and directed her to the stone bench behind the bathhouse, a secluded spot that would suit her needs perfectly. Ivy's mind raced with satisfaction at the prospect of the privacy it offered for her dark ritual of consuming the rabbit's blood.

'Well, I'll leave it in your capable hands,' Freya remarked, relieved to be rid of the task. With a swift turn on her heel, she made her way back to the warmth and comfort of her home, closing the door firmly behind her.

As Freya disappeared from view, Ivy realised she lacked a knife and called out in a sudden panic, 'Oh, dear!' her shrill voice cut through the air, causing Freya to reappear, looking surprised.

'I'm terribly sorry to bother you, but could you do one more favour for an old woman?' Ivy's voice quivered with false frailty, a façade that sickened her to her core.

Freya's concern flickered in her eye's, hoping Ivy hadn't changed her mind and now required assistance in killing and dismembering the rabbit.

In response, Freya swallowed hard and asked, 'Yes, what do you need?'

Ivy replied with sickening sweetness, 'I seem to have forgotten a knife.'

Relief washed over Freya, and she hurried back inside to fetch one, her Scottish accent echoing as she apologised for the oversight.

Returning fast, Freya handed Ivy the knife with a bone handle before retreating once more. Unseen by Freya, a wicked smirk crossed Ivy's face, her eyes gleaming with anticipation at the thought of fresh blood, a sinister glint betraying her true intentions.

Ivy hobbled with determination as she navigated her way to the rear of the bathhouse, her injured leg throbbing with each step. Despite the discomfort, the allure of the rabbit's warm blood eclipsed her physical distress. Swiftly, she snapped the rabbit's neck and made a precise incision, ensuring not a single drop of its precious essence was wasted as she savoured every last bit. The gamey richness flooded her parched throat, sending waves of pleasure through her, causing her eyes to flutter in pure ecstasy. In a fleeting moment, her craving was satisfied.

Effortlessly skinning and dismembering the rabbit, Ivy basked in the thrill of her cunning actions, a sinister chuckle escaping her lips. Setting aside a portion of the meat for her companion Luna, she deftly wrapped the remainder in the pelt. Before long, she indulged in consuming the rabbit's heart and tender eyes, relishing the visceral experience as they slid down her throat with minimal resistance, requiring little more than a cursory chew.

Ivy's lips curled into a devious smirk as she entertained the idea of extinguishing Freya once the latter had served her intended role. With the sun now casting its full radiance, Ivy's grin widened as she re-entered the enchanting witch's abode. Freya, noticing the remnants of the rabbit, felt a tinge of surprise at the scarcity of what was left. Perhaps the cat had been ravenous beyond expectation. Shrugging off the thought, she resolved to craft a delightful rabbit stew, immersing herself in the preparations with focused intent.

Ivy luxuriated in the glow of the roaring fire, its comforting heat easing the ache in her weary bones. Observing Freya, she resolved to request additional rabbits from the woman, recognising the necessity of more blood to speed her recovery. Hoping for Freya's acquiescence, Ivy envisioned a swift return to her quest to locate Raven. Satiated and content after her meal, she extended her limbs and closed her tired eyes, surrendering to sleep's embrace without delay.

***

Freya observed Ivy in her deep slumber, a tinge of compassion washing over her as it appeared that even the simplest tasks had left the woman utterly depleted. Leaving Ivy to the solace of her dark reveries, Freya discreetly tended to the rabbit shank. Ivy's enigmatic presence lingered in Freya's thoughts, igniting a fervent curiosity about the woman who had divulged so little about herself thus far. Resolving to explore this mystery at a more opportune time, Freya considered initiating a conversation over a steaming cup of rose tea, hoping to coax Ivy into sharing her secrets. Ivy seemed guarded, her privacy a fortress yet to be breached.

Unbeknownst to Freya, the peril Ivy posed loomed large. If she had only grasped the imminent danger, Freya might have resorted to poisoning the tea and utilising Ivy's remains to nourish her garden.

Room to Breathe

In the quiet of twilight, Ivy stirred from her slumber, her movements deliberate as she stretched her arms skyward and released a lingering yawn. As her gaze wandered, she caught sight of Freya diligently working at her bench. At the sound of Ivy's awakening, Freya turned with a warm smile and a playful greeting, 'Why, hello there, sleepy head.'

With a subtle flicker of defiance in her eyes, Ivy silently vowed to show Freya what true weariness felt like. A faint, strained smile graced her lips as she pushed herself upright and fixed her gaze upon the crackling fire, its warmth casting a comforting glow across the room.

'I've been waiting for you to rise. You must be parched by now. How about a soothing cup of hot tea?' Freya's enchanting emerald eyes sparkled in the firelight, a hint of mischief dancing within them.

Suppressing a flicker of distaste at the mention of tea, Ivy yearned for a different kind of sustenance, craving the taste of blood instead of the herbal concoction Freya insisted upon. Determined to broach the subject of acquiring more rabbits, Ivy seized the opportunity presented before her.

'Ah, that sounds delightful. I find myself quite thirsty,' Ivy purred in her velvety voice, masking her true desires beneath a veneer of compliance.

Freya, ever the proactive hostess, didn't linger for Ivy's response; she busied herself crushing fresh ginger in her mortar, having prepared the other ingredients beforehand. With practiced ease, she set the water to boil and allowed the fragrant herbs to infuse, the aroma of ginger and honeysuckle mingling in the air.

After a few minutes of brewing, Freya presented Ivy with a beautifully crafted cup of steaming ginger tea. Ivy approached the cup with caution, her senses keen as she tentatively took in the delicate notes wafting from the brew. A subtle hint of vanilla teased her nostrils, offering a surprising contrast to her expectations.

Watching Freya closely, Ivy observed as the young witch took a sip of the tea first. Only once Freya had sampled her own creation did Ivy allow herself a sip, blowing gently on the steam rising from the cup before taking a cautious taste. To her astonishment, the tea proved to be far more palatable than she had anticipated. The flavours danced on her tongue, the warmth spreading through her aching body. A small smile tugged at the corners of Ivy's lips, a grudging acknowledgement of Freya's skill in brewing a drink that surpassed her initial reservations.

With the two of them reclining comfortably in front of the crackling fire, Ivy felt a flicker of curiosity stirring within her. Leaning in slightly, she gently broached the delicate topic with the red-headed beauty beside her. 'So, my dear, forgive me for prying, but I can't help but wonder what led you to dwell in solitude at such a tender age?'

Taken aback by Ivy's directness, Freya's initial composure wavered. Subtle tension crept into her features, her expression shifting imperceptibly as a veil of melancholy descended. Her emerald eyes, illuminated by the dancing flames, reflected a deep well of sorrow as she began to recount her tale.

Freya's mother, a fearsome witch shrouded in darkness, was consumed by inconsolable grief upon learning of her daughter's innate gift as a white witch. Condemned by her own coven and marked to live a solitary existence, Freya's very essence defied their attempts to purge her of her white magic. Cast out at the tender age of sixteen, she was exiled not just from her homeland, but from her kin. The modest castle that now sheltered her had once served as a sanctuary during the harrowing days of the witch hunts.

The journey from Scotland to her secluded haven in the English countryside had been fraught with anguish and despair. Initially, the weight of her isolation felt like a punishment more severe than death itself. Yet, with time, Freya forged a new existence for herself, embracing her role as a healer while steadfastly shunning the allure of the dark arts. Tears traced silent paths down her cheeks, her gaze fixed unwaveringly on the flames as she wiped them away, seeking solace in the warmth of her tea.

Ivy, though concealing her inner jubilation at unearthing Freya's hidden anguish, recognised an opportunity to secure their seclusion from prying eyes. The notion of extinguishing the perceived threat Freya posed flitted briefly through her mind. 'Oh, my dear, what a heartbreaking ordeal,' she murmured sympathetically, her smile tinged with a hint of concealed malevolence. 'It's always admirable to stay true to oneself, don't you think?'

As the fire crackled softly in the background, a subtle tension lingered in the air, veiled beneath the façade of camaraderie between the two women.

Ivy, emboldened by her craving for more sustenance, decided to make a daring request for additional rabbits, her appetite for blood already stirring within her. With a voice that dripped like liquid gold, she approached Freya with feigned sweetness, her eyes gleaming with hidden desire. 'I wonder if I may impose upon you for another favour,' Ivy began, her words laced with a subtle charm that belied her true intentions.

Observing Ivy's demeanour closely, Freya's thoughts swirled with suspicion.

What now? she pondered, bracing herself for the impending request.

As Ivy artfully wove her tale about Luna's affection for the rabbits and the potential solution of a weekly offering, a flicker of discomfort crossed Freya's features, much to Ivy's concealed delight.

The request for a rabbit per week caused Freya to shift uneasily in her seat, her complexion paling slightly under Ivy's watchful gaze.

Stammering slightly, she reluctantly agreed, 'I guess I could do that.'

Ivy, quick to capitalise on Freya's tentative agreement, assured her of their imminent departure, painting a picture of swift resolution to put her at ease.

Relieved at the prospect of reclaiming her sanctuary by the fire and restoring normalcy to her quiet abode, Freya concealed her inner turmoil. The constant presence of Luna and Ivy, their scrutinising gazes, unsettled her deeply, evoking a sense of something she struggled to define. Ivy's resemblance to her dark and malevolent mother stirred unwelcome memories within Freya, prompting her to shake her head in a bid to dispel the haunting thoughts that threatened to engulf her.

A half hour later, Freya decided it was time to head to bed. A sudden wave of exhaustion washed over her like a scorching inferno. With Ivy tended to, she ascended the spiralling staircase, each step weighed down by an oppressive darkness that seemed to envelop her. Nestling under the comforting warmth of her covers, she drew them tightly around her chin. Despite her efforts, a lingering sense of foreboding lingered, prompting her to shut her eyes and silently plead for sleep to claim her.

In her restless slumber, Freya found herself running, her legs burdened by an unbearable weight. Abruptly, a thick rope coiled around her neck, its fibres painfully digging into her delicate skin. Frantically clawing at the constricting noose proved futile as unseen captors dragged her towards a distant town pyre, the searing heat already seeping through to scorch the soles of her feet. A piercing scream tore through the night as Freya jolted awake, her body drenched in sweat, her nightdress clinging to her shivering form. Clutching her knees to her chest, she shuddered in the aftermath of the vivid nightmare that had seized her.

Struggling to shake off the lingering horror, Freya pondered the significance of such haunting visions plaguing her subconscious. The memory of her dream's intensity left her unsettled, prompting a disquieting question: What mysterious forces were at play in her mind? Suppressing the terrifying sensation of being consumed by flames, she buried it deep within, alongside the other demons that lurked within her psyche.

Ivy emerged from her trance-like state, her gaze sharpening as it settled on the smouldering embers of the dwindling fire. A sly smile graced her lips as she contemplated the effortless success of her intrusion into Freya's mind, a feat that had proven to be even simpler than she had anticipated. The thought of it brought a soft, knowing chuckle to her lips. *White witches are so pathetic!* Her amusement danced in her eyes. With a tender gesture, she affectionately stroked Luna's fur, her quiet laughter fading into the night as she succumbed to the embrace of sleep.

***

As the first hints of dawn painted the sky in soft hues, Freya stirred from the depths of her slumber to the melodic symphony of birdsong.

'What, already?' she grumbled, her mind still heavy with the remnants of sleep. With a reluctant sigh, she cast off the warmth of her covers and rose from her bed, a sense of weariness clinging to her every movement. Despite her fatigue, she had made a promise to hunt for Ivy, and she intended to honour it.

The morning was young, the air crisp and still, as Freya readied herself for the task ahead. She swiftly dressed and gathered her essentials, her trusted broom by her side. Stepping out into the cool morning air, she cast a fleeting glance back at her dwelling, a pang of unease gnawing at her insides. Was it the lingering shadows of a sleepless night, the haunting echoes of a nightmare, or something more sinister that unsettled her?

Pushing aside her doubts, Freya set her gaze skyward and soared above the clouds, her hair streaming behind her like a silken banner. Her destination clear in mind, she flew towards the rolling meadows, intent on her mission. With practised stealth, she captured a rabbit, its unsuspecting form caught unawares. Hanging precariously from her broom, she swiftly secured the creature, its protests falling on deaf ears as she bound it tightly.

Returning to her abode, Freya presented the captured rabbit to Ivy, fulfilling her end of the bargain. A flicker of hunger danced in Ivy's eyes as she snatched the offering, her fingers closing around the creature with a primal grip. Freya's gaze lingered for a moment, unsure of the emotions that flickered across Ivy's face, before she turned away, her duty discharged.

Retreating to her chamber, Freya sought solace in the quiet confines of her room. A forgotten tome lay abandoned on her nightstand, its pages whispering of long-lost tales and forgotten knowledge. With a sense of longing, she turned the pages, craving the solace and escape that only a good book could provide.

Upon closer examination of the ancient scripture within the tome, Freya furrowed her brow in concentration, attempting to decipher the cryptic language that danced across the pages. Some of the symbols appeared so alien and enigmatic that all she could do was to stare at them in awe and wonder. Yet amidst the unfamiliar glyphs, there were a few that stirred a sense of recognition within her. These were the same symbols her mother had once inscribed in the air, weaving potent spells of binding and protection.

A sense of foreboding crept over Freya as she pondered the implications of these ancient incantations. Was there a reason she might need such powerful magic? Thoughts of Ivy, the enigmatic visitor in her midst, lingered in her mind like a shadow. Doubts gnawed at her, whispering of unseen dangers and hidden truths. Could it be that Ivy was not the helpless old witch she appeared to be?

Listening to the insistent tug of her instincts, Freya made a difficult decision. She resolved to confront Ivy and bid her to depart. Despite the woman's seemingly miraculous recovery and unnerving demeanour, Freya's unease only deepened. Ivy's rapid healing and mysterious behaviour posed a puzzle that defied explanation, casting a shadow of doubt over her intentions.

Exhausted from the morning's events and the weight of her thoughts, Freya sank into a deep slumber, the forgotten book slipping from her grasp and resting gently on her chest.

Throughout the remainder of the day, she slept soundly and undisturbed, her dreams veiled in a shroud of mystery and uncertainty.

As Freya drifted in the realm of dreams, a sense of unease lingered in the air, whispering of secrets yet to be unveiled and challenges yet to be faced. The quiet of her chamber enveloped her, offering a temporary respite from Ivy's enigmatic presence and the mysteries that surrounded her.

Three Warriors Return

Raven awoke from a deep slumber, a rare occurrence for her as she seldom slept past daybreak. The previous night had been taxing, and the group was exhausted from their intense encounter with the blood witch. Despite their eagerness to return home, they decided that an extra day of travel would not make much of a difference.

Stretching her limbs, Raven surveyed their makeshift shelter, noticing that both Otter and Silent Wolf were already up and about. The tantalising aroma of breakfast wafted into her nostrils as she emerged from the shelter's entrance.

Otter, as usual, was busy preparing their morning meal. 'Here she is,' he greeted her with his trademark cheerful smile.

Meanwhile, Silent Wolf was methodically packing up some of their gear before joining Otter by the crackling fire. 'Don't let the meat get too well-done, now, will you?' he said, with a relaxed grin.

'Have I ever?' Otter retorted with a playful tone. 'It looks perfectly cooked.'

Silent Wolf chuckled as he playfully prodded the sizzling venison. They all enjoyed their breakfast in silence, their senses alert to the peacefulness of the surrounding forest.

With a sense of urgency, they swiftly dismantled the camp and readied themselves to continue their journey. Working together seamlessly, they moved with a precision reminiscent of a team of soldier ants. As they set off along the forest trail, Raven gazed up at the sky, awestruck by the beauty of the day. The weather was perfect for taking to the skies, but she resisted the temptation to shapeshift and soar through the clouds, focusing instead on the path ahead.

They journeyed along the meandering trail, the sun casting shifting shadows as they rode tirelessly for the better part of the day. Since their last confrontation with the warring party, a palpable tension hung in the air, keeping them on edge. Every rustle of the leaves or snap of a twig set their hearts racing as they remained vigilant, ears tuned for any hint of impending danger.

Their age-old conflict with the Mohicans lingered in the background, a constant source of concern. However, murmurs of a new menace had begun to circulate among the council members. Whispers spoke of white men arriving in great numbers on their shores, driven by a desire to expand their dominion and exert their influence. Now, not only did they have to contend with encroaching neighbouring tribes vying for their lands, but also these unfamiliar adversaries from distant lands.

As if these challenges were not enough, a figure from the past had reemerged after years of silence. The blood witch, long hoped to have met her demise despite the prophecy about Raven, had returned to sow menace and chaos once more. Many had fervently wished her reign of terror to be over, only to discover that the rumours of her demise were greatly exaggerated. It was a cruel twist of fate that her malevolent presence had resurfaced, casting a shadow of uncertainty over an already precarious situation.

As they entered the glade, a vast open expanse where they had previously camped during their journey south, a sense of familiarity washed over them. 'Well, this is a welcome sight,' Otter exclaimed, breaking the silence. Raven couldn't help but share in the sentiment, feeling a wave of relief wash over her. With only a few more days of travel ahead, they would soon return to Laughing Bear's village.

Finding a suitable spot, they secured their horses before settling down. Raven recalled that pine needles could be used to make a refreshing drink when the young needles were harvested, and they still had a small amount of bush honey to sweeten the concoction.

As they began to eat, Silent Wolf returned from his scouting mission, entering the shelter he changed back into his human skin and donned his fur attire.

'Just in time, I see,' he said, taking in the scene before him. Brushing his shaggy hair away from his eyes, he observed the surroundings with a practiced eye before sniffing the drink Raven had prepared.

'Hmm,' he mused, eyeing Raven suspiciously, a hint of amusement in his gaze. The moment was light-hearted, and Raven struggled to contain her laughter. 'One of your concoctions, I presume?' he inquired.

'Not half as dreadful as your tonics,' she retorted.

Curious, Silent Wolf took a sip, his expression shifting from scepticism to surprise. 'Not bad at all,' he admitted, acknowledging the unexpected delight of the drink. The camaraderie among them was palpable, a brief respite in the midst of their challenging journey.

Content with a belly full of food, they lounged in front of the crackling fire as Otter proposed sharing one of his captivating tales.

'Sure, that would be wonderful,' Raven responded eagerly, her anticipation evident. It had been quite some time since they had been enchanted by one of Otter's stories.

Silent Wolf simply nodded in agreement, his gaze fixed on the flickering flames. Raven couldn't help but wonder what thoughts lay behind his enigmatic eyes.

As Otter rubbed his hands together to ward off the night's lingering chill, he began to recount the ancient tale of the Badger and the Bear. 'Long ago, deep in the heart of the dark woods, a badger family dwelled,' he narrated with passion, drawing his companions into the mystical world he painted with his words.

While Otter's storytelling enthralled his listeners, Raven's mind drifted, consumed by thoughts of her own abilities and the weight of her potential fate. The idea of permanently transforming into a bird troubled her deeply, even if it was supposedly her predestined path. Determined to defy this foretold destiny, she resolved to seek guidance from Saskia once more, yearning to explore any possibility of shaping her own future where she could embrace both her human and avian forms, defying the constraints of prophecy and shaping her own destiny.

After two more days of arduous travel through rugged terrain and verdant forests, their journey culminated at the threshold of the Red Wood Forest, the gateway to Laughing Bears village. A wave of relief washed over Raven as they approached their destination, the weariness of their long expedition momentarily eclipsed by the promise of rest. Her muscles ached from the extended hours of travel, and the monotonous routine of sitting atop Crow for three consecutive months had left her feeling as if her very bones had melded with the saddle.

Yearning for the comfort of familiar surroundings, Raven's thoughts drifted to the mineral pools that beckoned invitingly at the far end of the village. The mere prospect of soaking in the soothing warmth of the waters stirred a deep longing within her, a primal desire for relaxation and rejuvenation after the rigours of their prolonged journey. With a single-minded focus, she set her sights on indulging in the pools, determined to wash away the accumulated fatigue and tension that clung to her like a cloak.

Amidst the bustling activity of Laughing Bear's village, with its colourful stalls and lively chatter, Raven forged ahead, ignoring the cries and calls of her kin as they were welcomed home.

Dismounting Crow in haste, she handed over his reigns and continued through the village, her steps quickening with eagerness. Everything else could wait. Her weary body craved the solace of the warm waters, a sanctuary where she could unwind and surrender to their healing embrace.

Raven's only wish as she neared the pools was for solitude. She hoped fervently that she would find the pools empty. She had no desire to engage in conversation about their journey just yet.

Above all else, Raven yearned for peace and quiet. As she approached the mineral pools, her mind was a tumultuous sea of questions and uncertainties regarding her destiny and the cryptic prophecy of the witch. A witch she'd secretly hoped was already dead – despite her years of training with Silent Wolf. The incessant whirlwind of thoughts and doubts weighed heavily on her spirit, a relentless storm that threatened to consume her inner peace.

As she gazed upon the tranquil surface of the mineral pools, a glimmer of hope flickered within her heart. Perhaps in the tranquil depths of the warm waters, she could find reprieve from the ceaseless chatter of her mind.

The thought of submerging deep within the soothing embrace, letting the gentle ripples wash away the troubles that plagued her, held a promise of temporary escape from the burdens that now plagued her.

Raven clung to the fragile hope that the sanctuary would silence the clamour of her mind. Peering inside, she was delighted to find the pools empty. With a heavy sigh, she stepped inside.

Shutting the door firmly behind her, Raven swiftly undressed and immersed herself in the welcoming warmth of the mineral waters. A wave of instant relief washed over her as the heat enveloped her senses, melting away the tension that had coiled tightly within her muscles. With a deep, cleansing breath, she let the soothing waters cradle her body, allowing herself to sink into a state of tranquil bliss.

Closing her eyes, she surrendered to the healing embrace of the water, letting go of the weight of her worries and uncertainties. In that moment of serenity, all that mattered was the gentle caress of the water against her skin and the rhythmic beat of her own heart, offering a precious respite from the tumult of her thoughts.

***

After a brief celebration of their return with their clan members, Otter and Silent Wolf bid their farewells and ventured towards their respective teepees, seeking much-needed rest before the night's festivities. Their arrival coincided with the full moon ceremony, a revered event marking the awakening of spring. During this time, Mother Moon was honoured, and offerings were made in the hope of bountiful crops and robust health.

As Otter made his way to his teepee, his thoughts lingered on Raven and the allure of the mineral pools. A yearning to join her tugged at his heartstrings, yet he understood the importance of granting her the solitude she sought. He decided to give her the space she needed and trusted that they would reunite later at the solstice celebration, where they could revel in each other's company once more.

As he settled into the comfort of his bedding, he allowed the upcoming celebration to stir a flicker of excitement within him, eager for the solidarity and shared moments that awaited under the watchful gaze of the full moon.

Death of a White Witch

In the stillness of the house, not a sound stirred from the upper floors. The silence shrouded the space, granting a cloak of secrecy to her actions. This was Ivy's moment to excel in her craft, the art of administering poison to her unsuspecting victim.

Ivy had overstayed her welcome; Freya had already extended a polite request for her departure, observing the remarkable recovery of the elderly woman. Her injuries had nearly vanished, thanks to the nourishment provided by the rabbit's blood. Ivy seethed with resentment at the flimsy excuse given, finding it utterly preposterous. Nevertheless, such details were inconsequential now that she had regained enough strength to undertake the arduous task of dismembering Freya once she had been drained of her life's essence.

With a fluid motion, Ivy removed the woollen scarf securing her hair, allowing her dreadlocks to cascade freely around her. As a sigh of relief escaped her lips, she savoured the feeling of release from the confines of the scarf.

Eve emerged stealthily from her hiding place and uttered a soft whisper in Ivy's ear. Amused by the spider's bold suggestion to ascend the stairs and administer the poison to Freya, Ivy stifled a quiet chuckle. 'How kind of you, my clever little fanged friend,' Ivy murmured in response, concealing her amusement behind her hand. 'But it would be far more convenient to have her downstairs for the scheme I have in mind.'

With a swift movement, Eve retreated under the shelter of Ivy's hair, seamlessly blending into the dark tangle of dreadlocks once more, camouflaging herself within the messy strands.

Ivy located the vial of poison, bringing it close to her failing eyesight as she marvelled at the enchanting blue hue it emitted. A jug of water conveniently awaited her on the nearby bench. With a delicate touch, Ivy carefully manoeuvred her way towards it, allowing a solitary drop of the potent substance to trickle from the glass vial. Mesmerised, Ivy observed as the iridescent blue dissolved into the water, leaving no visible trace behind. A broad grin spread across her face, he eyes gleaming with silent triumph.

Securing the glass vial between her withered breasts, Ivy nestled it protectively against her heart, ensuring its safety and proximity. With the poison integrated into the water, all that remained was to await Freya's final unwitting sip. Resting comfortably by the fire, Ivy closed her eyes, though sleep eluded her. Like a patient predator biding its time, she lay in wait. Visions of Freya's lifeblood danced through her corrupted thoughts, eliciting a purr of anticipation. The longing for the taste of human blood coursed through her veins, a desire unfulfilled for far too long. The promise of satiating that thirst stirred her with a wicked delight; soon, very soon, she would revel in her grim feast.

***

It was early morning when Freya stirred from another restless night, plagued by dreadful nightmares. Despite the ancient protection symbols she had carefully inscribed on the floor beneath her bed, the hellish torment she'd endured seemed resistant to such defences. The arrival of Ivy, the weathered old hag, had marked the onset of these terrifying dreams, unlike anything Freya had ever experienced before.

180

The nightmares had grown increasingly frequent, haunting her slumber with relentless intensity. As she rubbed her weary eyes, a deep fatigue settled within her. Freya longed for the day when Ivy would finally depart from her home, hoping that with her absence, the nightmares would subside and grant her respite from this nightly ordeal.

Rolling over in her bed, Freya peered out of her bedroom window and observed the dimly lit morning, shrouded in a heavy fog that seemed to linger solely over her house. The unusual phenomenon was particularly striking now that spring had arrived. Puzzled by the eerie mist that surrounded her home, Freya reluctantly abandoned the warmth of her cosy bed, draping a plush woollen shawl around her shoulders for comfort and warmth.

Descending the stairs, Freya felt a sense of urgency to start her day with her customary cup of tea, a cherished morning ritual that brought her a sense of calm and routine. Intent on dispelling the lingering unease that accompanied Ivy's presence, she made her way to the hearth to stoke the fire before venturing out into her garden. Pouring water from the jug into a pot, she set it over the flames to heat.

As Freya patiently waited for her tea to brew, little did she know of the lurking danger concealed within the comforting beverage she had just served herself. The toxic presence of Ivy's insidious plan lay hidden within the innocent liquid, poised to unleash its fatal effects upon its unsuspecting victim. Oblivious to the treacherous scheme that had been set in motion, Freya sat in quiet contemplation, unaware of the imminent peril that awaited her with each passing moment.

Freya cast a concerned gaze at Ivy, who appeared to be lost in a deep slumber. 'Oh well,' Freya mused to herself, 'she can have a sip when she wakes, although I highly doubt she will.' Ivy never truly appreciated her tea, and on the rare occasions she did partake, Freya could sense her distaste. Settling herself as comfortably as possible on her small stool by the fireplace, Freya noted Ivy's complete stillness. She opted to abandon her initial plan of pressing Ivy further about her departure; it could wait a while longer, she reasoned.

Blowing gently on her tea, Freya eagerly sipped it down. Suddenly, an impulse seized her to nudge Ivy and rouse her from her slumber, a wave of irritation washing over her about the current circumstances. As she observed Ivy's serene sleeping form, a seed of suspicion sprouted in Freya's gut, gnawing at her insides like a voracious rat. Was it merely anxiety, or could it be the unsettling effects of some unknown poison taking hold from what she had unknowingly consumed?

Freya's world spun as the poison tightened its grip on her body. Dizziness enveloped her, and she sensed her throat constricting, making it difficult to breathe. Panic surged within her as she grappled with the sudden onset of sickness and excruciating pains that seemed to come from the depths of her being.

With a desperate attempt to rid herself of the toxin, Freya doubled over, but no relief came. Weakness washed over her like a relentless tide, leaving her immobilised and gasping for air. Struggling to vocalise her distress, she found her voice stifled by the poison's cruel effects. Fear consumed her as she felt her body succumb to paralysis, every movement thwarted by the treacherous substance coursing through her veins.

In her hunched and helpless state, a chilling realisation pierced Freya's mind: the tea! Ivy must have orchestrated this betrayal. Questions swirled in her mind as she grappled with the reality of what was happening to her. Despite all she had done for Ivy, the motives behind this treacherous act remained shrouded in mystery.

Regret and despair flooded Freya's thoughts as she lamented her failure to heed the warning signs that had nagged at her for weeks, hinting at Ivy's deceitful nature. Writhing in agony, unable to expel the toxic contents plaguing her, a desperate idea flickered in her mind: the knife on the nearby bench. If only she could muster the strength to reach it, perhaps she could yet turn the tide against her betrayer.

***

Ivy's malevolent laughter echoed through the room as she revelled in the success of her scheme, delighting in the sight of Freya's weakened state. With a wicked gleam in her eyes, she approached Freya, her movements swift and purposeful. A sharp pinch to Freya's arm yielded no reaction from the incapacitated woman, solidifying Ivy's satisfaction.

Leaning in close, Ivy peered into Freya's once vibrant emerald eyes, now clouded and unresponsive. A smirk played on Ivy's lips as she observed Freya's dilated pupils, a telltale sign of the poison's grip on her victim. Inhaling deeply, Ivy savoured the scent of Freya's essence, her predatory instincts sharpened by the smell of young blood coursing through the woman's veins.

'Ah, yes,' Ivy remarked, her voice laced with malice, 'Young blood! I'm thirsty too.' A chilling laugh escaped her lips as she taunted Freya, no longer needing to conceal her true nature. With a sudden release of inhibition, Ivy let out a piercing, blood-curdling cry that reverberated through the room, echoing her wicked delight and newfound freedom to unleash her dark desires.

Without delay, Ivy emptied the pot of water and meticulously cleaned it before setting it down next to Freya. Retrieving a sharp knife, she made a deep incision along Freya's wrist, tracing the path of a vein. Ivy finally tasted the young witch's blood that she had so long desired. Her eyes darkened in pleasure as a wave of ecstasy washed over her. Consuming the blood voraciously, Ivy indulged in great amounts like a famished beast. When Ivy had satisfied her thirst, she carelessly dropped Freya's arm into the nearby pot, treating it as if it were a discarded object. Using the sleeve of her dress, she wiped the blood trickling down her chin, a devious smile lingering on her face. The pot slowly filled with Freya's blood.

With an evil gleam in her eyes, Ivy continued to taunt Freya with a twisted sense of satisfaction. 'It won't be long now, my red-headed beauty! Perhaps in your next life – if you're fortunate enough to return – you'll learn to be more cautious and less trusting. Remember, never,

ever, trust an old witch,' she scolded, her voice dripping with venom as she loomed over Freya.

In that moment, a wave of euphoria washed over Ivy, filling her with a sense of joy she hadn't experienced in ages. With a vow whispered silently to herself, she swore that once she reclaimed her powers, and after stealing Raven's magic, she would never deprive herself of human blood again.

***

As Freya's lifeforce drained from her, she realised that her time was coming to an end. She didn't want to die, especially not like this, but there was absolutely nothing she could do about it.

Freya's heart slowed, and a sudden wave of sadness surged through her chest, as if her heart may explode. She cast her failing mind away from the horror unfolding, wanting her last thoughts to be of something beautiful. Focusing her mind, she ignored Ivy's ramblings and thought about the rolling meadows in summer.

Wildflowers bloomed, rabbits frolicked and majestic stags bellowed through the forest. The little red foxes and their inquisitive natures.

Flowers – oh, how she loved the flowers. Crocus, dandelions, daffodils and where the grass was damp and green, and where shallow streams were flowing, cowslip buds would be on show.

Daisies everywhere opened upon daylight to greet the sunshine, their little petals closing at dusk tightly. Buttercups, with their silken yellow glossy cups sitting perfectly upon a sturdy stem. In the tall grass, so small, little blue forget me nots would show their tiny faces, by streams the bigger ones grew.

What better flower to remember in my final hour, forget me nots.

Freya's spirit ascended from her lifeless body, transcending the earthly realm as she gazed down upon her physical form with a sense of detachment. Absent of pain or animosity towards her tormentor, she found solace in her newfound freedom. Hovering momentarily, her essence transformed into a radiant, shimmering golden light, exuding a sense of peace and tranquillity.

Unwilling to witness the macabre scene any longer, Freya bid a silent farewell to her home, casting a final glance before embarking on a journey guided by a distant, haunting melody that resonated with her soul. Drifting gracefully above, she recognised the ancestral song that beckoned her, drawing her closer to the luminous lights that served as beacons leading her homeward to Niflheim. A place of mist and ice, where the dead converge, especially if the fallen have died without honour.

As she followed the ethereal trail, love poured forth from Freya's being, enveloping her in a warm embrace of light as she twirled and danced in her spiritual form. Engulfed in a burst of radiant energy, she intertwined with the shimmering lights, their brilliance intensifying as the merged and intertwined in a harmonious symphony.

Calling upon all white witches that had gone before her with a Gaelic cry that echoed through the ages, Freya's essence expanded, inviting their spirits to bask in her luminous aura. Together, they became a tapestry of golden light, their collective energy pulsating with ancient wisdom and boundless love, creating a celestial spectacle that transcended time and space.

Blood and Bone

Ivy moaned a low and horrifying sound at the thought of stripping the fat from Freya's body. She would require flying ointment to return to Canada in the blink of an eye. Elated with joy, and on a high after the consumption of the white witch's blood, she danced a little jig, the pain from her wounds gone.

Inspecting her hands, she peered at them closely, noting how much softer in appearance they already seemed. She had drunk a lot of Freya's blood, and it was indeed starting to have the desired effect.

Once she could suck the marrow from the bones, she would be even more youthful. She prodded Freya's cold body, as if to make sure she truly was dead, taunting the woman further, as if death wasn't enough.

Happy with the amount of blood she had collected, she sat the two pots on the stone bench and covered them with a cloth. It had been almost four months since Ivy had felt this relaxed.

She needed to work quickly with Freya's body, as rigor mortis was already setting in, rendering the job harder than it needed to be.

Eve, her fanged familiar, crawled out and sat on her shoulder also happy at no longer needing to stay concealed.

Ivy held up a bloody finger in front of Eve, giving her a taste of the glorious blood as well. Eve then sprang off Ivy's shoulder and ran up into the corner of the rafters. She inspected her new surroundings, with her many eyes, as it had been a long wait for the spinner. The sooner she spun her web the sooner she would have a juicy moth to suck the guts from.

Ivy looked around and called a command to Freya's broom. It had been stored away in the back of a cupboard at the far end of the room, behind the staircase. The door shot open, and the broom hovered in front of Ivy. 'Oh, my,' she scoffed, 'it's been too long now, hasn't it?' Tenderly brushing the broom, she wiped the bristles, running the length of the tangled mess through her fingers.

The broom did Ivy's bidding and flew under Freya, assisting to lift her onto her bench. Before she started with the laborious job of dismantling Freya's body, Ivy wanted nothing more than to destroy her broom. Having no need for it, she saw no point in keeping any magical remnants of the white witch's, and she didn't want to be reminded of the ridiculous witch, with her ever-so-loving nature.

Ivy spoke a spell and the broom snapped into several pieces, then she burst into laughter.

Quickly retrieving the broken pieces, she threw them into the fire, and the dry elm wood caught alight quickly. It sparked and spat as if in defiance at being destroyed.

'Ah, now, to the job at hand,' she said as she glanced over at Freya's corpse.

Freya's blood had tasted so sweet, she could hardly wait to taste the fatty marrow. Her lips smacked together, making a loud popping sound.

Luna meowed, as she knew exactly what that sound meant. She too would soon have her fill of the young witch's organs, and if she was very lucky and her mistress was feeling generous, she would share some of the smaller bones with her. She rubbed up against the bottom of her mistress's legs and meowed again.

'Yes, yes, my little friend. It won't be long now.'

First and foremost, the fire needed to be roasting hot, so she threw plenty of logs on. It would burn long into the night. Ivy then got a soup ladle and scooped several spoonsful of Freya's fresh blood. She placed it into a smaller pot, which she then put inside the large cauldron that was suspended over the fire. This would allow the blood to keep at a perfect temperature and not burn.

'How nice of Freya to keep her cauldron so clean,' Ivy said under her breath.

Quickly cutting Freya's clothing from her body, she poked and prodded her tender flesh, feeling for the fattiest part on her slim body. She lifted one of Freya's arms and glanced at Luna. 'Look at it, the skinny bag of bones,' she mused as she dropped her arm in frustration.

'Slim pickings of fat from this one,' she begrudgingly said as she rubbed Luna behind her ears.

Ivy didn't want to be bothered with removing all the young woman's skin to remove her fat. It would take too long, and she was in a hurry, so she went straight to the organs.

Once she had removed her organs and stripped as much fat from around them as possible, she located a good amount of fat around Freya's belly and thighs.

Ivy laughed as she sampled pieces of every organ, savouring each morsel, like it would be her last. 'So soft, the taste is almost perfection. The only thing that will be better than this is Raven.'

Looking into the bowls of fat, she felt happy in her resolve, as she had collected enough to render down and make a flying potion.

Working long into the day, she did not stop and rest as per usual when skinning large animals. Freya's blood gave her the sustenance she required. She felt the best she had felt in a long time.

Ivy scratched her nose with a long finger. She peered at the back of her hand. A low, guttural sound escaped her as she witnessed less wrinkles and slightly plumper skin. The more blood and offal she consumed, the better the results would be.

Feeling much more recuperated, the only remnants of pain that remained was the memory of her failing to catch Raven that fateful night. It pained her greatly to think of it. A single drop of blood fell from her eye and rolled down her face. No longer needing to hide her bloody tears, she let it fall.

Knowing the human anatomy well, Ivy dispatched the largest bones as the bigger the bone the more delectable marrow she would reap from within. Smashing a thigh bone with just enough force to split the bone open, she exposed the golden marrow from within. Wasting no time, she dug it out with her razor-sharp fingernail, and her eyes rolled back in her head. Pure ecstasy. The bone being licked clean, she tossed it on the stone floor, along with everything she had discarded.

Staring at Freya's face, she murmured, 'So very pretty, weren't you.' The sea green eyes were now dull. But she would not waste this delicacy. The eyes were a favourite of hers. Savouring the texture of the jelly like substance as it popped, a jelly explosion squirting out. The centre of the eye was harder to chew but she liked it nonetheless.

Delving into her dress pocket, she deftly retrieved her pipe and settled on the sofa, ready to indulge in a well-deserved smoke. With each puff, she enjoyed the rich, sharp flavours of the herbs dancing on her tongue, enjoying every moment of the experience.

As the day slipped away and the night's embrace beckoned, Ivy knew it was the perfect moment to concoct her flying ointment. The crackling fire provided the ideal heat for melting the fat as she carefully placed it within the suspended cauldron. With a sizzle and a spit, the fat instantly started to render down, filling the air with a tantalising aroma that hinted at the potent magic to come.

With a sense of clandestine satisfaction, she retrieved her concealed bag and delved deep within until her fingers closed around the glass vial. A sneer crossed her face as she beheld the contents within – the most crucial ingredient essential for facilitating her swift transportation across the continent in the blink of an eye.

Ivy carefully added the full vial of rare starlight dew, its shimmering essence infusing the potion with a celestial glow. A few calculated drops of toad's venom followed suit, adding a touch of potent magic to the concoction. She knew that without these two powerful ingredients working in harmony, the elixir's transformative magic would simply remain dormant, unable to fulfil its intended purpose. As Ivy added the final ingredient to the potion, she felt the energy within it shift and swirl, as if awakening to its full potential. With a delicate touch, she crushed the dried waterlilies, allowing their essence to merge seamlessly with the other components. A strange and enchanting aroma permeated the air around her, tingling her senses with its otherworldly fragrance.

Ivy closed her eyes and inhaled deeply, relishing the potent scent that enveloped her. The brew was now ready, its magic palpable and potent. With a satisfied smile, Ivy knew that her work, for the time being, was complete, and the stage set for the unfolding of her next plan.

Revenge.

Omens

As Raven reached the hub of Laughing Bear's camp, it was alive with excitement. Everyone was busy preparing for the night's festivities, and she was looking forward to finally relaxing around the ceremonial fire above all else and watching the dancers.

Reaching Otter's tepee, ever so quietly she opened the flap. Otter was sleeping deeply by the look of it. She entered and was light of foot so not to wake him. Laying down beside him she listened to his breathing and longed to curl up next to him, but given the heightened feelings that now were ever present, she thought it best to keep her distance.

Wrapping herself tightly in her fur, she laid down and closed her eyes. Raven drifted off and ventured into the dreaming realm once more. She was walking through the forest and felt a familiar presence. It surrounded her in darkness, and she felt the pull to shapeshift. Crouching down she leaped into the air, changing into her avian form once again. Flapping her wings hard, she flew up into the safety of the forest canopy.

Scanning the forest with her keen eyesight, she searched for Ivy. Feeling her presence this time, she knew the witch was close. Sitting quietly, Raven cloaked herself in magic. Focusing her intention, she called forth her shield, the usual white light that surrounded her, which was a luminous blue hue this time. Unsure of what had changed within her, she could feel the magical power of the veil as it shifted. The protective barrier would keep her well hidden from the dark eyes of the spying witch. Sniffing the air, Raven detected a familiar scent. The pungent smell of blood, and the metallic taste that burnt her throat when the dragon was upon her, was present again.

A laugh she knew all too well echoed out around her, reverberating in the quietness of the forest. It was Ivy. The blood witch swooped into view, hovering gracefully above where Raven remained concealed. Her dress billowed around her like a dark, swirling storm cloud, trailing behind her in a mesmerising dance of shadows and whispers.

Raven observed intently as Ivy cast her piercing gaze over the forest below, causing a shiver to run down her spine. *How did she always manage to find me?* The question lingered in Raven's mind, planting a seed of doubt. A realisation slowly dawned on her: perhaps this encounter was more than just a dream – could it be a forewarning, a glimpse into a possible reality? Or was it merely Ivy, with her eerie abilities, once again insinuating herself into Raven's subconscious, haunting her in the most unsettling of ways? The boundary between reality and the supernatural seemed a blur in the presence of the enigmatic witch. It seemed Ivy was indeed alive and searching for Raven once again.

Raven observed keenly, her gaze locked on Ivy as the familiar storm of foul temper clouded the witch's features once more. Despite the tumult of emotions, Ivy seemed to exude an aura of vitality and youthfulness that belied the passage of time. Was this a manifestation of Ivy's potent sorcery at work, weaving illusions of vigour and rejuvenation around her? Or had she truly healed herself better than when Raven had last encountered her?

Ivy's enraged scream pierced the air as she swiftly vanished from view in the blink of an eye, her descent a blur of motion and speed. Raven watched in awe at the witch's incredible swiftness, realising the urgency of the situation. With a sense of uncertainty, she still understood the need to act swiftly. Raven knew she must alert the others of the imminent danger looming on the horizon, for Ivy's presence signalled a threat that once again loomed over their peaceful lives.

Raven jolted awake as Otter shook her gently, her eyes fluttering open to meet his concerned gaze. 'What's wrong? You were murmuring and trembling in your sleep.'

Rubbing her hand over her face, she felt beads of sweat on her brow and upper lip. 'Oh, you know, just another dream,' Raven muttered, a sense of unease in her voice. 'It's always the same when that witch is on the prowl. If my dream holds truth, she lingers among the living. I can't decipher if she cloaks her age with magic or if she has somehow turned back time. Yet, she again haunts my dreams.' Her words trailed off as she pondered the implications of her vision.

'Let her come,' Otter whispered, in a soothing tone. 'I relish the day when I drive a fatal arrow through her despicable heart. She will not take you, Raven, not without the fight of her life from me.' His eyes blazed with fierce determination.

They embraced and she buried her face into the nape of his neck, taking a deep breath and inhaling his familiar smell.

'We should get ready and head out. I don't know about you, but I could literally eat a buffalo,' he joked, trying to make light of the situation. Otter was right of course, as they needed to get ready for the spring ceremony.

Raven moved away and opened her gift from Ash. The most beautiful white suede dress was folded within the bundle, along with a pair of white suede boots and a bright blue-black sash, to complement her hair. Tiny turquoise, obsidian and coral beads were inlaid on the front in the shape of a raven. A little gasp of appreciation escaped her. Raven held it up for Otter to see.

'Wow,' was all that escaped him, his eyes wide, as he looked the outfit over.

Raven ran her fingers over the little beads, admiring the skilled work that had gone into making such a fine dress. It fit her perfectly and hugged her small frame.

Otter had been gifted a white suede shirt and pants, tassels fell down the sides of the legs and arms, the shirt was open at the front so that he could show off his beaded breast plate. Two hawk feathers swung off an abalone shell in the centre. White Moccasin boots, with a bright red head band, finished off his outfit nicely.

Otter painted two red stripes across his cheeks with red ochre. He certainly looked like the fierce warrior, and a handsome one at that.

Raven wore a white snowy owl feather in her hair, and the contrast against the colour of her blue-black hair was stunning. They both admired one another, before stepping out for the night's festivities.

Otter gathered his weapons, and they walked hand in hand along the pathway to the feasting lodge.

Laughing Bear and Ash were already seated waiting at the head of the table with Silent Wolf seated closest beside them. The atmosphere was intense as they entered the longhouse. Two seats beside Silent Wolf had been reserved for them. Cheers were called out and pats on the back given as they passed the young braves.

Otter looked proud, and he smiled and thanked them for their appraisal. They made their way to their seats and greeted the elders.

Laughing Bear stood up and everyone present became quiet. 'Three warriors left us on a dangerous quest, and three warriors return as heroes,' he bellowed out, his loud voice reverberating through the longhouse. Cheering echoed around the great hall.

Otter's smile never left his face throughout the entire evening. They were held in the highest of esteem and were served their meals first. Something that had never occurred before that night. Otter wiped his mouth with the back of his hand and slurped down a berry drink, then he grabbed a handful of nuts and tossed them into his mouth. He looked at Raven and rubbed his belly. 'I am stuffed, and I think I had better stop now before I burst,' he said.

Raven just laughed as she stuffed her mouth full of as many berries as she could fit in, wiping the red juice from her mouth as it overflowed down her chin. She didn't care that all eyes were on her.

After everyone had had their fill, Laughing Bear rose to his feet once more, his towering figure commanding attention as he lifted his cup high above his head. 'Oh, Great Spirit,' his voice thundered, resonating through the gathered crowd. 'We humbly express our gratitude to our revered ancestors, whose wisdom lights our way and leads us on the path to righteousness. Once more, we beseech your divine protection and benevolence, seeking your abundant blessings and prosperity upon us. As the season of spring envelops us, we offer our prayers for a plentiful harvest and the gift of robust health for all.'

In unison, every member of the gathering raised their cups as one, their voices blending in a harmonious chorus as they drank together in shared celebration. The resounding claps of their hands striking the table echoed through the hall, a rhythmic cadence of unity and camaraderie that resonated with the spirit of the moment.

'We shall venture forth to the ceremonial fire,' Laughing Bear declared. Following their revered leader, the assembly stepped into the enchanting embrace of the moonlit night, their hearts uplifted with hope. Proudly adorned with his magnificent headdress, Laughing Bear led the way, a beacon of wisdom guiding their steps towards the flickering flames that awaited them.

The great fire blazed brilliantly, casting its warm glow into the depths of the night and illuminating the faces of all who had assembled. As if drawn by a mystical force, the attendees formed a perfect circle around the roaring flames, their shadows dancing in mesmerising patterns upon the ground. In the flickering light of the fire, a sense of unity and reverence enveloped the gathering, binding them together in a shared moment of connection with the ancient spirits that dwelled within the flames.

Raven's gaze lifted towards the heavens, where the velvety night sky stretched endlessly above them, adorned with a tapestry of twinkling stars. The air was crisp and still, carrying with it a sense of ancient wisdom and serenity. In that moment of quiet contemplation, Raven reached out to Otter, drawing him near, urging him to join in her silent communion with the celestial lights above.

'Look,' Raven whispered, her voice soft yet filled with reverence, 'see how brightly our ancestors illuminate the night sky? Their eternal presence lights our path. They watch over us with love and protection, guiding us through the darkness on our way forward.'

Otter's eyes followed Raven's gesture, his gaze tracing the constellations that seemed to dance with a celestial grace, a reminder of the timeless bond between the living and those who had come before.

'You know what lies beyond those shimmering stars, don't you?' Otter's voice was filled with a gentle curiosity as he tenderly clasped Raven's hand. Raven met his gaze, her eyes reflecting a deep sense of wonder and contemplation.

'Everything,' Otter's words carried a profound weight in the stillness of the night. 'Eternity stretches infinitely, its vastness a realm that knows no bounds. Our ancestors dwell in that endless expanse, just as we will one day join them when our time comes.'

As much as Raven felt a sense of peace wash over her at Otter's words, she couldn't help but think about the spirit realm she often visited in her dreams. 'That sounds wonderful and all, but there is a realm out there where I'm sure the darkness wants to swallow me into its abyss. I venture there often in my dreams, and to be totally honest with you, as much as I hate to admit it, it scares the hell out of me.' Her amber eyes flickered in the firelight.

'What if it's just the old hag planting those seeds in your dreams? What if it's not real?' Otter questioned, sounding quite sure of himself.

'Only time will tell, I suppose.' Her voice hitched, and she turned away, not wanting to dwell on the topic any further. She only hoped he was right.

Just of late, Raven couldn't help but question her own beliefs. She knew that death was not an end but a transition – a gateway to new beginnings. What if there was something else, something other than a spiritual ascension, something dark, full of horrors? She shuddered at the thought and focused on the dancers and the music. Oh, how she loved the music. Pushing all thoughts and feelings of the blood witch to the depths of her mind, she swayed back and forth and lost herself in the rhythmic beat. The witch would not have the satisfaction of ruining her night – not tonight; it had been a long wait, to dance, to feel free from her restraints and really let her hair down.

As if he could sense her every thought, Silent Wolf sat before the great council fire, drawing long drags from the bone pipe. Smoke swirled around him as he exhaled, then rubbed the fragrant smoke through his shaggy grey hair. His gaze locked onto Raven, his expression unreadable as he observed her closely.

The drummers persisted in fervently beating out their laments, sending resonant rhythms echoing through the air, while melodic songs and ancient chants wafted into the night. Meanwhile, exuberant dancers leaped and twirled in a mesmerising circular motion around the blazing flames, their movements imbued with an infectious energy. Adorned with magnificent feathered headdresses that gleamed in the flickering firelight, they presented a breathtaking spectacle.

Otter joined the dancers brandishing his golden arrow above his head as he reenacted the kill of the fiery dragon. After many dances, Otter returned to rest with Raven, the paint on his face streaming down his face with sweat.

Laughing Bear passed them a bone pipe, which they both took several puffs of, before coughing and spluttering and firmly handing it back.

Otter rose to his feet, still clasping Raven's hand, and gently lifted her up alongside him. Grasping both of her hands in his, he guided her into the dance, seamlessly blending into the rhythmic movements of the other dancers around the blazing fire. Together, they twirled and swayed with the music, losing themselves in the euphoria of the moment. As the night wore on, they danced with such fervour that they gasped for breath, eventually collapsing in a contented heap upon their soft fur blankets. Despite their exhaustion, a sense of joy and relief washed over them, grateful for the rare opportunity to revel in the familiarity of their homeland once more. Though they knew deep down that this fleeting respite would soon come to an end, for now, they embraced the moment with all their hearts.

The younger braves converged around Otter, tugging at his shirt and pleading for more of his stories. Unable to refuse the excited lads, he looked at Raven, his eyes asking without so much as whispering a word.

Raven gave him a wide grin, she wanted to visit with the seer any-way and had had quite enough dancing for one night. 'Go,' she said, lightly pushing him onto his feet as the braves relentlessly pulled and tugged at him. 'I will go visit Saskia and meet you back at your camp.'

He briefly had time to peck her on the cheek before they boys laughed and patted him on his back, handing him a bone horn to drink from, as they led him away.

Raven made her way to the seer's tepee. Her fire was still burning, and it glowed faintly through the skins, casting shadows in the dark-ness. Raven stood quite still, gathering her thoughts.

'Come in, my little bird,' Saskia called out. Her voice soothing and calm as always.

Raven entered, and it was warm and inviting from the small fire that was situated in the centre of her dwelling. Surrounding the fire in a circular formation were black volcanic rocks. Large sage sticks hung from the apex, smouldering and filling the space with an earthy aroma. Saskia gestured for her to sit beside her.

Raven sat down and noted she smelled like Trillium, and a light and delicate floral scent filled her senses, which was quite lovely.

'So, you overcame your fear?' Saskia asked, smiling as she searched her face.

'I buried it deep, just like I was taught,' Raven replied.

'The dragon was killed, and Ivy was greatly wounded, I saw, but you were wounded too,' Saskia said, concern in her eyes.

'The flames almost had me. I was burnt, but Silent Wolf and Otter nursed me back to health. And I had some help from the Great Spirit too.'

The seer nodded and stared at the flames that seemed to dance within the pit.

'I had a dream – well, a vision, I think? If it's correct, Ivy lives, and she still searches for me.' Raven paused for a moment before continuing, her eyes cast towards the dancing flames as though she were caught in a hypnotic spell. 'Ivy appeared younger. But knowing what a trickster she is now, she taught me a valuable lesson. Never trust a witch, ever.'

Saskia watched the fire without breaking her gaze for some time before she answered.

'The blood witch indeed lives, yes, this is true, and your dream was correct. I have seen this also. Ivy dabbles in the dark arts and reverses her age for a time, by consuming human blood. When she drinks the blood of someone special, say another witch, or someone with powers, this is when she absorbs the power of that person, taking on their strengths and some of their youth. Maybe you have seen in your dream something that is yet to come to fruition.'

'Well, if that's true, then you are in danger with us as well. Your visions are powerful, Saskia. Are you not afraid?' Her voice laced with genuine concern for the elder.

'Did you bring the dragon's tooth?' Saskia asked, without so much as blinking at Raven's question.

Raven untied the suede pouch that was tied to her waist and produced the dragon's tooth. The ivory glimmered in the firelight.

Saskia's eyes narrowed as she peered at the massive incisor. 'How did you manage to pry it from Otter's grasp?' she asked with a cheeky grin.

'He gave it to me for safe keeping.' She ran her fingers over the smooth exterior, almost protectively.

'If you're willing to part with it, we would be able to easily spy on the witch, should you desire it, little bird?' Saskia's words dripped with intrigue and a hint of mischief.

Raven looked at the tooth and then at the seer, her eyes glinting as she held Saskia's intense gaze. 'But can't you do that anyway, without the tooth?' she queried, not quite sure how Otter would feel about her handing over his prized possession so soon.

The seer nodded. 'I can, but it takes great concentration, and my visions don't always allow me to see everything, not exactly. It's also very taxing. The tooth, being imbued with Ivy's magic, will make it much easier. I only wish Otter had removed all the fangs. Just imagine.' Her eyes sparkled with delight.

Raven nodded, understanding all too well the fatigue she endured after her dreams and visions. Handing over the tooth, she placed it gently in Saskia's open palm.

The seer closed her hand, forming a fist. Her eyes closed and she whispered something in an unspoken language – an archaic spell, perhaps.

Without warning, Saskia's hand moved swiftly, releasing the tooth from her grasp, sending it hurtling into the heart of the popping fire. As the tooth met the flames, a cascade of fiery tongues leaped skyward, dancing with an otherworldly zeal. The air crackled with energy as sparks exploded, painting an enchanting display of light and shadow. The wood beneath seemed to shudder and sizzle in protest, as if possessed by a life force of its own.

From the heart of the inferno, a great dark cloud began to unfurl, its tendrils reaching and twisting in a spectral dance. Slowly at first, then with increasing speed, the cloud spun in a circular motion, taking on the form of a swirling vortex. Its shape seemed to morph and re-form with each passing moment, defying logic and reason. Bursts of brilliant violet light erupted from within the cyclone, illuminating the surrounding darkness with an ethereal glow. Beams of sizzling lightning pulsed and surged through the swirling mass, casting eerie shadows that flickered and danced across their faces. As the spectacle unfolded, it felt as though a gateway to another dimension had been flung open before their very eyes. Suddenly, a part of the vortex cleared, revealing a circular black hole that seemed to pulse with a malicious hunger. It loomed like a yawning void, an endless abyss that beckoned with a chilling, irresistible pull, hinting at unfathomable depths.

In a sudden and chilling turn, Ivy's image emerged from the shadows of the spinning vortex, her presence casting a sinister aura over the scene. Her tall frame hunched over, she hovered over the slumped figure of a red-headed woman, her movements deliberate and unsettling as she prodded and poked at the woman's still form.

Saskia and Raven sat in a stunned silence, their eyes fixed on the unfolding horror before them. The air around them seemed to thicken with a palpable sense of dread.

As Ivy's sinister intentions came to light, a sense of dread gripped Saskia and Raven. With a twisted and malevolent purpose, Ivy began to siphon the very life force from the helpless woman, her gnarled fingers acting as conduits for a dark and forbidden power.

Powerless to intervene, Saskia and Raven sat rooted to the spot, their hearts heavy with a mixture of horror and disbelief as they watched the macabre scene play out. The air grew thick with a suffocating aura of malice, as if the very darkness of the night had converged upon this unholy act.

As the woman's life force ebbed away, a chilling stillness settled, broken only by the sound of Ivy's whispered incantations and the faint, desperate gasps of the woman as her vitality drained away. Each passing moment seemed to stretch into eternity, each heartbeat a painful reminder of the helplessness that bound Saskia and Raven in place. In the face of such unfathomable evil, all they could do was bear witness to the unholy ritual unfolding before them, their souls weighed down by the enormity of the darkness that had been unleashed.

Unable to bear witness to the macabre scene unfolding before her eyes any longer, Raven's seething anger boiled within her veins, a fiery tempest raging beneath her skin. As she turned away from the grisly spectacle, a deep and abiding hatred festered within her. Every fibre of Raven's being resonated with a profound loathing for Ivy, her contempt burning like a relentless flame deep within her core. Her jaw clenched tight, muscles taut with the tension of her suppressed rage,

Raven struggled to contain the emotions swirling within her. The very air around her seemed to vibrate with the intensity of her fury, a tangible aura of boldness radiating from her being.

Saskia, having seen enough, decisively shattered the spell and sealed the spinning vortex with a determined gesture. In a mesmerising display, it vanished as though the hungry flames of the fire eagerly devoured its very essence.

They both sat in heavy silence for a while, their eyes fixed on the flickering flames of the fire. The lingering horror of what they had just witnessed etched into their memories like a haunting spectre. The crackling of the fire seemed to underscore the weight of the darkness that had descended upon them, casting a sombre pall over the night.

As they stared into the dancing flames, the images of the grisly scene played out in their minds like a twisted nightmarish reel, each detail seared into their consciousness like a brand.

Saskia shattered the heavy silence with a solemn declaration, 'I knew she was of foul making, but I never. . .' Her voice trailed off into a whisper, the unfinished words hanging in the air like an unanswered question.

'She's coming, so let's put an end to her once and for all!' Raven's voice dripped with venom; her tone laced with a fierce determination. 'I'm putting everyone, especially you Saskia, in danger by staying here,' Raven declared with a sense of urgency. 'I believe we should seek a strategic vantage point within the forest to confront her.'

Saskia nodded thoughtfully. 'Yes, that could work. Or, you could stay here,' she suggested. 'I am certain that when I bring this proposal to the warriors, they will gladly offer their assistance. We all share the common desire to rid our lands of the witch's presence.'

'I believe the risk is too great, and let's be honest, ultimately it's me she's after,' Raven said, her eyes gleaming in the firelight like two fierce flames. As her anger intensified, a fiery blaze seemed to ignite within her eyes, blazing with fierce resolve. 'I came here tonight with another question in mind, but now it feels less significant,' Raven revealed, her brow furrowing slightly with a hint of concern.

'Ask away. I will answer to the best of my ability,' Saskia replied, her voice gentle and reassuring despite the looming presence of evil.

'It can wait. If I manage to survive this ordeal, we can speak again,' Raven reassured, attempting to sound confident despite the fear creeping up within her.

'As you wish, little bird,' Saskia cooed softly, a sense of understanding and warmth in her tone.

'You, know, it's "Little Feather", don't you?' Raven said with a hint of amusement in her tone. 'Shikoba means Little Feather.'

Saskia chuckled softly. 'Yes, dear. But I do prefer "Little Bird" for you, considering you are quite a petite raven, aren't you, Shikoba?' Saskia flashed her an affectionate smile, a silent gesture of reassurance.

Raven tried to smile, though it was a rather feeble attempt on her part, betraying the weight of the impending danger and uncertainty that hung in the air.

'I'm feeling weary. I think I will retire for the night as my furs are calling me,' Raven said, embracing the seer warmly and expressing her gratitude before heading off to rest.

'I'm here whenever you need me, little bird,' Saskia called out after her as Raven disappeared into the night under the luminous glow of the full moon.

Raven made her way back to Otter's teepee, her mind reeling with visions of Ivy's evil nature. Taking several deep breaths, she calmed her burning fury before entering. Otter was lying on his furs, arms crossed behind his head, looking most relaxed. His smile was as infectious as it was captivating.

Sitting up, he gestured for her to join him. Raven plonked down, her worries pressing down on her like a heavy burden.

'Is everything okay? Did you get the answers you were looking for?'

Raven shrugged her shoulders, locking eyes with Otter as she gently took his hands in hers, recounting the chilling details of the vision she had just experienced. 'I'm sorry, but the seer required the dragon's tooth for a vision, and… well, it's gone.'

Otter's eyes widened with a mix of shock and concern. 'I think you're onto something, to be honest. Venturing into the forest will at least divert Ivy away from here and, ultimately, Saskia. She's in danger, whether she wants to acknowledge it or not.' Otter's voice was firm with determination.

'We should inform Silent Wolf and depart at first light. We must gather our arsenal and secure the best vantage point before Ivy's inevitable return. Make no mistake, she will come back, and with a vengeance. She's more powerful than ever, so we must be at the top of our game,' Raven said, her eyes flashing with a fiery blue hue – a simmering rage that threatened to erupt.

Otter nodded in agreement, encircling her protectively in his arms as he attempted to soothe the raw power he sensed radiating from her. He had never seen Raven in such a wild state before, and it unsettled him slightly – her burgeoning powers were akin to a gathering storm, with the ever-present blue light cocooning her, especially in moments of anger. He felt her tremble against his chest, a deep sigh escaping her as she struggled to contain the tempest brewing within.

Spells and Bindings

Ivy puffed thoughtfully on her ancient bone pipe, the tendrils of smoke curling around her like whispers of the past. Every now and then, she muttered incantations beneath her breath, her words carrying a weight of power. Her long fingers traced the intricate patterns of the ancient amulet hanging around her neck, each touch leaving a trail of dark energy in its wake. Her eyes, as black and unyielding as the void, remained fixed on the dancing flames of the fire. Her stare as stark as her face, she looked menacingly cold, betraying no hint of emotion. However, Luna her faithful companion, knew better.

Luna understood that beneath Ivy's stoic façade lay a mind teeming with dark intentions. The subtle flicker of malice in her mistress's gaze spoke volumes to the perceptive feline. A sense of foreboding hung in the air, a silent warning of impending mischief and hatred aimed at Raven.

If cats could laugh, Luna thought wryly, she would have revelled in the chilling sound of Ivy's wicked laugh, a sound that sent shivers down the spines of those who knew its true meaning. As Ivy's laughter erupted into uncontrollable fits of demonic mirth, Luna braced herself for the chaos that was sure to follow. In that moment, evil glittered in the shadows, a harbinger of dark deeds yet to unfold.

The blood witch's eyes gleamed with a demonic light as she chanted the ancient incantation, each syllable dripping with dark power. The air around Ivy crackled with an otherworldly energy, as if the very fabric of reality shuddered at her command. With each repetition of the spell, she beckoned forth shadowy entities and malevolent forces, forging unholy alliances that thrived in the depths of night.

The veil between worlds thinned under the cover of darkness, allowing Ivy's magic to reach its zenith during the witching hour. At the stroke of three o'clock, beneath the full moon's haunting gaze, her spells held unparalleled potency, weaving a tapestry of darkness and despair that few could withstand.

Having recently absorbed the essence of Freya, a source of white power, Ivy felt her strength surge, fuelling her insatiable hunger for more. Impatience gnawed at her, but she knew that her true might would be unleashed under the impending full moon. Until then, she would content herself with haunting Raven's dreams, again sowing seeds of fear and despair in the young girl's mind.

Ivy delighted in the psychological torment she inflicted, knowing that fear was a potent weapon, a herald of downfall for those who succumbed to its insidious grip. She thrilled at the terror she would sow, knowing that in fear lay the key to her ultimate triumph.

With a gaze that seemed to penetrate the very essence of the flames, Ivy locked eyes with the flickering inferno, her black orbs reflecting a darkness that mirrored her intentions. In a solemn gesture, she made an offering to the dark forces she now courted again, an omen of the greater tribute to follow. With a deft flick of her fingers, she cast a piece of Freya's heart, ensnared within a tress of her fiery red hair, into the heart of the fire.

As the sacrificial offering touched the hungry flames, a sudden burst of intense heat consumed the delicate strands of hair, transforming them into a blazing inferno that crackled and hissed in response. The scent of singed hair mingled with the acrid tang of magic as the fiery blaze devoured the offering, casting eerie shadows that danced across Ivy's features.

A cruel sneer twisted the corners of Ivy's lips, revealing a glimpse of the evil that thrived within her dark soul. The sight of Freya's essence consumed by fire brought a twisted satisfaction to her, a prelude to the grander schemes she had woven in the shadows. In that moment of grisly communion with the flames, Ivy's pact with darkness grew stronger than ever before, setting in motion a chain of events that would herald untold chaos and despair.

As the march of time carried the night deeper into its embrace, a perceptible sense of foreboding descended upon the surroundings, shrouding everything in an unsettling veil of unease. Despite the warmth coming from the fire, Ivy's sinister presence seemed to chill the very air around her, casting a spectral mist that coiled and twisted in the flickering light.

The back of the house lay cloaked in impenetrable darkness, a void that seemed to devour all traces of light and warmth. Within this abyss, shadows danced and whispered, their movements inscrutable and filled with a sense of lurking malevolence.

The frigid air clung to the skin like icy fingers, a stark reminder of winter's relentless grip refusing to yield to spring. Each breath hung in the air like a ghostly apparition, visible puffs of mist that mingled with Ivy's own wicked exhalations, creating a chilling tableau of darkness and frost.

In this desolate scene, where time seemed to stand still and the night held its breath, the boundaries between reality and nightmare blurred, leaving a lingering sense of dread that whispered of unseen terrors lurking just beyond the edge of perception.

As the witching hour drew near, Ivy stoked the fire with a determined hand, the flames leaping higher in response to her cruel energy. With a deep drag from her pipe, she exhaled a cloud of smoke that twisted and curled like serpents in the night. The time had come to unleash her evil intent upon Raven's unsuspecting dreams.

Rising from her seat with an air of purpose, Ivy approached the bubbling cauldron, its contents simmering with a venomous energy. With practiced precision, she sliced her palm with a sharp blade, the darkened blood welling forth to bind the spell with its potent sacrifice. The potion, as black as the abyss, swirled and seethed, its potency reaching its zenith.

Removing the wooden spoon from the cauldron, Ivy watched in silent fascination as the potion continued to churn of its own accord, a testament to the hostile forces at play. Uttering ancient incantations in a language long forgotten by mortals, she imbued the potion with the essence of her intent, each word carrying the weight of centuries of old magic.

Seated once more upon the sofa, Ivy crossed her ankles and closed her eyes, entering a trance-like state where the boundaries between the physical and the ethereal blurred. In the flickering light of the fire, her features contorted with concentration, the whites of her eyes gleaming with an otherworldly light. In her previous weakened state, how she had missed this power and communion with the darkest of forces.

A sudden flapping sound filled the air, like the beating of a thousand wings in unison, heralding the arrival of unseen forces drawn by Ivy's call. Undeterred, she focused her will, directing the tendrils of her spell towards Raven's slumbering mind, where her darkest nightmares awaited to be unfurled once more. In this moment of unholy communion, Ivy's power surged, a tempest of ill will poised to descend upon the realm of dreams.

As the veil between dusk and dawn grew thin, the liminal hours ushered forth a wicked legion of spirits, drawn to Ivy's beckoning call like moths to a flame. With a voice that echoed through the realms, she invoked the dark forces, weaving her will into the fabric of existence at Satan's behest once again.

In the shadowed expanse of the spirit realm, where boundaries blurred and reality twisted, the demons heeded Ivy's summons, their amorphous forms coalescing from the void with an insatiable hunger for souls. Like a nightmarish orchestra, they converged, their shapeless silhouettes taking on substance as they clawed their way from the depths of their infernal domain, eager to fulfil the blood witch's bidding.

A cacophony of high-pitched cries pierced the ether as the demons, Satan's legionnaires, took flight, their massive wings casting ominous shadows that sped through the ethereal darkness. With predatory intent, they scoured the unseen realms, seeking out lost or lingering souls to sate their unholy thirst, their unearthly presence instilling dread in all who crossed their path.

From the depths of Ivy's being, a guttural sound rumbled forth, a feral utterance that bordered on a purr, a chilling testament to her communion once again with the forces of darkness. With a gesture of her hand, she unleashed the ghouls of the night, their ghastly forms surging forth like a tide of malice, ready to carry out her immoral will in the twilight hours between worlds.

Demons and Dreams

Raven tossed and turned restlessly in her sleep, her subconscious guiding her into the ethereal realm she frequented. Amidst the familiar dark void of her dreams, she pondered the possibility of encountering the white witch's spirit. The enveloping darkness embraced her, while the gentle wind tenderly brushed against her feathers, akin to delicate kisses. Her piercing call resounded through the infinite expanse as she soared into the uncharted territory once again.

'I refuse to succumb to fear,' she whispered resolutely. Despite her efforts, fear often insidiously crept into her mind in this realm, clutching her like a vice around her throat, threatening to snuff out her essence. But the atmosphere felt pristine and pure, devoid of any foul scents, and devoid of any traces of Ivy's presence.

Banishing all thoughts of Ivy from her mind, she directed her attention towards seeking out any trace of her ancestors instead. Her melodic call echoed through the void, bouncing off what seemed like a nearby rock formation, the sound hinting at the presence of solid structures in the darkness. Flying onwards with determination, she navigated through the seemingly boundless cave system, the profound darkness evoking thoughts of endlessness that raced through her mind's eye. Urgency fuelled her search as she accelerated, gaining momentum while her repetitive caws echoed throughout the surrounding space, a persistent beacon in the vast unknown.

In the distance, a familiar voice reached Raven's ears, stirring a sense of recognition and longing within her. It had been so long since she'd last heard that voice, a voice she knew all too well. Clearer and more purposeful, the voice resonated with the essence of her mother. Unmistakable and comforting, it cloaked Raven with feelings of warmth, familiarity and love. Fuelled by a surge of joy, she eagerly scanned the abyss, searching fervently for a glimpse of her mother. The sound of her mother's voice calling out, 'Shikoba, where are you?' vibrated around her, echoing through the emptiness as Raven pressed on in her quest to reunite with her beloved mother.

Little Wing's voice beckoned once more, calling out to Raven with reassurance. 'I'm here, Raven. Fly to me, I'm right here.'

Despite Raven's keen eyesight, her search yielded no sign of her mother. Confusion and frustration mounted within her – where could her mother be? Why was she unable to locate her? With a sense of desperation consuming her, Raven's calls transformed into mournful cries, echoing through the darkness.

Abruptly, a deep, ominous rumbling sounded from the shadows, its low, guttural tone drawing closer with unnerving swiftness. Fear, which she had fought to suppress, surged back with a vengeance, constricting her throat. Struggling to vocalise, her attempts to cry out were met with silence. The sound of a multitude of beating wings surrounded her, like a cacophony of impending doom as they closed in from all directions.

As dread flooded her, a familiar, pungent scent filled the air – reminiscent of blood and smoke – assaulting her senses and tightening its grip around her. Raven's realisation dawned too late: Ivy had once again ensnared her in her deceitful web. Attempting to muster her magic for defence, she found herself inexplicably powerless, bewildered by the unexpected turn of events. Trapped and exposed, she frantically employed every skill at her disposal in a desperate bid to evade the clutches of the blood witch once more.

In a sudden and chilling turn, ominous black shadows materialised before Raven, hurtling towards her with alarming speed. Splitting apart into giant avian forms, these monstrous birds descended upon her, their massive wings enveloping her in a vice-like grip as they ensnared her in their mighty talons. Paralysed and defenceless, Raven found herself unable to break free from their hold.

The creatures' wings thrashed violently, their razor-sharp claws tearing at her feathers, while their beaks snapped and gnashed, inflicting searing pain as they drew blood. Agony coursed through her body, and her once-pristine wings became soaked with the crimson evidence of her suffering. Amidst the chaos, Ivy's sinister laugher echoed through the air, sending shivers of dread down Raven's spine.

Instinctively, she pulled her wings tightly around herself, seeking refuge from the unyielding assault of the demonic birds' talons. Despite her efforts to shield her face, the creatures persisted, their claws gouging at her protective barrier. Their grips tightened, causing anguished screams from Raven, her cries echoing into the abyss.

'You are mine, Raven!' Ivy's chilling words pierced the chaos, adding to Raven's terror as the onslaught continued. It disoriented her, causing her to plummet earthward like a falling comet, her torn and bloodied form hurtling towards the unforgiving ground below.

In her rapid descent, the wind tore at her tattered body, bloodsoaked feathers clinging to her in a grisly embrace. Gripped by the fear of impact, and with her magic inexplicably absent, Raven had no choice but to hurtle towards the earth below. Each time she dared to open her eyes, the grotesque visages of the demonic birds twisted and contorted, their birdlike forms warping in and out of their true nightmarish shapes.

Blood-red eyes locked onto her; jagged teeth bared in a feral display of aggression as these creatures vied for dominance. With a sickening thud, Raven collided with the solid ground, her body skidding across jagged rocks as she emitted gut-wrenching screams of agony, shielding her face from the onslaught of rocks and dust.

Gasping for breath, Raven jolted awake, her body drenched in a cold sweat as she frantically attempted to break free from the imaginary grip that seemed to linger on her shoulders, the remnants of the harrowing nightmare still haunting her senses.

***

Otter and Silent Wolf were in a state of panic, desperately shaking Raven with trembling hands, their grip tight on her shoulders. They could feel the intensity of her terror as she thrashed violently in her sleep, as if ensnared in a nightmare beyond imagination.

'It's as if she's trapped,' Silent Wolf declared, his voice strained with emotion, a look of deep concern crossing his mismatched eyes. Otter held on firmly, his heart breaking as he witnessed her struggle, her body drenched in sweat, her screams piercing the air with sheer terror.

In that moment of helplessness, Otter could only imagine the unspeakable horrors that tormented her in her dream. He shook her even harder, desperation driving his actions. 'Raven, wake up, wake up now!' His words, drowned out by her nightmarish cries, seemed futile. The sound of her screams was unbearable, sending shivers down their spines.

As the situation escalated, Otter felt a rising sense of panic threatening to consume him. Just as he was about to join her in screaming, a sudden breakthrough occurred. Raven, with a gasp, broke free from their grips, her eyes wide open as she sat up abruptly, finally awake from the depths of her terrifying ordeal.

***

Raven's eyes slowly refocused, the familiar voices of her friends gradually becoming clearer. Her eyes stung as if filled with grit, prompting her to rub them vigorously in an attempt to dispel the phantom discomfort. Squinting against an imaginary glare, she anxiously scanned her body, half-expecting to find it covered with wounds and blood.

To her relief, only sweat clung to her skin, a physical reminder of the nightmare that had just seized her.

The experience had been so real, so intense, that Raven couldn't shake the pain and fear still clinging to her, even though she was now wide awake. Fear, the emotion she tried so hard to overcome, was now wrapped tightly around her throat. Shaking her head in disbelief, she turned to her friends, their expressions mirroring a mix of shock and concern.

'It's the witch,' she said, her voice laced with urgency. 'She's on her way, bringing with her a legion of dark forces. We must prepare for the battle of our lives.' Her eyes flickered with a fierce blue light, a telltale sign of her rising temper, a force to be reckoned with despite her fear.

In that moment, the sense of danger hit them all, and Raven's resolve grew stronger. Still shaking but with a determined heart, she braced herself for what was to come, her friends standing by her, ready to face the threat head-on together.

***

Silent Wolf and Otter stood resolute, their determination clear in the way they held their ground. Deep in the heart of the Canadian wilderness, they had found refuge in a vast cave system that offered both protection and a sense of security. But now, all they could do was prepare for the inevitable clash with the blood witch and her dark army.

As they waited in tense silence, Otter carefully checked his weapons, making sure his enchanted arrows, knives and spears were within reach. The thought of facing the undead gnawed at him—*how does one fight the dead?* he wondered, grappling with the terrifying reality of their supernatural enemy.

In the midst of his thoughts, Otter found comfort in the belief that Raven's magic could be their salvation. He clung to the hope that her powers would be the shield they needed against the darkness closing in. If her magic failed them, though, like in her nightmare, their fates would be forever changed, their survival uncertain, as they prepared for a battle unlike any they had ever faced.

Book 2
Shadows of the Blood Witch

The Scottish Highlands – 1758
Lochmore Castle

Elspeth Tadhg, a figure of imposing beauty and presence, sat in solemn contemplation, her mind consumed by the passing of her daughter Freya. As the esteemed leader of the notorious Black Fang coven, a weighty responsibility hung upon her shoulders – the pursuit of retribution against the blood witch accountable for the heinous murder. Despite the painful history of Freya's exile from the Scottish Highlands fifteen years prior, the unwritten law among witches stood firm: No one could harm their own kind with impunity. It was a code deeply ingrained in their traditions, a code the blood witch should have honoured. Yet, in the face of this crime, Elspeth pondered whether the blood witch's audacity stemmed from the indifference of unyielding confidence, perhaps, daring Freya's kin to confront her and exact the justice they sought.

Elspeth's heart ached with the knowledge that her daughter had inherited the gift of white magic, a truth that weighed heavily on her soul. Struggling to reconcile this reality with her own dark past, she often found herself questioning why fate had dealt them such a cruel hand. In moments of despair, she couldn't help but contemplate whether things would have unfolded differently if Freya had embraced the shadows instead of fiercely battling against them. The memory of Freya's defiance haunted Elspeth, and her daughter's stubborn determination had ultimately led to her tragic demise.

Elspeth admired her talon-sharp fingernails with a sense of satisfaction, noting their flawless state that mirrored the perfection of her obsidian fangs. In her 100 years of existence, not a single chip had marred their sleek surface. Her pointy black teeth glistened in the flickering candlelight, a reflection of her immortal essence that shone through her unchanging, depthless eyes.

The chilling howl of the wind echoed through the castle walls, carried by the icy gusts from the frigid waters below the rugged cliffs, threatening to shatter the bravest soul with its bone-chilling cold. In this perpetual state of cold and wind, the conditions were perfect for flight as the elements danced in a wild symphony around the castle.

The fortress stood as an impenetrable bastion, its high curtain walls, sleek towers and fortified battlements encircled by a deep, forbidding moat. Despite the passage of centuries, the castle remained untouched, preserving its ancient grandeur since the coven of witches had claimed it as their own.

During the height of the witch huntings, thirteen Black Fang witches had descended upon the unsuspecting castle like shadows in the night, their arrival as effortless as plucking fruit from a tree. With ruthless precision, they'd silenced the soldiers, leaving a trail of destruction in their wake as they overpowered the keep. The massacre had unfolded with terrifying ease, leaving no survivor to recount the harrowing tale of the kingdom's tragic demise that fateful night.

Bound by blood or distant kinship, the thirteen women bore the unmistakable mark of their dark lineage: murderous-looking teeth and nails that spoke of their deadly heritage. For those born without the telltale signs of obsidian nails, a grim fate awaited them as offerings to the Goddess of the night, ensuring the continuation of their unholy covenant.

Upon Elspeth's shock at the sight of Freya's silken white nails at birth, she was seized by a primal fear that gripped her very soul.

Desperation had clawed at her as she screamed and pleaded with her sisters, her voice raw with anguish, to spare her daughter's life. In the depths of her being, Elspeth harboured an unwavering belief in her power to alter the course of Freya's destiny.

Over the course of fifteen gruelling years, the members of the coven relentlessly delved into their darkest arts, weaving spells of malevolent intent in a desperate bid to break the bonds of Freya's white magic and set her free. Throughout this arduous trial, Freya stood firm, her emerald-green eyes ablaze with defiance. Her fiery red hair streamed out behind her like a silken banner in the relentless wind as she descended from the cliff's edge, severing ties with the evil of her lineage and seeking the white light instead. With a heavy heart, Freya did not spare a backward glance at the horrors she left behind.

Elspeth, a silent witness to her daughter's departure, had watched as Freya soared into the mist-shrouded skies and vanished into the veil of clouds, her depthless eyes devoid of tears, her heart as dark as her blackened soul.

Returning her mind to the present, Anya, Elspeth's second in command appeared, exuding a breathtaking beauty that rivalled that of her sister's. Her appearance was a weapon in itself, as much as her teeth and nails. Draped in a sumptuous cloak of rich velvet green, she moved with a grace that commanded attention as she entered the room. Without casting a glance in Elspeth's direction, she positioned herself in front of the small stone pond that lay in the room's centre, fixating her gaze on the inky depths of the water.

A long, gleaming nail delicately grazed the surface of the pond, causing ripples to disturb the previously mirrored stillness. In a voice that was as cool as it was deliberate, Anya broke the silence with a question that hung heavy in the air.

'Are we to attack?' Her eyes, flecked with violet and as dark as the moonless night, remained transfixed on the water's surface as Elspeth silently joined her sister's side, a silent understanding passing between them.

Following a prolonged silence, Elspeth's voice sliced through the stillness like a blade.

'This is my battle, and you are well aware of it!' she declared. 'Freya was my daughter and, it is I, and I alone, who will claim retribution by tearing the blood witch's throat from her traitorous head.' Elspeth's upper lip curled back, revealing her menacing obsidian fangs, a stark warning of the primal rage simmering within her.

The display of her fangs should have been enough to give Anya pause, to halt her in her tracks. However, the younger witch, harbouring her own dark desires and ambitions, refused to be deterred. Despite the significant age gap of twenty years between them, Anya remained unfazed by Elspeth's dismissive demeanour, her gaze unwavering as she contemplated the older witch's stance.

'Oh, what a delightful notion,' Anya purred, her tongue darting across her gleaming black fangs at the tantalising prospect. 'To spill blood with purpose!' Her words dripped with a macabre playfulness.

Elspeth fixed her second-in-command with a piercing gaze, a silent warning.

Anya's casual demeanour and flippant words danced dangerously close to the edge of provocation, treading on thin ice that threatened to shatter beneath her if she dared to push the matter further. Tension lingered, hinting at the volatile power dynamics at play within their coven.

Anya's eyes narrowed ever so slightly in a silent display of defiance, a flicker of disbelief dancing within their depths. How could her sister possibly intend to exclude her from what promised to be a moment of glorious triumph and wicked delight? The prospect of the impending conflict stirred a hunger within Anya, a craving for the thrill of battle and the taste of victory that she yearned.

Silent tension between the two witches simmered. Anya grappled with a decision that could alter the course of their shared destiny. Accept Elspeth's decree and bide her time, or dare to seize the opportunity for glory and revel in the chaos that awaited them? The choice loomed before her, a test of loyalty, ambition and the depths of her own dark desires.

With a keen intuition that seemed to penetrate her sister's thoughts, Elspeth gnashed her obsidian teeth together, the sound cutting through the atmosphere like a crack of thunder in a quiet storm. 'Is that envy in your eyes?' she hissed, her words laced with a venomous edge that conveyed her understanding of Anya's thoughts.

The accusation hung heavy in the air; a barb aimed directly at Anya's heart. Elspeth's sharp words cut deep, exposing the raw nerve of rivalry and ambition that simmered beneath the surface of their relationship.

Anya flicked the water's surface, a wordless retort to Elspeth's cutting accusation. Spinning on her heel, she strode purposefully out of the room, her graceful movements belying the storm of emotions raging within her. Each step she took exuded elegance, her figure gliding across the stone floor as if untouched by gravity, a vision of beauty in motion. For despite their obsidian fangs and nails, all thirteen witches possessed undeniable beauty.

Her fiery auburn hair billowed out behind her, as if caught in an unseen storm that echoed the fierce winds battering against the castle windows. The heavy door swung shut in her wake, the sound of its closing rumbling through the room and leaving a stifling hush in its aftermath.

***

Anya's frustration simmered beneath a veneer of poise and grace. She knew that now was not the time for confrontation, but rather a strategic retreat to allow the heat of the moment to dissipate. As she navigated the labyrinthine corridors of the ancient castle, her thoughts raced with a daring plan forming in her mind – a plan to challenge the age-old law that had long bound them, a law that she was now determined to defy.

With each step echoing in the empty corridors, Anya knew that the time for change had come, and she, with her cunning mind, was poised to be the catalyst for a transformation long overdue.

***

Elspeth stood in solemn silence, her gaze fixed upon the still, black waters of the pond, a mirror to her own inner turmoil. The reflections of the castle stones danced on the surface but offered no solace to her troubled mind. Night after night, she had come to this enchanted spot, hoping to catch a glimpse of her daughter, Freya, seeking any hint of deviation from the righteous path she had set for herself. Yet, each time, her vigil ended in disappointment.

Then came the day that shattered Elspeth's heart — a day etched in her memory with a darkness that eclipsed all others. She watched in helpless horror as Ivy, in her cruel and evil way, tormented and betrayed Freya, draining her life and defiling her remains without mercy. The act was an unforgivable atrocity, a grievous offence that ignited a ferocious fury within her. Elspeth's head throbbed; what a shame, all her sweet remains were scattered across the room. Guilt now filled the empty place that resided in her chest. Buried so deep, so she could hide the pain, that her soul daughter, was gone.

Her teeth ground together, a stony hardness settling in her features as thoughts of vengeance consumed her. The image of ripping open Ivy's throat and drenching herself in the witch's blood flickered through her mind like a dark flame. It had been far too long since Elspeth had last taken the life of another witch, and the prospect of this kill stirred a long-dormant hunger within her, a thirst for retribution that begged to be sated.

With a quickened heart she reached for a goblet filled with the deepest red wine, a hue so dark it bordered on black, mirroring the shadows that lurked within her own soul. With each sip, the wine's bitter sweetness tingled on her tongue, a taste as dark and rich as the depths of her soul. In that moment, Elspeth embraced the darkness that coiled within her, steeling herself for the bloody reckoning that lay ahead.

Acknowledgements

There are many people who inspired me to continue with this story, if it were not for them, the first chapter would still be sitting in rough draft in the bottom of a cluttered cupboard somewhere. Thank you, to all of you for your encouragement and telling me to finish my story.

For my daughter Tessa-lee Rose, who is my biggest inspiration with her free spirit and positive attitude. Thank you for being the kind-hearted and amazing little person that you are. For picking me up when I was down, and for reminding me that Brent and Poppy are watching over us now.

For my brother Brent, who received his wings far too early. You were my strength and my biggest protector. I miss and love you so much. Fly high, my Bro.

For Mum and Dad, who allowed me to believe in whatever I wanted and always supported me no matter what. I am so lucky to have had you both.

For my brother Alan, who I have shared so many great adventures with, here's to many more! Thank you for everything you have done and continue to do. My life would not be the same without you.

For my brother Dean, for instilling the warrior within and giving me the strength to overcome my fears.

For Donna, my BBF, I love you endlessly, thank you for all your support and encouragement, you are the best, straight up honest and down to earth. I love you.

For Petra, for all your guidance and wisdom, you are as wise as you are beautiful, inside and out. Thank you.

For Robyn, for continuing to assist me when I was ready to give up! You are without a doubt a force to be reckoned with. You are stronger than you know. I love you.

For Erin, thank you for all your support during my writing journey, you are much appreciated. I think you may have a couple of stories of your own to tell. Maybe one day?

For Carmel for always being there for Tessa and I especially during some of the most challenging health issues I have faced recently. I love you, my friend. Thank you.

For all my lovely female friends who kindly read a chapter and gave an honest opinion. Tya, Eleanor, Josie, Gemma and Renee. Thank you so much for believing in me and telling me to finish my story. You have no idea what it means to me. I love you all.

A huge thank you to my editor and independent publisher Dr Juliette Lachemeier for the tireless work that you invested in my story. Without your expertise and guidance, this book simply would not be. You are a true master. Namaste 🙏

A big thank you also to Judith San Nicolas for bringing my book cover to life. You absolutely nailed my vision, and it exceeded my expectations.

A wise prophet once said, 'There are two things we should give our children, one is roots, the other is wings.

Flying

Her soft down blows in the gentle wind; her feathers touch my
milky white skin.
Together we fly, no one else, just her and I.
Above the breeze to the Crystal Seas, she shows me what she sees.
Our eyes engage, it's so pure, sweet euphoria.
The snow-white clouds engulf us, flying higher and higher we soar,
into the distant evermore.

ABOUT THE AUTHOR

Wendy Pym is a talented artist and storyteller with a passion for creating vivid worlds inspired by Native American history mixed with mythology and magic. Honouring a promise to her late brother Brent to share her stories with the world, she has poured her creative vision into her debut series, Bloodlines of Destiny. The first book, *Raven and the Witch*, blends themes of identity, magic and the eternal clash between light and darkness, with a touch of YA horror.

With a painter's eye for detail, Wendy crafts fascinating tales while pursuing her dream of becoming a full-time artist and writer. When she's not writing or painting, she finds inspiration in outdoor adventures and her lifelong love of sport, which fuel her creativity and determination. She earned three belts in Kung Fu before taking up Muay Thai kickboxing, with Martial Arts teaching her confidence, respect, honour, and dedication – all qualities reflected in her main protagonist, Raven Shikoba – a heroine not to be messed with.

Wendy Pym has always been fascinated by Native American culture – their deep connection to nature, respect for the animals they hunted and their spiritual beliefs. As a child, she would collect bones and feathers to craft ornaments, long before she understood their cultural significance. Her passion led her to travel solo to America many years ago, where she visited reservations and brought home treasured jewellery and carvings that continue to inspire her work today.

Enjoyed the book? You can follow Wendy Pym at:

Facebook: www.facebook.com/wendy.pym.9?mibextid=ZbWKwL

Instagram: wspym

Email: wendyspym.13@gmail.com

TikTok: tiktok.com/@wspym13

If you liked the book, please leave a review on Amazon, Goodreads or with the author directly. Reviews are invaluable in supporting an author's hard work and are greatly appreciated.